Terrace Books, a trade imprint of the University of Wisconsin Press, takes its name from the Memorial Union Terrace, located at the University of Wisconsin–Madison. Since its inception in 1907, the Wisconsin Union has provided a venue for students, faculty, staff, and alumni to debate art, music, politics, and the issues of the day. It is a place where theater, music, drama, literature, dance, outdoor activities, and major speakers are made available to the campus and the community. To learn more about the Union, visit www.union.wisc.edu.

A Winsome Murder

A Winsome Murder

James DeVita

Terrace Books
A trade imprint of the University of Wisconsin Press

Terrace Books
A trade imprint of the University of Wisconsin Press
1930 Monroe Street, 3rd Floor
Madison, Wisconsin 53711-2059
uwpress.wisc.edu

3 Henrietta Street, Covent Garden
London WC2E 8LU, United Kingdom
eurospanbookstore.com

Printed in the United States of America

Library of Congress Cataloging-in-Publication Data

DeVita, James, author.
A winsome murder / James DeVita.
pages   cm
ISBN 978-0-299-30440-9 (cloth: alk. paper)
ISBN 978-0-299-30443-0 (e-book)
I. Title.
PS3554.E928177W56   2015
813'.6—dc23
2014042916

For
Brenda,
Gale,
and
Sophia

A Winsome Murder

A humid night in August, after midnight. Helga Steimel was walking her dog, Fred, a tiny yelp of a poodle. The stars were out and a mild breeze was beginning to cool the evening.

Fred, happy to be himself, barked and tugged Helga farther and farther away from town, past the Legion hall, past the church, past the high school and the cornfields behind it, and down the empty streets of the new development being carved out of the last forty acres of farmland out by the highway. There were no houses there yet. No streetlights. The asphalt roads were laid, as well as the sidewalks, chalk white and unscuffed in their newness. Mounds of lumber and roofing materials lay stacked along either side of the street, and every fifty yards or so numbered stakes sectioned off the hayfields soon to be bulldozed into residential lots.

Fred kept yapping at the air, pulling Helga along, and she let him, gazing skyward occasionally at the clusters of brilliant stars above. On a night as dark as this she could even make out the wispy thin sheen of the Milky Way, which was exactly what she was doing when Fred suddenly stopped.

He did not bark.

He did not shift from his mark.

What Helga saw first was a shadowy darkness in the tall grasses to her left, a deeper darkness than the rest of the field. Everywhere else the hay was moving, the long grasses swaying back and forth beneath the light night breeze, but not where Helga was looking. There, nothing moved. There, the grasses had all been matted down, leaving a sort of dark impression. She moved closer. Within the dusky void there seemed a thing of whiteness on the ground, a colorless form, silent and—

Helga stopped. Her mouth opened, but no sound came out. She backed away, slowly, carefully, as if she'd stumbled upon some act of horrific intimacy that she knew she should not be looking at.

A body.

Its arms and legs bent and pointed in ways arms and legs should not be able to go.

Melissa Becker was the first girl that Deborah Ellison ever kissed.

She'd kissed girls before, of course, when she was little, at sleepovers, lying under blankets on living room floors or sleeping in the same bed

3

with a playmate, but that was always practice, as they giggled it, practice to kiss the boys. But for Deborah, it wasn't practice. She enjoyed it. She craved the tingly feeling she felt when a little friend's hand accidentally brushed her body while whispering sixth grade secrets. There, nested into each other, so close that each could smell the other's candied breath, Deborah felt an overwhelming desire to *be* the other girl, to be all of her, to dissolve within her. She didn't know what this meant at the time, only that it felt right and true. And although some part of her, the part that was not truly her, told her that what she wanted was sinful and wrong, another part of her told her that it was right and good.

So she knew, even then, that she was different. This difference walked before her like another person whom only she could see, leaving herself always trailing slightly behind. She wanted to catch up to her own self someday, to be the person in front of her, the person she'd been trying to pretend wasn't there.

And then she kissed Melissa Becker.

Melissa was Deborah's first love. The kind of love that marks you for life, the kind of love that can damage you. She'd felt this way about Melissa ever since middle school, but never dared to say a word. Slowly, though, as they grew up together, Deborah began to think that maybe Melissa felt the same way—something in her eyes when they said good-bye after volleyball practice, or when they ate lunch together, or when Melissa combed her hair on the bus. Deborah's chest tickled at her touch, a flutter of hummingbird wings within her heart. She was so scared, though, so scared to say anything, to do anything. What if she were wrong? What if Melissa didn't have the same feelings? What if she would think her disgusting and never talk to her again?

Then Melissa got sick. The kind of sick you read about in newspapers.

Deborah could barely breathe. She could not imagine a world with-out Melissa, without the person who made her look forward to waking. Just to glance her way in the hallway made day worth being day. How could this be? How could whoever does such things do such a thing?

It happened in the high school gym.

Deborah and Melissa were putting away volleyballs in the storage room. Melissa, in loose blue gym shorts, sitting on a rolled-up gymnastic mat, showed Deborah her leg, where the cancer was. Deborah knelt and put her hand on Melissa's knee, hating what was beneath the skin, the unseen sickness inside, the other thing that was in the room with them now. She could feel its presence. She stroked Melissa's leg, feeling for it, but felt only smoothness and warmth. She bent and kissed her knee. Holily. She kissed it again and again and again and again and prayed to God to make the disease go away and leave Melissa alone. When she looked up, Melissa was smiling.

Deborah's neck and chest blushed warm. She rose higher and kissed Melissa on the mouth. No hesitation, no awkwardness. A naked, unbound, long kiss. And Melissa kissed her back, all wanting, all willingness, all acceptance and ease, all which cannot be said, all which cannot be described in words, was in that kiss. Deborah's body felt as if it should burst. She could not stop kissing Melissa, barely could she find time to breathe as her hands touched her every part. She wanted to travel the whole of her, every turn and curve and rise of her body, to feel it and taste it and sear it into her memory. She wanted herself and Melissa to be inside each other, to pass into one another; she wanted to devour her and keep her safe and whole within her own belly, safe from the cancer, safe from the world. It was all heat and breath and love and giving and generous and natural—and, god, so easy, so, so easy—so like the person that Deborah had always known she was. She had finally become the person walking before her, the one who had always been just a few steps ahead, waiting for her to catch up.

She had arrived now, and she and her other self breathed as one.

And she and Melissa breathed as one.

And now this had happened.

Tom Ellison finished up his paperwork and headed home. He pulled the squad car into his driveway and got out, noticing for a moment what a warm, listless night it was. He went into his unlocked house, placed his car keys on a table just inside the front door, and fingered through the mail.

He walked down a short hallway lined with family photographs, oak framed and neatly arranged on the wall. He took a moment to look at them. In one, his daughter, Deborah, was wearing a white lace dress and a flowered veil, her hands, gloved in white, held before her in prayer. She was smiling. She had an amazing smile, wide mouthed and full. The picture hung slightly askew next to a silhouette profile she'd made of herself in the third grade, cut out of black construction paper. Beneath these two pictures, on an oak side table polished to a golden sheen, were three photograph albums: one for Deborah, the cover hand-colored by herself; one for her brother, Braden; and one for the family. Tom's wife, Deanne, was an avid scrapbooker.

If you had been standing there, in Tom Ellison's quiet hallway, on the freshly cleaned carpet, and you had reached down and flipped open Deborah's photo album, you would have seen a picture of her in diapers, straddling a baby walker, playing in the ankle-high water of the lake in Winsome Bay. Even as an infant, her smile is what you would have noticed first. If you looked down a little farther, on the same page, you'd have seen a photo of her at three years old, standing in the same lake, a clump of marsh weeds balanced on her head. Two plastic-covered pages farther in, Deborah wears a sparkly red dress, red leotards, and tap shoes. If you kept turning and reached the high school pages, you would have seen her at fourteen in a blue-and-white Wildcats uniform, her softball cap pulled down low on her forehead, prepared to bat and trying to look very serious, but you'd still have been able to see the grin beneath. On the next page, at fifteen, she holds a twenty-three-inch walleye, caught while vacationing with the family at Lake Sinissipi, her hair wildly fat and funny, her cheeks burnished red from the wind, smiling a smile that would have made you smile to look at it.

At sixteen she stops smiling.

Tom Ellison continued down the hallway into the kitchen. He flipped on the light. On his way to the fridge he saw the flashing red button on his answering machine. The ringer is always off after midnight because so many people call his house directly instead of the police station. He's told people time and again to call the nonemergency number or 911, but having grown up in Winsome, and knowing just about everyone there, he still gets calls for everything from stray cats to drunks at the Dew Drop Inn to shot-up mailboxes. A rash of lawn globe thefts had been the big case last year.

Tom went over to the answering machine and tapped the Play button. The message was garbled. He played it again. Jotted down the time. Deanne leaned into the kitchen doorway, shielding her eyes, and Tom apologized for waking her.

"You coming to bed?" she asked.

"Not just yet."

"Why, what now?"

"Nothing. Go on back to sleep. It's only Helga." Tom headed back down the hallway for his keys. "I couldn't make out what she was saying. I don't know, a dead animal or something out by the highway. Be back in a bit."

Kevin Lachlan sat in his car and lit a cigarette. Parked in a clearly marked No Parking zone in front of the Bank Street Diner, he didn't care if his car got booted or towed away. Actually, he hoped it would so he wouldn't have to return to work and face the little bitch Mara Davies again, a spiky-haired witch who color-coordinated her eyeglass frames with whatever too-tight skirt she'd slithered into that morning, a woman too old for her hip hairdos and too short for the three-inch spike heels she liked to *ka-lick* around in every day. One stupid night, a drunken night he couldn't even remember, and he'd been paying for it ever since.

Lachlan cranked the AC and opened the window. He wanted two minutes of peace and quiet. The day was only going to get worse, he could feel it. Mara had set the meeting up without asking him and the last thing he wanted to do today was listen to some hack children's book writer perform a dog and pony show she'd probably memorized out of *Guerrilla Marketing for the Writer*. Give me grownups, for fuck's sake, he thought, flicking his cigarette out the window, I want to work with grownups. He shouldered open the car door and headed into the diner.

The Bank Street was the only place in Chicago Lachlan knew of where you could still smoke. Not that it was legal there, they just didn't care. Somebody on the payroll somewhere. He spotted the woman he'd come to meet right away. She was sitting in a booth and waving at him as if she knew him. He gave a half wave back as the owner of the diner took off his glasses and stepped from behind the register. He whispered something in Lachlan's ear.

Jillian McClay had allowed enough time for traffic jams, flat tires, wrong directions, road construction, lack of parking, and unforeseen acts of God—none of which she encountered—and arrived in downtown Chicago an hour before her meeting with Kevin Lachlan, editor of the *American Forum* magazine. The first thing she did when she got there was buy a pack of cigarettes. Whenever she traveled more than an hour from home she became a smoker again. Like tax deductions, rules were different out-of-town.

Walking into the Bank Street Diner, she first thought that she either was in the wrong place or had wandered onto the set of a Quentin Tarantino movie. The Bank Street looked like the scene of some Slovakian mob hit waiting to happen. When she came through the door, the entire staff paused in their routines and stared. The cook, watching her, set two dishes on the countertop so slowly that neither plate made a sound. The waitresses, staring, kept doing whatever it was they were doing—serving, counting cash—only they did it slower. Even the overhead fans turned with deliberateness. Bad country music was playing, and dying aloe plants were splayed against the windows of each booth as if gut shot.

Jillian stood by the door and waited to be seated. A man with a face like work walked toward her. Middle aged and oddly handsome in the way that ugly men can sometimes be handsome, he sipped his coffee and nodded to her. He wore black-rimmed glasses, a black suit, gray tie, and gray sweater. A charcoal man. He handed Jillian a menu heavy with plastic. "Sit, please, where you like," he said in a soft accent that, although pleasant, somehow conveyed the sense that he was a person one was never to screw around with, like one of those quiet neighbors you read about who work in their garages late at night carving tiny wooden Santas and are later discovered to have been guilty of genocide somewhere in the Balkans.

Jillian slid into a booth, avoiding the tangle of dead plant limbs hanging off the windowsill, and took out her cigarettes. An older man in a black suit, gray vest and tie, looking much like a twin of the charcoal man, slipped in from between the kitchen's swinging doors. He circled the room silently, paused near the front door, looked out the windows, and then glided, shark-like, back into the kitchen. Jillian dragged over an ashtray, lit her cigarette, and scanned the room. She couldn't write a place like this if she wanted to. The employees all looked as if they belonged to some vaguely Slavic mafia with an enforced dress code of black and gray and instructions to move more slowly than normal people. They sported runway-worthy scowls and smoked cigarettes like they were inhaling sex. Jillian envied the fact that they still smoked in restaurants in Chicago. And still had sex.

A pretty waitress, late twenties maybe, walked past Jillian's booth. She had dark waist-length hair and wore a gray polo and black spandex pants. She had a pot of coffee in each hand and drifted through the diner topping off customers' cups. She walked over to Jillian's booth, well aware that every man in the place was staring at her and looking like she could care less.

"You know what you like?" she asked in a weary Euro-something accent.

"Just coffee, please," she said, reading *Fenyana* on the girl's skinny name tag.

The waitress filled Jillian's cup, spilling coffee into the saucer beneath and looking completely bored. Bored and beautiful. Not Hollywood beautiful, deeply beautiful. A plain face, new and undented, and breasts that whispered, "We're young, we're young." As she walked away, Jillian snuck a look down at her own breasts, adjusted her blouse, nostalgically, and sucked her belly a little farther behind the waist of her jeans.

On her second cup of coffee she saw Kevin Lachlan walk in. Not quite fat, pudgy, a bright red face, salt-and-pepper hair. He was dressed well: suit, dark blue and double-breasted. She'd seen his picture in the magazine, but he looked older in person. Jillian caught his eye with a wave just as the man in gray walked from behind the counter and whispered something to him. Lachlan smiled at the man and then headed toward Jillian. She stubbed out her cigarette and stepped out of the booth.

"Jillian McClay," she said, holding out her hand.

"Kevin Lachlan," he said. "Thanks for driving in."

Lachlan took off his jacket, and they both slid into the booth. He'd already sweated through his shirt. "So," he said, "Mara speaks highly of you." He set his iPhone down on the table and turned up his coffee cup. "You two been friends long?"

"We met at the book expo about fifteen years ago."

The waitress with the beautiful everything came over and filled Lachlan's cup without asking. "Cream," he said, not looking up. He was about to say something else when his iPhone spun in a half circle on the table before him. He groaned slightly. "Sorry, I have to get this."

Jillian waited as he listened to the message. Lachlan smiled, trying to fill the awkward silence, saying, "Mara really likes your books, by the way. I haven't had a chance to read them yet."

Neither has anyone else, Jillian thought.

The waitress brought over a tiny bowl mounded with containers of cream.

"Eat?" she asked, setting it down.

Lachlan, still listening to his messages, glanced at his watch and said no.

"You?" she asked Jillian.

"No, thanks."

The waitress left and Lachlan put down his phone. "Sorry about that." He emptied a few creams into his coffee. "So," he said, "this idea, this story of yours. Talk to me."

Jillian lit another cigarette. "Mr. Lachlan," she said, "I'm sure you're very busy. I drove three and half hours and I have to be back by five, so here's the pitch. If you don't like it, thanks for your time."

Lachlan took a long sip of his coffee, and said, "Go."

"Winsome Bay, Wisconsin. Bucolic small-town America. Apple pie, county fairs, Corn Queens, unlocked doors. Then a murder. The brutal killing of a young girl. First murder in the town in sixty years. A sort of *Fargo* meets *Northern Exposure* meets *In Cold Blood*. A killer on the loose. Will it happen again? Weekly installments written in chapters. Creative nonfiction." Jillian leaned into the table. "A true crime story evolving in real time. The reader gets *my* point of view, not some famous author who churns out a book a month, or brilliant about-to-retire detective on his last case, but me, someone who usually writes children's books and has never even been on a crime scene before. Someone who doesn't like dead bodies. Someone who is scared to even put this murder down on paper."

"What murder?" Lachlan asked.

"Deborah Ellison. It happened a week ago."

"I've heard the name."

"The girl in Wisconsin."

"I read about it."

"They found her body in the town right next to mine."

Despite his best efforts not to, Lachlan began to listen more closely. "Tell me more."

"Here's the angle. I don't apologize for my lack of experience, or my fears, I *write* about them. I write about the very same fears my reader has. This story is bound to get ugly, lurid, unimaginably horrific, and I want to make the reader complicit with every turn of the page, just as I'm complicit every time I write one. Our reader doesn't have to go on. They can put the story down. I don't have to write it. I can stick to children's books. But neither of us stops. Just like the killer who could have stopped, but didn't." Jillian mashed her cigarette into the ashtray. "That's what I want to write about."

Lachlan waved for more coffee. "Any suspects?"

"No. But I've already interviewed a few people from the town who knew the victim and her family, and I've got a meeting set up with the chief of police there."

"You think there's enough to make a serial out of it?"

Jillian took a thin manuscript out of her bag and placed it on the table. "This is rough. There's enough there for two, maybe three installments."

Lachlan took up the pages and leafed through them, silent for a moment. Small-town murder, he thought, rural Midwest, it might sell. Might even increase sales in Iowa and Minnesota. He could make an offer: option to publish upon approval, no advance. Not much risk.

"Mr. Lachlan," Jillian said, "I can write this."

Lachlan looked across the table and held out his hand.

"Call me Kevin."

•

J. McClay/Killing/American Forum

The Killing of Deborah Ellison

Three and a half hours northwest of Chicago, deep in the hinterlands of Wisconsin, I drove past a sign that said Welcome to Winsome Bay, Home of the Wildcats. As I took the next left, a rural, angled lane, the inside of my car suddenly shadowed and cooled as an endless emerald wall appeared out my driver's-side window: Corn, corn was everywhere, thick leaved, rainforest green, eight to ten feet tall. Every square foot of earth in Winsome Bay that didn't have a house on it seemed to have corn growing on it. If not corn, then soybeans or hay: timothy grass, bluestem, red clover, alfalfa. I continued driving, passing field after field of green gridded farmland, the crops pushing right up to the backyards of homes and businesses.

West of the Wisconsin River, just below Friendship, Winsome Bay doesn't have a bay at all but a medium-sized lake, one of over fifteen thousand left behind after the glaciers melted away some ten thousand years ago. No one in the town seemed to know why the lake was called a bay when it wasn't one, and no one really seemed very interested in the question. The town had a population of 632 and boasted a high school, a public swimming pool, three churches, and four bars. A sign on the local liquor store said Wine, Cheese, and Bait.

Night crawlers were $2.50 a dozen.

Jillian saved her document, scrolled up to the top, and began editing the first few paragraphs of her new story. At five that morning, she had hobbled into her sweatpants, hustled down the stairs to the kitchen, poured a thermos of coffee—preperked on a timer—and headed out the back door, wide awake and ready to work. She'd tugged open the creaky barn door of her writing studio, a converted carriage house in her backyard, and made her way up the stairs, avoiding whatever spider webs and bat guano had accumulated overnight. She unlocked the door and hit the lights. She had tried writing in the house when Michael was little, but found it torture. At fourteen now, he was used to waking up alone. He'd been making his own breakfast since he was seven. In the days when he still liked Jillian, he used to take breakfast out to her studio: badly microwaved eggs, cold toast, too chocolaty chocolate milk, and a small alp of ketchup. A lifetime ago. Before iPhones and puberty.

Jillian poured another cup of coffee.

She hadn't been this focused and ready to write in a long time.

Farther into Winsome Bay the farmland was interrupted by a smattering of residential streets and a small downtown. The streets there, double-wide with angled parking stalls, were lined with a modern Midwest mix of pickup trucks and minivans. The oldest building, a restaurant called the Grainery, has been in business since 1873.

I drove past a fabric store with a quilt and an American flag hanging in the window. I passed the Dew Drop Inn tavern, a sign on its door touting the Friday night fish fry and prime rib special. I continued on, out of the downtown area, past Saint Francis church, a gorgeous red-stoned cathedral in the style of Frank Lloyd Wright, whose architectural school, Taliesin, only two hours from Winsome Bay, still functions today. I thought the church to be quite modern looking for a small Midwest town: single storied, sleek and low to the ground, its lengthy run of roof dipping gently in the center and gradually rising to peaks on either end. One wall of the building, from peak to foundation, was made entirely of stained glass, in deep cerulean blues and ruby reds.

I stopped and got out of my car to take a look, catching the faint smell of pig manure in the air, or, as it's more commonly referred to here, "the smell of money." Walking into the hushed lobby I felt as if I were in somebody else's house and they weren't home. Behind glass doors to my right I could make out the altar and a wide expanse of pews before it. The room was streaked with the colors of the stained-glass windows, their beams drifting silently across oaken pews in steep angles as the sun flitted in and out of clouds outside. The sacristy was made of numerous panes of glass, framed in golden oak, as was everything in the church. Oak abounded, honey colored.

Its splendor stilled me.

I took a few notes, returned to my car, and as I pulled away I noticed a new playground going up beside the church, donated, as a sign said, by the Elks Club. A flight of boys on mountain bikes squealed by, popping wheelies and laughing, trying to outrun the last few weeks of summer. On the corner of Erlanger and Mill Road a brown-haired girl, maybe twelve, in an orange tube top and denim shorts, sold sweet corn pyramided high before her on a rusty-legged card table. All this and many other such summer sunset scenes were playing out along the peaceful streets of Winsome Bay. I saw no signs, however, that this was a town where a young girl had recently been horribly, brutally murdered.

At the end of their senior year, Gary and Neal Peterson posted a comment on Facebook saying that Melissa Becker and Deborah

Ellison should run for "Queen and Queen" of the prom. Until then the relationship had been pretty discreet, but still, people talked. Plus Gary and Neal had had no luck trying to have sex with Deborah or Melissa all through high school so they had to find some other reason for being turned down besides their own inherent repulsiveness.

The summer before senior year, Melissa lost her leg to the cancer. Deborah had stayed with her as much as possible through the whole ordeal: the follow-ups, the chemo, radiation, physical therapy. Insurance covered only the most basic prosthesis, so Deborah helped organize a fund-raiser to buy Melissa a top-of-the-line artificial leg. She even got along with her mother then, and despite the cancer, it was a good time, a close time, when everyone in Winsome seemed to be a little more thankful for the things they had, when people acted just a little kinder. But that was before it all came out and the town discovered that there was "something going on" between Melissa and Deborah.

"Why are you doing this to us?" her father screamed at her. "Why?"

"Oh my god—this has nothing to do with you!"

"It doesn't? You know what they're saying about us? The whole town?"

"I could care less what this stupid town thinks!"

"Well, you're going to start caring." He grabbed Deborah's scrapbook off the hallway table. "This is done! You hear me? It's over!" He tore out the pictures of Melissa.

"Dad, please, no! Dad, stop!"

Deborah's mother stepped into the hallway, "Tom! Tom, what are you—"

He whirled on her, "Shut up! Get the—just shut up!"

She retreated to the kitchen, noticeably smaller. The incredible shrinking woman. All fog and vodka. Deborah tried to grab the book from her father, but he wrenched it away, knocking her to the ground. He raised his hand to strike her, but stopped suddenly, his arm trembling. "When you're eighteen," he said, calmly, "you do whatever you want, but until then, while I'm feeding you and putting clothes on your back, you do what I say. Do you understand me?"

Nothing from Deborah.

He laid out each word for emphasis. "Do you understand me?"

She nodded.

Her father left the house.

Deborah gathered up the pieces of Melissa's pictures.

Her mother stayed in the kitchen the rest of the night.

Later, when things calmed down, Deborah's mother tried to reason with her husband, tried to get him to understand his daughter, or at least to have a mature discussion about the situation. It didn't work. He wasn't built for that kind of conversation. Each attempt quickly escalated into what Deborah called an adult version of a temper tantrum, born of an inherited ignorance, which, tick-like, only burrowed deeper when challenged.

Her mother then brought over the local priest to talk with Deborah and her father. Maybe he could help, she'd thought. But no. The subject was far outside his scope of practice, and the painfully awkward counseling sessions invariably ended up with a generic prescription to pray. So Tom Ellison, devout man that he was, dragged his daughter to church every Sunday and knelt beside her on the bishop's spanking new and improved kneelers and made her pray for forgiveness. And she did. She prayed just as she'd been taught. She prayed with every cell in her body and her mind and her heart, and she squeezed her thin fingers together till they hurt and she dug her skinny knees into those friggin' kneelers and she asked her God, with an open heart, she asked him or her or whomever, she asked to know that if this was wrong, if what she felt for Melissa was evil, if it was this horrible abomination that her father kept screaming about, then he or she or whoever should let her know it right then and there.

He or she or whoever made no response.

It was the great scandal of the town, that shithole town with all its petty, ignorant people who had nothing better to do with their time than trying to justify their own worthless existences by trashing everybody else's. Nobody posted comments on Facebook about the not-so-secret drunks in Winsome Bay, or the women sleeping with other women's husbands, or the men having sex with girls twenty years younger than them, or the graying front-pew couple in church who never missed a Sunday but watched hardcore porn behind locked doors while their kids machine-gunned people into masses of bloody flesh on the newest Xbox slaughter game; nobody posted comments about the girls who drank, or did pot or meth or coke, or who had been having sex since they were twelve—no, nobody called Father Ryan and tried to help *them*.

That summer the girls were kept apart. Deborah worked at the Subs 'n' Spuds sandwich shop. Dropped off, picked up, and curfewed. Melissa was sent to a camp for disabled athletes in Pennsylvania for six weeks. She returned in August, and still, the families kept them apart. And after the graffiti on the school walls, and the prank phone calls, and Facebook, and the textings, after the looks and the sneers and the laughter from the righteous and religious, Melissa Becker's family moved to Minnesota.

Deborah went off to college in La Crosse.

Melissa died in November.

The cancer had come back. In her lymph system and lungs.

Something spilled out of Deborah that day and never filled again. She had sex, she had relationships, but she never felt that thing again, that flutter in her heart. Her parents had been paying for college and now it made her physically sick to take their money. She dropped out of school and moved back to Winsome. She didn't know why; it was the last place on earth she wanted to be. To spite her parents maybe, she thought, to spite the whole town. She lived in a rundown apartment by the lake. She avoided her parents. Avoided friends. Her father tried to make contact with her. She wouldn't respond to him or anyone. And then the drinking started, and the drugs, and the tattoos, and the piercings—she wanted to do things to her body, to brand it, to cut it, to use her body like a huge fuck you scream. She slept with women. They meant nothing. She slept with men. They meant less. She hitched rides to Chicago and whored herself there to pay for drugs and rent. She had sex with Winsome men on drunken nights back at her apartment, thinking, *How's this, Dad? Is this better? Are you happy now? Huh? Are you and Father Ryan and God okay with me now?!*

And it might have gone on like that.

But that she met someone.

On a good day of writing, when the ideas were really coming, 5:30 in the morning couldn't come quickly enough for Jillian. On a bad day, she dreaded the eerie blue numbers on her digital alarm more than estimated taxes. On this morning, out in her office, writing, coffee in hand by 5:38, the ideas were coming. She'd had a phone interview the day before with a young officer on the Winsome Bay police force, Dan Ehrlich.

Winsome Bay has always been a great place to raise kids. People still leave their doors unlocked and the keys in their cars. You can forget your money at any of the stores in town and come back later to pay, and mail with just your name on it will still find its way to your house.

Mixed in with the local population of Winsome Bay are a lot of refugees, as officer Dan Ehrlich told me, an unassuming man who sounded too young to be a police officer. "Refugees," he elaborated, are people who have left big cities like New York or Chicago to settle out in the country. Some seem to be running away from something, others seem to be running toward something. They've brought a little diversity to the town too, which ethnically looks a bit like a modern-day Viking settlement: fair skinned, blond, and blue eyed. There are also a number of "hippie types" living around Winsome, said Ehrlich, quickly adding that he meant no disrespect by the term. He stammered the slightest bit before explaining further. A lot of them had moved into the houses of farms that had failed in the late seventies. The two-hundred-acre farms, chopped up and auctioned off into forty-acre lots, were ideal for growing organic produce. A pretty good crowd shows up every Saturday when these farm families come into town in their rubber boots, rain slickers, and Rastafarian hairdos to sell vegetables at the Winsome Bay Farmers' Market, which basically consists of two pickup trucks and a few old card tables. "They're a bit different at some things," Ehrlich said, "but if weren't for them, there'd be hardly any farming going on here at all."

This still beautiful community is in danger of being transformed into what most small towns outside of larger cities look like today: a jammed conglomeration of fast-food chains, gas-grocery-liquor stores, and used-car dealerships. Urban sprawl is spreading, quickly, and its negative impact on rural America is undeniable: reduced green space and animal habitats, pollution, economic disparity, petty crime, and drugs. Heroin has had an alarming resurgence here, as well as crystal meth and marijuana.

And now, a murder.

Today, there is a little less winsomeness in Winsome Bay.

Jillian took a break and went back to the house to make some breakfast.

Maybe all of her morning's work wouldn't make it into the final draft, but she thought that fleshing out the location and the feel of the town would help her readers get a greater sense of the world in which this horrible story happened.

The story.

Jillian had been waiting for it to show itself, for it to tassel itself out of the images she'd been living with for so long. That's the way it usually happened for Jillian: An image would strike her and, for some reason, would not leave her alone. It would hound her thoughts. Then she would start to see similar patterns everywhere she looked. The earliest promptings for her story had begun showing themselves long before the murder had even happened.

Jillian had been driving home from a swim meet with Michael. It was late. As they drove into town, they passed a carnival, one of those traveling companies you often see in school or church parking lots: kind of seedy, kind of fun, all the rides just a little too greasy and dirty, like the people running them. This one had been set up on a large expanse of lawn in front of the high school. A giant red-and-white-striped tent stood center, patched up and stitched together with wide knots of graying sutures, mendings from years of teardowns and put-ups. There were games and rides, loud mechanical music, food stations, barkers, a glittering of colored lights flashing on and off everywhere you looked—a mobile Chuck E. Cheese, only outdoors. As Jillian drove past, Michael asked if they could stop. It was late and she was tired, so Jillian said they could go tomorrow. They won't be there tomorrow, Michael complained, they'll be gone. Of course they'll be there, Jillian said. They've just set everything up. They'll be there for the whole weekend.

The next morning the carnival was gone. Completely. Nothing, not a piece of litter left behind. The only thing left was the massive impression it had made on the ground. The grasses had all been matted down where it once stood, a footprint the size of half a football field. For months Jillian had no idea why that image stayed with her. Then, over time, its meaning started to show itself—or she started to *give* it meaning—she wasn't exactly sure how it worked. She started to believe that the image had something to do with a *disappearing* of some kind. How could something so vibrant, so big, have vanished so quickly? The impression marks obsessed her, the matted-down image of the grasses, the *footprints* that people or things leave behind after their actual physical presence is gone.

Then she read about the disappearance of a young Chicago woman and the discovery of her body in the small town of Winsome Bay, not far from her home. In the article, the woman who had discovered the body described what she had first seen as a dark *impression* in a grassy field. The hay in this area had all been matted down, leaving a shadowy *footprint* of the body.

A body.

That's what her writer's mind had been hovering around. As soon as she'd read about the murder, the ideas in her mind started to click. She knew a story was there, a good story, and one that only she could write. It felt very odd when she'd first read about the killing in her local paper, but also very right. The words used to describe the discovery of the body were nearly identical to Jillian's own musings about the disappearing carnival. It was as if the image in her head had refused to leave until it found the story it belonged to, as if it somehow knew that Deborah Ellison was going to be murdered. In Jillian's still creepier Stephen King–like thoughts, it almost felt as if her image had caused the murder. A pang of guilt flitted through her as she thought this, but she chased it away. It was ridiculous. No, if anything, she was feeling more and more that she was being drawn to this story for some greater reason. Deborah Ellison's story needed to be told. A young life so horribly ended. And now her obsession had purpose. Yes, yes, she thought, realizing that it was a very different story she was writing this time.

And it wasn't for children.

Deborah stacked the plastic plates she'd bought at Saint Vincent De-Paul's into an empty, newspaper-lined, white cupboard. They reminded her of the miniature mess kit plates that she used to play with as a little girl, part of a collection of G.I. Joe accessories that she'd bought for twenty-five cents at a yard sale, for her Barbie doll. G.I. Joe's mini mess kit opened on a flimsy plastic hinge. One half of it was a frying pan and the other was a tiny gray tray divided into three separate compartments to keep G.I. Joe's—now Barbie's—food in order. There was a teeny fork and a teeny knife and an even teenier cup. Deborah used to take sandwich meat and tear off a little piece and put it into the largest section of the plate to look like a steak. A pea or a kernel of corn would go into the next largest section, and nothing for dessert. Even though Barbie hiked trails, built lean-tos, and chopped firewood, she still had to watch her figure.

Deborah's new used plates had three sections too, just like Barbie's, only Deborah's weren't battleship gray, they were bright orange. Everything else in the apartment was white, one of those Chicago flats that had once been trimmed out in natural woods and ornate moldings until the landlord painted over everything in a quest for maintenance-free living units. Year after year, new white paint had been slopped over old white paint until there were virtually no distinctions left—white walls fading into white cupboards fading into white doors fading into white rooms fading.

Featureless.

Until Deborah moved in.

On this day, approaching night, cardboard boxes littered the floor amid scatterings of old newspapers. Deborah sorted through the few belongings she'd taken with her and placed and hung and shelved them around the room: a crimson red picture frame, sky blue pillows, a penguin snow globe, a purple shower curtain with clownfish swimming across it, a bright green swath of remnant fabric she was determined to find a use for, and a gold acrylic candy bowl she'd made herself in ninth grade art class.

The apartment brightened.

She had met someone.

Even Lambeau, the lime green parakeet she'd brought with her, was happy. He chirped and chirped. Rooting for her, she liked to think. A Packers bird in Bears country. She grabbed up the remnant, draped it over the cage, and Lambeau fell silent. She unpacked her last box, taking out hotel soap bars and mini shampoo bottles, a thick clutch of Culver's napkins, a short blue-and-yellow kimono, socks—lots of socks, multicolored socks with individually colored toes—and her photo album. The cover on the photo album, hand drawn with crayons when she was in high school, read "Deb's Mems." It was empty now, but for a few old pictures that she'd managed to save. She would fill it soon, though, with other photos, she would fill it with a whole new life.

Deborah had been unpacking, and hitting garage sales and thrift stores, and cleaning all day. It was hot (no air-conditioning) and she was exhausted (no bed), so she cleared a space in the middle of the living room and stretched out on the cool hardwood floor. She took off her T-shirt and wiped the sweat from her face and neck. She took off her bra and stripped down to her lavender panties and lay there staring up at the white, cracked ceiling. She was so glad to be out of Winsome Bay, out of her shitty apartment by the lake, away from her father, and Gary and Neal, and everybody else there. Finally on her own.

She felt, and then could hear, the rumble of the "L" train. It trembled her body and felt good. She closed her eyes.

I feel like me again, she thought, and heard a door scrape open.

Fenyana came out of the bathroom. Deborah was lying in the middle of the living room like a magnificent nude figurine that had been un-packed from one of the boxes and not yet shelved. She lay there, very still, her eyes closed, like a brightly tattooed doll, a living matryoshka, vined and birded in rosehip reds and linden greens, her trimmed nest a soft lavender hill, her butterfly breasts, inked in monarch orange and blacks, her white thighs leafed dark lilac.

Fenyana walked over to Deborah, who smiled at the sound of her steps. She knelt beside her and whispered very softly, "Do not open your eyes."

Deborah stayed very still.

Fenyana grazed the little doll's lips with hers, but did not kiss them. Deborah's lashes fluttered to stay closed as Fenyana whisper-kissed the length of her body, letting her long hair drag slowly over the so small breasts, her soft lovely stomach, her hips, then down, down to her own self, and there, the arched backs pleading, and then, "Fenyana, Fenyana," cried the little doll as they lost themselves into one another, into feelings that swelled their hearts as if to burst and blushed their bodies red.

"I am filled with you," Fenyana said, barely breath enough to speak. "I am drowning in you."

Jillian sat at the Amish-built picnic table in her backyard talking with her friend Mara Davies and enjoying a much needed glass of wine. A beautiful summer afternoon, cool and still.

"Look at those clouds," she said, leaning back.

If Jillian wanted, she could have had many friends, but she tended to stay to herself. She had friends, of course, particularly since she was always hanging out with the other moms at Michael's swim meets and baseball games, but she didn't socialize much outside of that. Especially since the divorce. It had been amicable, as amicable as divorces can be, but Nick had always been the favorite of their friends. He was lightness and fun, he was the talker and the laugher and the planner. Not that Jillian couldn't be fun also, but she generally took a back seat to his enthusiasm. And she didn't mind that, no, actually she liked it. She was, by nature, a little more thoughtful and quiet, perhaps too pensive at times, so, socially, their combination worked well. Everyone assumed they had the perfect mix of personalities. And Jillian did too. So it was quite a knee to the stomach when Nick left her for a slightly older, but very lithe and blithe, yoga instructor. A *yoga* instructor? she'd thought. Really? Could you at least *try* to be original?

Jillian and Mara had met years earlier at the American Library Association's expo when Jillian's first book came out, when she still dreamed about a Newbery Award and the call from Oprah. She and Mara had been good friends ever since, long distance friends though, as Jillian rarely got to Chicago. But Mara's work often took her to the neighboring cities of Madison and Milwaukee, and when it did they always tried to get together somewhere.

Mara reached under the picnic table and lifted a large fabric book bag onto her lap. She pulled out a thick stack of magazines and spread them across the table: ten copies of the latest *American Forum*.

Jillian let out a small squeak of joy. Her second installment.

"So what do you think?" Mara asked. "You happy with them?"

Jillian fanned open one of the magazines and breathed in the glossy smell. "Yes, yes, yes!" She flipped through it and found her story. She loved seeing her own words in print, her name in the byline.

"It's going well," Mara said. "Kevin likes your writing."

"Really? He does? Really?"

"Yes."

"I can't tell. He doesn't say much, just sends me notes."

"He's not the most personable guy, but he's a good editor." Mara sipped her wine. "You meeting your deadlines okay?"

"Yeah, no problem. I mean, it's a lot different from writing a novel, but I love it. I don't wake up every morning thinking, 'Oh my god, I have to write a novel today.'"

The only problem Jillian *was* having was that she needed more material. She had to get to Winsome Bay for more interviews: the police, doctors, family and friends, teachers, maybe the coroner. But between Michael's swim meets and summer basketball camp, and working concessions at the games and helping the boosters, she hadn't been able to get away. On her first trip to Winsome very few people were willing to talk, but she'd gathered enough information from phone interviews, the local papers, and public records to piece together the first few articles. But she knew so little about Deborah Ellison. Nobody would talk about her. Jillian knew her readers needed to know much more about the murder victim—her life, her aspirations—to have any empathy for her, but all she could learn was that the victim had abruptly left Winsome and moved to Chicago some time ago, and that she was the daughter of a local police officer. Nobody would tell her anything else. No known address. No phone number. No visits home. Nothing. Her life, work history, relationships were all a mystery. Deborah Ellison had virtually disappeared from Winsome Bay two years before her body had been discovered there.

"Well, here's to you," Mara said, holding out her glass.

"You mean, to you."

"It was your idea. You pitched it."

"You set up the meeting."

"Well, yes, I did."

They clinked glasses.

"I'm so glad you're here," Jillian said. "I miss you."

"Move to Chicago."

"Move here."

"I wish."

"No, you don't. Not really." Jillian topped off her glass of wine. She took a glance toward Michael's bedroom window. "Light a cigarette so I can have a drag."

"He knows you smoke, Jillian."

"I quit again."

Mara lit a cigarette and passed it to Jillian, who took a few drags, holding it under the picnic table. "So," Jillian said, "how's Steven? You're still seeing each other, right?"

"Oh, yeah, we're fine, fine. We have a recreational relationship. It's fun. It's fine. It's not going anywhere. Works for both of us. It's very user-friendly." Mara looked up at the sky. "Maybe I should move out here," she said. "Find a nice country guy."

"You'd implode out here, Mara."

"What? I could do the rural thing."

"Mara. There's no Michigan Avenue here, no Grant Park, no cabs, no symphony. Our idea of clubbing is a Friday night fish fry, and there's not a good cappuccino for fifty miles. Believe me, I tried the country guy thing."

"How is Nick?" Mara asked. "You hear from him?"

"Sometimes," Jillian said. "We get along fine. He's good with Michael."

"Is he liking Florida?"

"He loves it. Never has to shovel a sidewalk again."

"Is he seeing anyone? Dating?"

Jillian tried to fill Mara's glass of wine. "Drink with me."

"Whoa, whoa," she said, covering her glass. "I'm driving."

"Oh, just stay, stay the night."

"I can't. I have to get going."

"Oh, come on. Please?"

"I can't. I'm meeting Steven at the Nite Cap. I promised."

The back door opened and Jillian thrust her cigarette at Mara. "Shit, take this, take it."

Michael came out, shirtless and in shorts. "Hi, Mara."

"Hi."

"I got a game tomorrow, Mom," he said. "I need my uniform washed."

"I already did it, honey. It's in the laundry room."

"Thanks," he said, walking away. "Bye, Mara."

"Bye."

He yelled back before he stepped inside. "Shouldn't smoke, Mom."

"Shit."

"I have to go," Mara said, laughing. "I love you. Call me."

The woman pulled her hair over to the side and took a long, lazy drag of her cigarette. Sitting on the edge of the bed, she searched the sheets for her underwear. Kevin Lachlan, tying his shoes, felt himself thicken again just watching her. She tugged on a T-shirt so gauzy thin that the dark puddle around her nipples seeped through. She leaned forward on her elbows, resting for a moment. Lachlan walked over and stood in front of her. He stroked her face toward himself, but she pulled away and dropped her head between her splayed knees, her T-shirt riding high up her swayed back, her beautiful back, her young back, with a zigzag of tiny moles across it. God, she was gorgeous. He wanted her again.

She didn't want him.

"No tip for you today," he said, trying to be funny.

He wasn't.

He tossed an envelope on the bed and made a pot of coffee.

The woman walked over to the window. The sun was just coming up over Lake Michigan, bulging the horizon and tinting the Gold Coast's high-rises pink. She watched it break free from the water, which kidnapped it every night, as her grandmother once told her, kidnapped it and held it deep in the depths where dragons slept and thunder was brewed, but at dawn each day the angry sun would turn the lake into a caldron and burn itself free, as it was doing right now, streaking the edge of the eastern sky red. She slid the tall window open a crack and flicked her cigarette out. It fell to the pavement below, hardly varying its course. Already the day was hot. She felt the sludgy air worming its way into the air-conditioned room.

"Hey," Lachlan called to her. "Let's go. I have work to do."

She slid the window shut. "Cab?" she asked.

"Take the Red Line."

"You are too kind." She bent over and gathered up her hair. She could smell him on herself. "May I please use a shower?"

"Sorry," Lachlan said. "I've got work to do."

She pulled on her jeans and tucked in her T-shirt, wishing she knew a curse to leave him with, wishing she'd listened more closely to her grandmother's tales, her grandmother who would stick a knife into a loaf of bread and spin it on the floor whenever there was lightning, her grandmother who liked to scare her with stories of the shadow monsters who lived in bottomless puddles and cut children to pieces and ate them.

"Come on," Lachlan said, taking up a pile of submissions. "This isn't the Playboy grotto. I work for a living."

She said nothing. She cursed her secret curses, grabbed the envelope off the bed, and left. Out the apartment door, down the windowless hallway, into the mirrored elevator, taking her 30 percent out of the envelope on the way down, through the lobby and the gawking security guards, outside, muggy, the walk to the "L", the Red Line to work, crowded, hot, the stench of him on her still. Into the Bank Street Diner, busy, she handed her money over to Savva, grabbed her uniform and a dish towel, went into the bathroom, kicked off her pants and underwear and soaped herself, washing between her legs. She took off her shirt and scrubbed her stomach and breasts till they blotched red. She scrubbed them again, put on her uniform, tightened her apron, and went to work.

In his Gold Coast condo, Kevin Lachlan poured a third cup of coffee and skimmed the opening paragraph of yet another magazine submission, hoping this time to discover an original thought. He didn't. He tossed it into the trash and reached for another submission.

"The hell?" he said, examining a thick envelope.

It was one of those padded envelopes that so many writers like to use, as if there's something fragile about their stories, for Christ's sake. It was sealed, and had no postmark. Just his name was written on the envelope. There was something heavy in the bottom of it. He opened it and reached in—

"Jesus Christ!" he screamed. He dropped the envelope and backed away, fumbling for his cell phone. "Jesus fuck! FUCK!"

At the end of a long hallway, on the second floor of Chicago police headquarters, inside a room known only as Room 70, detective James Mangan waited for the shitty coffeepot to stop gurgling so he could pour himself a cup of shitty coffee. Room 70 was off limits to the public and most other detectives. The door, always shut. A handwritten note in the hallway: No Press. The room was home to the Violent Crimes Task Force—the VCTF—which investigated bank crimes, drug violations, kidnappings, and extortion. Serial killings, murder, sexual assault, and other crimes of violence, however, were given the highest priority.

As Detective Mangan waited for his coffee, he sorted through a file of his open cases—two rapes, a North Side drive-by, a robbery gone bad with a baseball bat, and a dealer thrown off a roof in the projects—thank you, good morning. He fumbled with the teeny slivered clasp of a manila envelope, opened it, and slid out an eight-by-ten photograph of a dismembered hand.

A new investigation.

He tossed the photo on the table and went over to the half-sink, strewn with dirty plates and coffee cups caked with grime. He grabbed the least filthy cup he could find and cleaned it. He was sweating already. The air-conditioning had been out for two days now. He took off his two-button wool blazer, a jacket he was rarely without, even in summer. It hid his gun well and made him look as if he was in better shape than he actually was. It also obscured the extra flesh beginning to muffin out around his waist, a thing that mortified him. He'd complained about it so much that Dr. Brian Rhys, the forensic pathologist, had recently dropped a *Men's Health* article on his desk: "101 Ways to Lose Your Gut." Mangan was going to wrap a dead salmon in it and put it in Rhys's car, but on second thought he decided to give it a try. He quit after number two: "avoid foods that come in a bag or box." He was lazier now, and he knew it. He didn't like working out anymore, didn't like running or stepping on a scale, or having to watch what he ate, and hated that his doctor had made him quit smoking. He wanted his other body back, the maintenance-free one of his youth, the one like aluminum siding that he only had to hose down once in a while.

The shitty coffeepot hissed and pissed to a finish. Mangan poured a cup and denied himself a third packet of sugar—as if that was going to make a difference—and looked more closely at the photograph of the bloodless hand on the table. He put his glasses on and read the prelim notes attached to the photo. The hand had been severed from the basilar joint of the left thumb on a clean diagonal across the wrist between the metacarpal and the trapezium bones. It is this joint, where the metacarpal bone of the thumb attaches to the trapezium bone of the wrist, that

27

allows movement of the thumb into the palm, or *opposition*, a motion that distinguishes human beings from most beasts, as Rhys liked to say.

Mangan sipped his coffee and read on.

A small-toothed serrated blade had been used to sever the hand, no trace under the fingernails, no signs of decomposition. A female appendage. A ring still on the small finger. A five-leafed clover inlaid with a greenish stone, malachite. Detailed forensic analysis was pending.

Mangan wasn't holding out much hope of finding a one-handed woman strolling along Lake Shore Drive. He knew whoever the hand belonged to was dead. The body would show up soon, though, he thought. It had been hot as hell in Chicago for weeks now, over ninety, somebody would nose her up in a few days. He read the remaining notes. The hand had been placed in an envelope addressed to a Mr. Kevin Lachlan, a magazine editor, and discovered within a box of submissions. There was no return address on the envelope. No postmark. A clerk at the front desk of the building had found the envelope in the lobby and had put it with Lachlan's other mail. A note had also been found in the envelope, allegedly written by the perpetrator. Mangan took up a photocopy of it to give it a read, when a thought sounded in his mind—a question actually—a cadence of words singing quietly in his head.

And who has cut those pretty fingers off?

"Shit," he muttered, taking off his glasses. He listened more closely.

Thou hast no hands to wipe away thy tears.

And he knew, then, that this was going to be a case that would not leave him alone. It was going to haunt him until he caught or killed whoever had done this.

What accursed hand hath made thee handless?

"Shit," he said again.

These verbal quirks, these teasings of thoughts that pinged around in Mangan's brain on occasion, always began in the same way: snatches of words, lines of poetry, minisoliloquies in his mind. And when they came to him, he paid attention, because in some strange way he knew they were there to help him. They helped him to find murderers. And no, he wasn't crazy, this wasn't ESP or psychic detecting or voodoo magic, or any fruity woo-woo crap like that.

It was just true.

At about five thirty in the morning, her mouth still tasting of sleep, Jillian did as she did every morning: filled her thermos with coffee, hobbled out her back door, and headed to her writing studio. A hazy, warm morning, muggy. She tugged open the rotted wood door of the carriage house and tripped over a lawnmower.

"Damn it."

Michael had left it just inside the doorway again. The first floor of her carriage house was filled with more crap than Jillian knew what to do with. She'd promised herself that spring, as she did every spring, that she was going to clean it out. It was now late August, her next installment on the Ellison murder was due, and she didn't have time to clean her kitchen, never mind the garage. The summer was flying by. The first few installments had gone well, but for the last week or so her writing had begun to slow. This morning it was practically sloth-like. She needed more material, but her interview with the police chief in Winsome Bay was still a day away.

She poured a cup of coffee and read through the first few installments again to see what she'd already covered. Shit, she suddenly thought, has this been done before? This whole idea, which she'd been thinking was so original—true crime, creative nonfiction—had it already been done by someone else? There's probably a movie about it already, or a TV series with absurdly beautiful people playing the leads.

Relax, she told herself, stop it. The murder was original, it couldn't help but be. So were the characters. Besides, Lachlan liked her writing. She was being published. She was getting paid. It was all okay. She stopped the looser thoughts in her brain, which, monkey-like, had a habit of leaping around unexpectedly.

She looked at the framed quote she kept next to her computer.

Just write something, she told herself.

Anything.

J. McClay/Killing/American Forum

. . . .

Nothing.

Nothing was coming.

She started looking around her office. I should vacuum in here, she thought. She checked her e-mail. She called Mara, who didn't answer. She left a long message. She wondered if she should repaint.

Focus, she told herself.

Again she read through what she'd already written. It all felt wrong. The pacing was slow, there was too much back story, too many quirky details and locations and new characters, not enough action—

Stop it, she thought, scolding herself, don't start rushing. It's not a movie script, it doesn't need heart-stopping action in every chapter, it doesn't need the obligatory sex and violence scenes this early. Pace will come, action will come. *He* will come. Whoever murdered Deborah Ellison, that is, and when he's caught she'd have a wealth of material to write about: the arrest, the trial, maybe a jailhouse interview with the killer, his final words dictated to her on death row, then the call from Oprah—

A wisp of shame blurred Jillian's thoughts for a moment. She looked away from the computer and took a sip of coffee. Was she sensationalizing this girl's murder merely to make a buck? Was it only about fame and money? Was she becoming the kind of writer that she'd looked down at all her life, cannibalizing lurid tragedies, adding to the glut of garbage already out there, the "reality shows" of literature? No, she told herself. No. She felt a need, an uncontrollable urge, to write these articles. She was bound to them. She was bound to Deborah Ellison. And keeping the story of this girl's murder alive and vivid in the public eye might even help catch whomever had killed her.

Jillian heard a noise outside her office door.

She turned quickly in her chair. A slight chill trickled down her neck. She looked around the room. The door was unlocked. She waited a moment—no sound—then ran to the door and locked it.

Her heart was racing.

She was scared.

She'd heard authors say that writers should write about what scares them. What if this was what they meant? To write about a subject that literally terrified her. Murder. Random horror. Unspeakable evil. Maybe this was the very thing she needed to be writing in order to grow as a novelist. She'd been feeling inauthentic in her work for years now, uninspired, repeating things. She bored herself. She needed something drastic to push her into whatever was next.

"Then *use* this," she thought. "Write about the fear. Write about feeling bored and repeating things. Write about getting up from the computer and locking the door. It's true, so write it."

Jillian filled her coffee cup, faced off with the computer screen before her, and began to write.

Detective Mangan opened the door of Room 70, looked down the hallway, and slammed it shut. He called maintenance for the third time that day and badgered them until a janitor finally showed up outside the door. He set down a filthy, once-white, standing fan and walked away without a saying a word.

"Appreciate it," Mangan called after him as sarcastically as he could. He grabbed the fan and brought it into the room. "Hey, Coose," he said to his partner, "plug this in for me, would you?"

"In a second, I'm eating."

"I'm not asking you to stop eating, just plug it in. Is that so hard?"

"Why don't you do it then?"

"Oh, for—" Mangan said, starting to do it himself.

Coose grabbed the fan from him, "I'm just busting your ass." He pulled the fridge away from the wall and plugged in the fan. "Why you so pissy today?"

"Because I'm dying of the heat in here, we're out of coffee, my back is bugging me again, and this guy is pushing forty minutes late now." They were waiting for Kevin Lachlan to show up for an interview. "And that's just for starters." Mangan turned the fan on. It blew more dust than air for a moment, then settled into a noisy sweep of the room. "Where the hell is this guy, anyway?"

Coose shrugged, "I don't know," and peeled open a drippy sausage and pepper sandwich.

"They said he was on his way."

"Who's *they*?"

"Eagan and Palmer."

"Then he's on his way."

Mangan watched Coose devour half the sandwich. "Breathe," he told him. "Breathe between bites."

Coose mumbled something unintelligible.

Mangan opened a file, talking half to himself. "Look at this . . . like I've got nothing better to do than to track down the owners of errant limbs." He sorted through some papers. "I've got statements from officers on scene, a clerk in the lobby, and this Lachlan guy." Kevin Lachlan was the editor of the *American Forum* who'd had the misfortune of finding a severed hand in his mail. He'd been questioned by uniformed officers the day of the incident, but something about his statement didn't sit right with Mangan. He held out a clutch of papers to Coose. "Here, tell me what you think."

"*You* think. I'm eating."

"I already thought. It's your turn."

"In a minute."

Frank Cusumano (Coose), ten years younger than Mangan but with less hair, stood about five foot eight, 210 pounds. In great shape, and he hardly ever went to the gym. A fact which irritated the hell out of Mangan. The two of them weren't the tallest detectives ever to walk onto a crime scene, but they might very well have been the widest: Mangan, a short bull of an Irishman whose former V-chest was now something like a square block, and Coose, a tree trunk of an Italian with very little neck, who looked a bit like Sly Stallone in *Rocky* after he'd had the shit kicked out of him for four consecutive movies. What the two of them lacked in height they made up in thickness, physically and mentally. They bickered like an old married couple and enjoyed it.

"Would you finish eating already," Mangan said. "We've got work to do."

Coose wiped his chin. "I get agita if I eat fast."

"You get agita 'cause you eat crap."

"You're gonna talk about what I eat? Mr. Krispy Kreme four hundred calories a pop?"

"You and your calories—like a girl."

"You should count a few yourself, lose that gut. There's no real nutritional value in gin, you know that, right?" Coose negotiated another bite of his sandwich. "Moderation, James. Word o' the day."

"Moderate your mouth." Mangan held up a copy of the note found with the severed hand. "You see this yet?"

"I just got in, for Christ's sake. I haven't seen anything."

Mangan dropped the note on the table.

"You want agita? Read that."

COPY: Ref. D-M 5
#8912-Pending
Chicago VCTF
Det. Mangan 63

SHE WAS CHOSEN.
YOU WERE CHOSEN.

EVERY TICK OF TIME
SINCE THE UNIVERSE BEGAN
HAS GUIDED YOU TO THIS MOMENT,
RIGHT NOW, READING THESE WORDS.

YOU THINK YOU CHOOSE.
YOU CHOOSE NOTHING.

I AM THE CHOOSER.
I WILL FIND THEM OUT.
THE FIRST WAS WINSOME.

"Okay, that's, like, that's very weird," Coose said. "I hate weird. Why can't we just get normal murderers." He took another mouthful of sandwich and slid the note back across the table.

Mangan picked it up. "It's all greasy now."

"*The Chooser*?" Coose said. "What's that, his name? Did he anoint himself?"

"I don't know."

"The press will love it, once they get their hands on it."

"They're not going to."

Coose looked at the note again. "What's this word mean, anyway?"

"What?"

"Winsome."

"You don't know?"

"I kind of know. Generally. You're always telling me to be specific, I'm being specific."

"You're being lazy, look it up."

"Oh, don't start that again, for Christ's sake. Just tell me."

"Don't be lazy."

"I'm not lazy, I'm efficient. You know what it fucking means, so just—"

"If you read it, you'll learn it. You're being lazy."

"And you're being a pain in the ass," Coose said, "like always." He Googled the word on his laptop, muttering, "Mr. Literature-guy, always thinking you're so smart." He found the word. "Here, all right, you happy? 'Winsome: cheerful or pleasant. Often possessing a childlike charm and innocence, as in: He had a winsome smile.'" Coose looked up, feigning surprise. "Hey, just like you."

"Don't start. I smile enough."

"Yeah, you got a smile like a comet, James, it comes around every decade or so."

"You're not funny."

"Actually, I am. A normal person would have laughed at that."

"What do you make of the note?"

"I don't know . . . 'The first was winsome'? He enjoyed it?"

"Maybe."

"There's an implied threat there: 'The first was winsome.' Could mean that there are going to be others, or there *were* others. He might have killed before."

"Maybe."

"Anything on the prints? The fingerprints?"

"Not in the system."

"And we have no body."

"No."

"Who's this Lachlan guy, anyway? What's he got to do with it?"

"I don't know. That's what I'm going to find out if he ever gets here."

"He say anything in his statement about it?"

"About what?"

"The note."

"No. He didn't know it was there. Forensics found it at the bottom of the envelope."

Mangan walked over to the window and looked out. A pigeon was shitting on the window ledge. He read the note again, "I will find them out."

Coose went to the sink and turned the faucet on, letting the water run warm. "You know, James, it could be a kidnapping," he said, washing his hands. "This woman might be alive somewhere." He grabbed some paper towels and turned to Mangan. "Hey, you hear what I said? This woman could—"

Mangan wasn't listening anymore.

He was staring at the floor. Words were coming to him. Fractures of sentences. He cocked his head, trying to put them together . . . *and I . . . with tears . . . do wash . . . the blood away. . . .* He thought he recognized where they were from, but there were other words too . . . unfamiliar words . . . *in my heart . . .*

Coose started to say something but Mangan waved him quiet.

. . . vengeance . . . in my heart . . .

"Hey," Coose said, "you all right?"

. . . death in my hand . . .

"C'mon, James, stop it already. You creep me out when you do that."

"Shhh!" Mangan said. He stilled himself. He listened.

Vengeance is in my heart, death in my hand,
Blood and revenge are hammering in my head.

Where did they come from, Mangan wondered, these words, these literary inklings? His subconscious? His imagination? What was the other thing at work in his mind? He really didn't know, but he'd come to trust the poetical oddities that flitted through his mind. He'd trained himself not to dismiss them, not to judge the mind's ideas too quickly. It was part of his job, he'd come to believe, to let the words in, to listen to them, to let the creative mingle with the forensic, to encourage the fiction of it and dream the wicked dreams of murderers, who never played by day-waking rules.

"James!" Coose said, stepping closer.

The words were gone. "Do you mind?" Mangan said, looking up. "I was having a moment there."

"A moment of what?"

"A moment of—I don't know—of trying to catch this guy before he kills someone else."

"Someone else? We don't even know if the lady's dead yet. We don't have a body."

"We will, believe me. I got a bad feeling about this one."

"You got a bad feeling about everything, James. You were born with a bad feeling."

"All right, Little Miss Sunshine, just—" There was a knock at the door. "What?!"

Mickey Eagan stuck his head in the doorway. If you had to draw a caricature of what an overweight middle-aged Irish cop from Chicago looked like, it would look like Mickey Eagan. Reading made him sweat.

"Special delivery," Eagan said, winded. "Mr. Kevin Lachlan. I got him outside."

Out in the hallway, Kevin Lachlan was on his cell phone. He looked impatient and bothered. At a glance, Mangan didn't like him. He knew his type: the church-going North Shore businessman who liked to meet with associates in Chicago for conventions and trade shows, which were really just excuses for them to whore themselves for a weekend. And after the CEOs got tired of whacking their johnnies off to the twenty-four-hour porn stations, provided at their all-expense-paid hotels, they'd turn to the local escort services, just a computer click away, major credit cards accepted. Scum like Lachlan were all over Chicago, and Mangan couldn't do very much about them. If the girls were of age and consenting, he and his men left the tricks and pimps alone or turned them over to vice. But under-agers, or girls forced into the business, well, that was a very different story with Mangan. He'd seen girls beaten unconscious, arms broken, faces pounded into walls, skulls crushed. It angered him irrationally and brought out the worst in him as a cop, or perhaps the best—the distinction was always a little hazy.

Early in his career, he and his team had busted up a strip joint in west Chicago called the Blue Throat. Up on a second floor they'd broken down the door of a room called the Dessert Bar and found about a half dozen girls inside, mostly naked, slumped in wooden chairs. The girls barely moved when they crashed through the door. They didn't look scared or even surprised that the room was suddenly crowded with police. They looked dead. On a filthy mattress, on the floor, was a girl lying on her side, naked from the waist down. Blood stained her thighs and the mattress beneath her. She couldn't have been more than thirteen years old, maybe ninety pounds.

Not a man easily moved, Mangan had always prided himself on being inured to the things that would make most other officers lose their lunch. He'd seen horrific murders, mutilations, decaying corpses, mob slayings—things done to human bodies which no person should ever have to see or think about. *Habit, the great deadener,* had numbed him. But on the second floor of the Blue Throat that day, looking down at a listless blood-soaked little girl, a strange pressure pushed upward in his chest and throat. He felt nauseous and sweaty. He reached for the wall to steady himself. He was going to pass out, he knew the feeling, he was going to faint right in front of all of these other cops. He struggled to hold on—

And for the first time, he heard the words.

He didn't know why they had come to him, but when he listened to them they seemed to steady him. They stopped his mind and heart from shutting down. They helped him to somehow express the inexpressible. His nausea passed, and under his breath he actually spoke some of the words aloud.

I was not angry until this instant.

And then he nearly beat the club owner to death.

He had felt nothing but heat, a kind of heat in his stomach and balls as he sprinted down the stairs. He grabbed a liquor bottle off the bar and took it to the club owner's head. There wasn't much of the guy's face left when he was done—bottles don't break like in the movies. If Coose and another officer, Willie Palmer, hadn't stopped him, Mangan would have killed the man. That thing, that darker thing inside Mangan had a tricky on-off switch, and it didn't always work right. It was the same thing that helped keep him alive as a kid growing up on the streets of Chicago. It was the same thing that, when kept in check, made him a good cop. It was also the thing that would probably get him killed one day. It was a nasty line to walk, given his kind of work. Not a thin blue line, but a thick fat fucking black one. He'd waded through the shit of it all his life.

This thing of darkness I acknowledge mine.

After the episode at the Blue Throat, Mangan was suspended for six months and put on paid leave, then brought up on charges. He lied on the stand. Cusumano and Palmer swore to it. What had happened, they'd said, was that the club owner had rushed at Detective Mangan with a bottle of Slivovitz, which Mangan barely had time to grapple out of his hands. He was then forced to beat the man senseless with it in self-defense. Mangan was acquitted. He received the Cook County Distinguished Service Award and was offered complimentary anger-management counseling.

He accepted both.

Mangan knew there were plenty of things in his life that he wasn't very good at: The nicer things, the lighter things. Smiling, for example. They'd passed him by somehow, or maybe he'd refused to let them in, he didn't know. Shrinks would have a field day with him. A few of his friends, and most of the women in his life, had at some point taken it upon themselves to help fix him. He'd worked a long time at trying to change himself, and now, if he were honest, and he was, he was tired of it. His new outlook on life, arrived at through the wisdom of age—or sheer exhaustion more likely—could pretty much be summed up as, Fuck it, this is me. He was born with a little gloom around his heart, and he knew it. He'd fought it when he was younger. He'd set ideals for himself, honorable ideals, and tried to rise to them, but his other self, the kid from the street, was always tagging along just a few skips behind him, calling out, "And where do you think *you're* going?"

He often wished he'd have turned out to be a better man.

"And screw that too," he'd think in the very next second. He was a middle-aged cop and good at it. All right, so he'd missed out on some of the nicer things in life. All right, so he wasn't the oh so virtuous guy he'd started out to be. Guys like that don't always have what it takes to catch bad guys, the *really* bad guys: to roll around with them in the muck and the blood, to bite a nose off if that's what it took, or stick a gun into a meth-crusted mouth until the guy vomited and confessed where a missing child was. That's what it often came down to, because real bad guys eat good guys for breakfast. You blink, you're dead. This wasn't TV or some cock 'n' cunt crime novel with a vampire love triangle at the end. This was Chicago, and the sign over detective James Mangan's door said Room 70, Violent Crimes Task Force—emphasis *violent*.

Mangan stepped into the hallway when he saw Kevin Lachlan start to make another phone call. "Mr. Lachlan," he said, gesturing him into the room. "Thanks for coming in today."

"Sorry," Lachlan said, putting the phone away. "I have a lot going on at work."

"No problem. I'm Detective Mangan." He gestured to Coose. "My partner, Frank Cusumano." Coose pulled out a chair at the table and Lachlan sat. Mangan sat across from him. "Sorry it's so hot in here. The AC's out. I keep calling maintenance. They don't like me."

"Uh-huh," Lachlan said, glancing around the office. He stood, took off his jacket, and sat back down.

"You okay?" Mangan asked.

"I'm afraid I . . . I'm not feeling too well."

This is a subtle whore, echoed in Mangan's head, *a closet lock and key of villainous secrets.*

Coose asked him, "You want I should get you some water?"

"Please."

Coose took his cue and left the room. Mangan waited. He let the silence sit. He learned a lot about people from their silences. Lachlan kept wiping his forehead but there wasn't anything there. Coose came back in, gave Lachlan the water, and left the room. Lachlan sat up a little higher in his chair and drank.

"Better?" Mangan asked him.

"Yes. Thank you."

"Good. So. Look. I'll try and get you out of here as quick as I can, all right? So, to start with, Mr. Lachlan—is that Irish? You Irish?"

"Scotch Irish."

"Uh-huh," Mangan said, the words *we have scotched the snake, not killed it* darting through his thoughts. "So to begin, Mr. Lachlan, I want to apologize right off the bat because I'm going to have to ask you some things, and I'm kind of a straightforward guy in my work, because, you know, it just saves a hell of a lot of time." Mangan opened the case file and placed it on the desk. "And, tell you the truth, I got a friggin' blivit times three here that I'm trying to clean up. You know what that is, a blivit?"

"I'm sorry?"

"Ten pounds o' shit in a five-pound bag. My shop teacher told me that in seventh grade. Mr. Manfrey. Never forgot it." Mangan sorted through his notes. "So, help me out here if you could, Mr. Lachlan. Oh, and one more thing," he added in as pleasant a voice as he could muster, "don't bullshit me, okay? Because I might not catch it right now, you know? But I will, eventually. And then that's just not good for anybody. Because then I gotta get you back in here, and then I'm not so personable, and it's just, you know, it's just no fun all the way around. All right?"

"Excuse me, did I do something wrong here?"

"I don't know, did you?"

"What kind of a question is that?"

"It's just a question. I'm a detective. I ask questions."

"Look, I found a hand in my apartment. I called *you*."

"I understand that, Mr. Lachlan, and I'm very sorry for the trauma, the obvious emotional trauma which I'm sensing this has caused you. I apologize. You're right. You're very right. I was assuming. I was *projecting*. Bad habit of mine. And I think maybe I was doing that because I was starting to sense a kind of, I don't know, a kind of hesitancy in your demeanor. And I'm probably completely wrong about that. So, I apologize. Please, let me start again." Mangan took out a sheet of notes from one of the files on his desk. "And you understand, of course, that you don't have to answer anything, right? I just thought I'd try and get you in here early to talk, because there might be some things about this case—and there I go *assuming* again, so please correct me if I'm wrong—there might be some things that you'd prefer to maybe keep out of the newspapers." Mangan waited for a response. Lachlan's silence told him all he needed to know. "I'm nothing if not discreet," he said, skimming the preliminary reports. "So, this young woman, Mr. Lachlan. Who was she?"

"I'm sorry?"

"The woman who left your apartment at approximately six twenty-five that morning, jeans, T-shirt, midtwenties, long black hair, very attractive. You didn't mention her in your statement to the police."

Mangan paused a moment. "I'm assuming she wasn't your wife. Or your daughter."

Lachlan twisted the cap back onto his water bottle. "No."

"What's her name?"

". . . Fenyana."

"What's that, like Cher, Prince, or something? Just Fenyana?"

"I don't know her last name."

Mangan jotted the name down in a small notebook. "A professional, yes? The Slovak social club? Where's the *tochka* you picked her up at?"

"I didn't pick her up. She comes—I know her through a friend."

"This friend got a name?"

Lachlan hesitated. "I think I'd like to call my lawyer now."

Mangan stopped taking notes. He put his pen down.

"Mr. Lachlan," he said, "did you read the sign over my door when you came in? It says Violent Crimes. That's me. That's what I wake up for. You really think I care about some little *baruxa-bun* you're banging up in your apartment? No, the answer to that is no. Now when I talk to the press—which I'm going to have to do eventually—I really wouldn't want to slip and maybe mention something that I shouldn't, which unfortunately happens to me at times when lawyers get involved. They make me nervous. And here I go again *assuming*, but I'm thinking that maybe you might not want your wife and—let's see, how many kids you got?" Mangan flipped to a page in his notepad. "You might not want your wife and *three* kids to know that you're dicking a girl about the age of your youngest daughter in a very nicely situated and, if I might add, very nicely furnished apartment, which I *assume*—there I go again—is perhaps a business expense? Tax write-off? We wouldn't want the IRS to get involved in this, now, would we? That would be just terrible. So, if you could just help me out a little, I'd feel a lot better because I really wouldn't want to say something that I shouldn't say. Accidentally."

Lachlan slumped slightly in his chair.

"Tick, tock," Mangan said, tapping his watch.

"Savva Baratov. The Bank Street Diner. It's on the corner of—"

"*Bank* Street, right? Wow, I'm good at this." Mangan took a quick note.

"She, um, she works there, sometimes, and he, he arranges—"

"I'm way ahead of you, buddy. You been with her before?"

"Yes. About once a month. But not always her."

"Alrighty, we're cooking with gas now." Mangan ripped out a piece of paper from his notepad. "Coose!" Cusumano came back in and Mangan handed him the note. He took it and left again. Mangan watched Lachlan's eyes. "Did you read the note that was in the envelope?"

"Note? I . . . I'm sorry, I don't know what you're talking about."

"You didn't see what else was in that envelope?"

"No, I didn't. When I felt the, when I saw what it was, I dropped the envelope and got out of there and called the police."

Mangan pulled out the copy of the note. "Well, there was a note in it. This is a copy. I'd like you to read it." Mangan placed it in front of Lachlan. "Normally we wouldn't do this, but, well, this isn't very normal. Tell me what you make of it."

Mangan watched Lachlan read the note.

When Lachlan reached the end of it he mumbled, "Winsome." A puzzled look drifted across his face, then a shock of recognition. "Jesus, that's the name of the town. Winsome." He shoved the note back to Mangan. "Winsome Bay. We're running a series on it right now. That's where she was killed, the girl, that's where they found her. She was—"

"Slow down, Mr. Lachlan, slow down. What are you talking about? Who was killed?"

"The girl from Wisconsin. Deborah Ellison."

Sorry," Jillian said as she fumbled with her digital recorder. "I think it's the battery. I have another one here." She was new at interviewing people, more nervous than she thought she'd be. "Just a second."

Wesley Faber waited while Jillian dug through her purse. He had agreed to meet after his shift, at 8:00 p.m. Inconvenient for Jillian, yes, but she hadn't had much choice. When she called to confirm, Faber had tried to cancel the interview altogether, but Jillian gently reminded him that as well as being the chief of police in Winsome Bay, he was also the town's public information officer. They met at the police station, only blocks away from where Deborah Ellison's body had been found. Faber had been police chief for the last seventeen years. This was his first murder case.

"Almost got it," Jillian said, smiling at him.

He didn't smile back.

Balding, graying, and stiffly polite, Faber sat very erect and very still at his desk. Behind him, mounted high on a dark paneled wall, were two large, antlered deer heads. Next to them were some fanned-out turkey-tail mountings, and on a low shelf beneath were at least a dozen shooting trophies and a number of engraved gold plaques for police marksmanship.

"Okay," Jillian said, testing the recorder. "It works now." She placed it on the corner of Faber's desk. "Sorry." She read through her list of prepared questions. "Um . . . okay."

"You want anything?" Faber asked. "Something to drink?"

"No. No. Thank you. I'm ready now."

"Okay."

"So. Do you have much crime out here?"

"Not much. But some."

"Any violent crimes?"

"Bar fights mostly. A suicide now and then. Domestic abuse."

"Any drugs?"

"Well, drugs are everywhere, aren't they? We're no exception."

"What kind of drugs?"

"Marijuana and OxyContin mostly. In the high school."

"Heroin?" Jillian knew the answer to this. She wanted to see if Faber would answer honestly.

"Well, yes," he said, "we're starting to get the heroin out this way too."

Drugs, Jillian knew, were one of the dirty little secrets of small-town America. Well, not so much a secret as a profound misconception that things like that don't happen in small towns, as if all the rah-rah ball games, corn dogs, and flag-draped porches somehow granted rural America immunity from the horrors going on around the rest of the country. There weren't any fewer drugs, just less media coverage. Jillian had done her research before coming to Winsome for the interview. In 2007 Wisconsin had about thirty heroin deaths. In 2013, two hundred and twenty-seven. The drug is just too cheap. Oxy might cost forty or fifty dollars, while a hit of heroin might go for twenty. And with cheap drugs come the addicts, and with the addicts, crime. There's just no honest way to afford a three-hundred-dollar-a-day habit.

"What about crystal meth?" Jillian asked.

"Less of that now," Faber said. "It was a big problem for a long time. They can't cook the stuff in the city, the smell is too strong. So they all started coming out this way. Hard to know where they are, though. They move around a lot, setting up out in the woods and the old farms, campsites, hauling in gallons of hydrochloric acid, acetone, methanol, kerosene, propane."

An explosion waiting to happen.

"We generally don't catch them till they blow themselves up."

Jillian pressed the question now that she really wanted to ask. "Do you know if Deborah Ellison was involved with any drugs?"

Faber hesitated the slightest bit. "I can't comment on that, ma'am."

"The papers said her body had been mutilated somehow. Could you be more specific?"

"Nope."

"Can you tell me how long the body had been there?"

"Nope."

"Can you describe for me what the victim was wearing?"

"Nope."

"Did you know Deborah Ellison?"

"I believe I've already answered that, ma'am."

"I mean, personally. Did you know her well?"

"I've got a son her age. They went to school together. So, I knew her pretty well." He gestured to a photo on his desk of a young man kneeling, dressed in full camouflage, holding a rifle in one hand and a dead turkey in the other. "That's him there, Kyle." He pointed to another framed photograph. A family picture. "That's my wife there, and my other two boys, Carson and Matt, and my daughter, Jennifer. And that little peanut there in her arms is our first grandchild, Kayla."

"That's a big family."

"Not for around here. You get families of eight, ten, eleven, out on the farms."

Jillian tried to steer the conversation back to the murder. "Deborah Ellison was last known to be living in Chicago. Is that right?"

"I believe so, yes."

"What do you think she was doing back here in Winsome?"

"Don't know."

"Visiting family? Or friends?"

"Don't know."

"Do you think she was killed here? Or was her body just—was she killed somewhere else and then left here?"

"I don't know."

"Do you have a guess?"

"I don't guess, ma'am."

Jillian checked some of the notes she'd gathered from news reports. "The papers said that the victim's father, officer Tom Ellison, was first on the scene."

Faber nodded, barely.

"But he didn't identify the body." Jillian looked at the wall to her left. "That officer did." She pointed to one of the framed photographs hanging there. "Officer Schaefer."

"Yes."

"Tom Ellison didn't recognize his own daughter but Officer Schaefer did?"

Faber shifted in his seat and adjusted his bulletproof vest, the outline of which was clearly visible beneath his uniform. "From the condition of her body," he said, "it was obvious that death had occurred. So Tom, well, he stepped away as soon as he seen it and called for backup. He didn't get a good look at first."

"One of the papers said that she'd been beaten beyond recognition. How did Officer Schaefer know it was Deborah?"

"I can't say anything to that."

"Did anyone else on the scene know it was her?"

"No. After Schaefer told me who it was, I got Tom out of there fast as I could and sent for Father Ryan. He was the one who told Tom."

"Father Ryan?"

"Tom's priest over at Saint Francis. He helped out some with Debbie when she was younger."

"Helped with what?"

"Kid stuff, teen stuff."

"Can you be more specific?"

"Nope," Faber said, taking out his cell phone. It was buzzing. He looked at the number. "Excuse me," he said. He spoke to the caller. "Hello? Yes, sir, you're talking to him. Yes, sir. Yes, I will. Just a minute, please." Faber looked to Jillian and nodded toward the door. "I'm sorry, ma'am, I have to take this."

"Just a few more questions. Please?"

"No, ma'am, I think we'll be done here."

"But—"

"Careful driving. Lot of deer out this time of night."

•

J. McClay/Killing/American Forum

I drove to the north edge of the town after meeting with the Winsome Bay chief of police, Wesley Faber. He'd been less than forthcoming during the interview. I slowed the car as I approached the area where Deborah Ellison's body had been found. The sun, not quite down, cast a Creamsicle-colored tint across the still blue sky as I pulled into the unfinished development that would someday be the Deer Park Apartments, as a sign at the entrance promised. The site had the look of a vandalized Grant Wood painting: acres of still green hays and soybean fields, slashed and marred by asphalt roads and freshly poured sidewalks.

Just inside the entrance, two new houses had started to go up, framed out in bone-white two-by-fours, like a barn raising suddenly halted midrise. Piled high to the sides of the houses were stacks of plywood and roofing shingles. Behind the homes were acres of half-harvested farmland. Wide swaths of hays had been cut and raked together into long narrow windrows. They lay there, snakily, field curing. Some of the hay had already been baled into massive cubes and scattered about the earth like the droppings of some giant straw beast. Much of it, though, hadn't been cut at all. Waist high and willowy, the grassy fields rippled lazily beneath the breeze.

In the distance, a cloud of dust tumbled behind a slow-moving tractor.

I drove farther in, to the exact spot where the newspaper said Deborah Ellison's body had been found. I opened my window and turned off the car. There was a wooden stake stuck into the field there, just off the curb, with a white number 46 painted on it. A string of rosary beads and a blue-ribboned medal hung from it. Someone had propped up a ceramic cross at its base. Stacked on the ground around it were piles of weathered bouquets, their cellophane wrappings gently crinkling in the light breeze. A large square of yellow crime scene tape sectioned off the makeshift memorial from the rest of the field. I stared at the spot, wondering if the future owners of lot 46 would be told of what had happened on their property, or if they'd discover it years later, perhaps whispered to one of their children on a playground during recess.

Sitting there, I expected, I wanted, to feel differently.

I didn't.

A vague sense of sadness filled me, or perhaps it was disappointment. I expected something momentous to occur as I gazed at the actual spot where the body had been discovered, but I felt nothing. Everything looked so normal. Something unspeakable had happened in this place; there should have been some residue, some echo in the air of that awful night. God should not have allowed the sky to blue or the hay to green in such a place. Deborah Ellison's body had been dumped here like so much garbage. She may still have been alive. She may have breathed her last breaths not five feet from where I was parked. The grasses might have tickled her face in the warm wind that night, and she, unable to brush away the blades, may have lain there, staring up at some dark star, thinking her last thoughts. A human being had died horribly in this spot, something should be different.

But nothing, it seemed to me, was different. Except for my presence.

He may have been here too, parked where I was parked. He may have sat in his car, just like me, with his window rolled down, looking at what he'd done. If Deborah Ellison had still been alive, he may have been able to hear whatever dying sounds she'd still been able to make.

Jillian stopped writing. She saved her work and closed her laptop and placed it on the seat beside her. The Winsome sky to the east had turned a lilac purple now. She watched it for a time, still hoping to experience something, she didn't know what, just something: an act of coincidence, an image, a feeling. But nothing happened. She looked around her, up and down the yet to be inhabited streets, croplands to either side, driveways leading to nowhere, waiting for homes to be attached to them. A large black hawk glided across the road and into the field to her right, and Jillian thought for a moment that it was an omen of some kind. It wasn't; she could feel it right away, it didn't mean anything. It was just a bird in a field.

She took out a pack of cigarettes she'd hidden in her purse and smoked. She wrote down a few notes. Checked the time. She had to be getting home soon. She gave Mara a call and left a message on her voice mail.

"It's me again. Where are you? I've been calling you for two days. Look, I got some really great stuff. I want to tell you about it. So call me, okay? Even if it's late. Love ya. Bye."

Detective Mangan tracked down the Wisconsin murder victim that Kevin Lachlan had told him about: Deborah Ellison. He called the officer in charge of the investigation, Wesley Faber, the police chief in Winsome Bay. Mangan explained to Faber about the severed hand that had been found in Chicago, then queried him as to the condition of the Wisconsin victim's body, the details of which had not yet been released to the public.

Faber told him that Deborah Ellison was missing her left hand.

"Well," Mangan said, "guess I can stop looking for a body."

"I'm afraid that's right, sir," Chief Faber said. "We have her here."

Mangan spoke with Faber for a while. He was pleasant enough on the phone, but Mangan could sense that he was a bit overwhelmed by the case, and understandably so. This was his first murder investigation and he'd known the victim and her family.

"I'll send you everything I've got," Mangan told him. "Our forensic reports should be coming in soon, and I'll get them up to you. We'll keep following up on things here. If I find anything, I'll contact you."

"Thank you" Faber said. "I'll fax what we've got to your medical examiner. You have his number handy?"

Mangan gave him Rhys's fax number and wished him luck.

Why the severed hand of a murder victim from Wisconsin had been dropped off at Kevin Lachlan's apartment in Chicago was still a mystery to Mangan, but at least he had a corpse now, or rather Wesley Faber had one. It would be Faber's investigation now and off Mangan's plate, which was just fine with him. He had more than his share of open cases to keep him busy. He wondered, though, why he'd misread the case. The feelings had been so strong when he'd heard the words, *And who has cut those pretty fingers off?* That usually meant he was in for the long haul. But then again, occasionally his instincts were wrong.

Mangan completed the paperwork, filed it, and finished out the day reviewing his next case: the killing of a Sally-Boy Hicks, a heroin dealer in K-Town shot twice in the back of the head and tossed off a fifteen-story building. Redundant, Mangan thought, but obviously somebody was trying to make a point. After work he stopped off at the Melrose Diner and got dinner to go, eating most of it on the drive home. He headed up Lake Shore Drive, hitting the usual traffic, and continued north to Rogers Park.

The four-story townhouse where Mangan lived, built in 1920, still had a vintage charm to it, a phrase most often used to camouflage the more dilapidated shitholes in Chicago, but this building was actually in pretty good shape. He'd moved there not long after his wife died and had lived on the fourth floor, apartment 421, for three years now.

He pulled into his absurdly expensive parking space around back and grabbed what was left of his dinner. Built onto the rear side of the building was a tall zigzagging run of wooden stairs leading nearly to the roof. The stairs opened out onto landings off the back of each apartment's kitchen entrance. Pretty much everyone used these stairs as the main entrance to the building since the parking was out back. Mangan made his way up the wooden stairway—his exercise for the day—keyed open his back door, and walked into the kitchen. Quiet and dark. He kept his thick window curtains closed during the day. A room at the front of the apartment had a bay window that jutted out slightly from the building. If he stood at just the right angle, Mangan could spy a little piece of Lake Michigan at the far end of the street.

It was not a small apartment but one of those spaces where the square footage was three times as long as it was wide, like living in a skinny rectangle. There were two large guest rooms off a long hardwood-floored hallway that led from the back kitchen to the front room. There were no beds or dressers in these rooms, only a single chair in each, a short stepladder, and books—hundreds of books—shelved on every wall. There were books piled on the floors against the walls and stacked in the closets. Out in the long hallway, shelves had been built, floor to ceiling along both sides. They too, were filled with books. In the living room there was a couch and a large coffee table with books strewn on and around them and piled everywhere that there was space enough to do so. This was the other part of Mangan's world. Books. They were his Yale and Harvard. They cracked the quiet of an otherwise empty home, and he never had to feed them or take them for a walk.

Mangan ate what was left of his dinner and poured himself a gin. He headed to the front room and called his daughter.

"Hey, Katie, it's Dad."

"Hey, what's up?" she said. "Hold on a sec. Shit. Sorry. Okay. Hi. How are you?"

"What are you, exercising or something? You sound out of breath."

"No, just trying to get out of here. Working late tonight. What's up with you?"

"Nothing, just calling."

"Uh-huh."

"How's the job?"

"What?"

"Work, how's it going?"

"Oh, good. Crazy, but good."

"You still liking it there?"

"Uh-huh."

Mangan heard something fall on the other end. "You okay?"

"Sorry. Yeah, fine. What did you say?"

"What?"

"You just asked me something."

"Nothing. Look, I'll call later. You're busy."

"No, no, I'm fine, Dad, really. I'm just—hold on a second. Okay, I'm good now. I'm sitting. Go ahead."

Mangan could hear the preoccupation in her voice. When she was little and didn't want to talk to him on the phone because she was watching TV, she used to do the same thing. She sounded just the same now at twenty-nine.

Mangan lied, "Katie, honey, I forgot, I can't talk right now. I have to make a another call. It's work. Sorry."

"Sure. That's okay, Dad. Call me later."

"Okay."

"Love you."

"Love you too."

"Bye."

Mangan listened into the quiet cell phone for a moment, then flipped it closed.

He took up the copy of *Titus Andronicus* he'd started reading the night before. Most of the words that had been coming to him lately were from that play. He hadn't read it in years. He took a slow sip of his drink and started reading. The Lachlan/Ellison case was off his hands now, but he thought he'd finish *Titus* anyway.

I'll find a day to massacre them all,
And raze their faction and their family,
The cruel father and his—

His cell phone buzzed. It was Brian Rhys from forensics. The Wisconsin M.E. had faxed down the Ellison girl's fingerprints.

"Hey, Jimbo," Rhys said. "Got a little hitch. The prints don't match. It's not Debbie Ellison's hand."

Jillian McClay was driving home after her interview with Wesley Faber. She was less than satisfied with the results. She was almost to the interstate when she passed the Bar Nun Tavern on the edge of town. Parked in front were two pickup trucks and a police cruiser.

She checked the time.

Made a U-turn.

As Jillian opened the door to the tavern, two feed-capped heads sitting at the bar turned toward her. They lingered on her for longer than was comfortable, then went back to their drinks. The barmaid, tapping at a video poker machine, barely looked up. On the opposite side of the bar was a small back room with a pool table, a few men corralled around it in a haze of smoke. The dark carpeted floors smelled faintly of stale beer and urine. Sitting at a table near the back of the bar was officer Michele Schaefer. Jillian was sure it was her. She had seen the woman's photo on the wall of the police station while interviewing Wesley Faber. Schaefer was out of uniform and sitting with three other people. They appeared to be close in age, late twenties, maybe, early thirties, huddled around a table crowded with beer bottles, their conversation hushed.

Michele Schaefer was the officer who had identified Deborah Ellison's body.

Jillian sat at the end of the bar. She didn't want to approach Schaefer too quickly, didn't want her to shut down the way Faber had. She ordered a drink and texted her son. Might be late, make a pizza. She called Mara, but again she didn't answer. She left a long message and then lit a cigarette. The two men in feed caps stared over at her between their swallows of beer and fistfuls of popcorn, and the barmaid paid attention to no one.

The sound of cue balls cracked occasionally from the back room.

Eventually, Schaefer glanced Jillian's way.

Jillian nodded a polite, and slightly wary, hello. She waited a few more minutes, then ventured over, making an apology to the table, and asking if Schaefer was the officer she'd seen on TV.

Her friends, all a little drunk, started to object.

Schaefer waved them quiet. "Whoa, whoa, let her talk," she said. "What do you want?"

"I'm a writer," Jillian said. "I'm here doing a story."

"About what?"

"Deborah Ellison."

The two men scraped back their chairs and stood. "Come on," one of them said, "let's go." He was tall and well built, with a scruff of beard and short-cropped hair. The other man, just as big and scruffier, cleared the table of empties and took them to the bar.

"Cal," Schaefer called after him, "Cal, wait a second."

"I said let's go." He turned to Jillian. "Look, she's not talking to anyone, okay? Just leave us alone."

"Aw, don't be like that," Schaefer said. "You're not being very hospitable." Her last word was slightly slurred.

The man called Cal appealed to the other woman at the table for help. "Jeannie?"

She got up. "Come on, Michele." She was a tall woman, nearly as big as Cal. "We should go."

"I got a full beer."

"Come on," Jeannie said, "we're helping Dad tomorrow early."

"I'll be there. I'll be there before you."

Jillian felt awkward in all kinds of ways, not knowing whether to stay or leave. "If this is a problem, I can—"

"No, it's all right," Schaefer said. She looked to the two men, who were glaring at her. "Go shoot pool or something. Stop looking at me. I'll be done in a minute."

Jillian heard Jeannie whisper to Cal, "I'll stay with her."

The men headed to the poolroom, not happy.

Schaefer waved for Jillian to sit. "Come on. Join me."

"Thanks." Jillian extended her hand and sat. "I'm Jillian."

"I'm drunk. This is my sister, Jeannie."

"Hi."

"Hi."

"That's was my brother," Schaefer said, pointing to the poolroom, "the rude one, Calan. The other guy, the cute one, is Jeannie's husband. Bobby. She always got the nice guys. Me? Not so much."

"I need another beer," Jeannie said. She asked Jillian, "You want something?"

"No, thanks."

Jeannie went to the bar.

Jillian, unsure what to say, nodded toward Schaefer's brother. "He's a big guy."

"Yeah, he is."

"Is he the oldest?"

"No, just the bossiest. There are seven of us."

"Seven?"

"Yup. My sister and me and five boys."

"That's huge."

"Not for around here."

"I'm an only child. I can't even imagine."

"You don't want to."

Jeannie returned with her beer. A short awkwardness followed and then Schaefer said, "So what newspaper are you with?"

"Well, uh . . ." Jillian said, "actually, I'm not a reporter. I'm a freelance writer, and I'm working on an article, a series of articles, for a magazine."

"About Deborah."

"Yes."

Jeannie leaned into the table. "My sister's a cop, you know. She can't talk about the case."

"No, I know that. I'm really just researching the town, the people. It's a beautiful town."

The two sisters both let out something that sounded like a snort. Schaefer took a long guzzle of her beer, eyeing Jillian's cigarettes. "Can I have one? I'm out."

Jillian slid the pack across. "Sure. Help yourself."

"You smoke too much," Jeannie said.

"I know."

Jillian didn't ask any real questions at first. She wanted to gain Schaefer's trust. She started out by saying that she was sorry for what had happened and went on a little bit more about how beautiful Winsome Bay was. She casually dropped that she had already talked to Wesley Faber and Dan Ehrlich, and that they'd been very helpful. Then she began asking easy questions about Schaefer's own background, her family, her career. Her brothers eventually stopped staring over at them, and from the sound of it, were involved in a pretty heated pool game. Jeannie, wary, listened closely and drank steadily.

Finally, Jillian got the nerve to ask, "So what can you tell me about Deborah?"

Schaefer picked at the label of her beer bottle and glanced at her sister.

"Nothing about the case," Jillian added, "something personal about her."

"Why?" Schaefer asked. "Why do you want to know this?"

"I'm . . . it just, it seems wrong to me," Jillian said. "Nobody's talking about Deborah, about who she was. Who she *really* was. Everybody's talking about how she died. It's good headlines, it sells. But nobody has written about her life. We hardly know anything about her. And I just think that's wrong. We should know what she wanted to be, what she liked to do, the things she loved, her dreams. That's how people should remember her."

Both Jeannie and Schaefer seemed moved.

Schaefer spoke quietly, not making eye contact. "I'm, uh . . . I'm a good bit older than her, but we spent some time together." She concentrated on peeling the label off her beer bottle. "I knew her pretty well."

Jillian took out her digital recorder. "Do you mind if I use this? I have a terrible memory."

Schaefer shrugged and took another of Jillian's cigarettes. "I don't care."

Jillian put the recorder on the table behind a small wicker basket of popcorn.

Schaefer spoke hesitantly at first, eyeing Jillian often, but after another drink she started talking, and once she did, she wasn't shy about it. By the time Jillian arrived home that night, she had more than enough material for her next article.

She wrote late into the night.

•

J. McClay/Killing/American Forum

The Bar Nun Tavern

I was sitting at a table at the far back of the bar. In the darkened corner, a tall, electronic dart board flickered red and played celebratory chimes every few minutes, even though no one was playing it; a Siren song of gaming, sung to a near-empty bar.

Sitting across from me was officer Michele Schaefer. She wore a flannel shirt rolled up at the sleeves, blue jeans, and beat-up cowboy boots. Her hair, unfussily shoulder length and natural. Her eyes, a piercing hazel-green, that seemed to pronounce, "I will not suffer fools." She wore no makeup that I could see. Her skin, burnished and smooth, had that natural look usually reserved for the very young or for those who can afford daily facial treatments and tanning booths. I thought Schaefer was in her late twenties. She is thirty-seven. She's also tall for a woman, nearly six foot. She hunts deer, turkey, and pheasant; works the Fireman's Smelt Feed each year; target shoots with a .44 Magnum; and will icefish on occasion. She's between relationships at the moment. Boyfriends, she said, tend to get in the way during haying season, when she helps out on the family farm. She's never married because, she said, husbands tend to get in the way *all* the time. Schaefer's dad, a cop for twenty years, retired early to run an organic dairy farm.

Her sister, Jeannie, who was with her during my interview, is thirty-one and has a similar look to her, a hardened beauty born of the fields and more than a bit of grit. You wouldn't say either of these women was pretty, but they're striking nonetheless. She, like her sister, is not a small woman. This is solid stock around here. Her ancestors cut trees, pulled stumps, and wrestled boulders by hand, trying to grapple out tillable land in this Driftless area of southwest Wisconsin. Schaefer's brother, Cal, was in the bar too. Cast in half shadow by a too-bright plastic beer sign, he and his brother-in-law stalked a hazy pool table in the back room like mini-Agamemnons. This family could sack a city. They were all born and raised in Winsome Bay, and are determined to stay there.

They, too, are, in a way, driftless.

Schaefer drank a lot during the interview, her speech often slurred and sloppy. She seemed aware of this at times, but continued to talk through it, rough and rambling, and at times angry. She frequently went off on non sequiturs: small-town life, domestic beers, the press, deer season coming up, bow hunting turkeys, the flooding last spring, being a cop. The hardest thing about being a cop in a small town, she told me, was that you know just about everyone you have to deal with. They're your friends, your relatives, neighbors, people you like or don't like. Most of the calls are minor, she said, but there's always the farmer who rolls his tractor or gets caught on a power takeoff shaft, the neighbor kid on crack, the hunting mishap, the drunk driver, the domestic abuse, and now, the murder. Schaefer and officer Tom Ellison, the father of the victim, had worked together for the last four years.

"Tom," she said, speaking about the victim's father. "He was just crazy about Deb."

"How's he doing?"

She took a long, hot pull off her cigarette. "Not good. Not good."

"Is he back to work?"

"No, no. He's, uh . . . no. He goes to church a lot. He's—Tom's a very religious guy. Always has been. His family too. Never missed a Sunday. Always wore a suit, did the collection at Mass, the prayers before eating, you know, the whole nine yards. He'd pray in the cruiser over a turkey sandwich. I'd tease him about it. And now . . ." Schaefer crushed out her cigarette. "Things just aren't adding up for him." She reached across the table and grabbed another cigarette from my pack. "You mind?"

"No, go ahead."

She looked to her sister. "I know, I smoke too much."

Jeannie stood and said, "I have to pee," and headed down a long dark hallway.

Schaefer's mood darkened suddenly. I wasn't sure what to ask next. I didn't want to scare her off. So I lit a cigarette too and said nothing. A long silence followed, one of those uncomfortably long pauses when you know somebody should say something but nobody does. It seemed to go on forever. I was just about to say something to break the awkwardness when Schaefer glanced toward the ceiling and said, "A policeman was just born."

"I'm sorry?"

"Huh? Oh, nothing. Just something you say when nobody knows what to say. You know, like 'an angel just passed over' or something. Deborah used to say it."

"Oh." I waited another few seconds. "So you said earlier that you knew her. Deborah."

"Yes." She held up the cigarette. "Thanks."

"And you said you knew her pretty well."

"Hold on." Schaefer grabbed her empty beer bottle and went to the bar. Turning back to me, she asked, "Want one?"

"No, I'm good."

She called the bartender out of a cloud of smoke. The woman twisted open a beer, poured a shot of something, and pushed it in front of Schaefer, who slammed it down. Schaefer took a guzzle of her beer and headed back to our table. "Sorry," she said, "what were you saying?"

"You knew Deborah well, you said. Was this before she moved to Chicago?"

"Yes."

"Was she living at home while she was here?"

"Home? No, she had an apartment by the lake. She was pretty messed up back then."

"In what way?"

"I can't really go into that, but, uh, this wasn't a good place for her to be. She needed money, there were no jobs here, she was getting into some bad things."

"Didn't her parents help her?"

Schaefer didn't answer. She shrugged and looked around the bar. I could tell she was uncomfortable with my last question, so I asked, "But you and Deborah were friends?"

"We didn't really hang out together, but I took her to Chicago with me sometimes."

"Before she moved there?"

"Yeah, this was a while ago. My old boyfriend and me, we used to drive in a lot. And one time, we were on our way there, and we see her hitchhiking out on the beltline. I pulled over, I was like, what the hell are you doing? You're going to get yourself killed. She was trying to get to Chicago. So we took her with us. After that, I started telling her whenever we'd be going in, and sometimes she'd come with. We'd drop her off at a club or something and she'd meet up with us later, or crash with us."

I took a sip of my drink. "Wesley Faber mentioned some kind of trouble Deborah had been in, when she was younger. Something Father Ryan helped with? Do you know anything about that?" Schaefer shook her head. Her eyes were glassy. I pressed her. "Is that why she moved to Chicago? Because of whatever this trouble was?"

Schaefer squinted and waved away smoke from her cigarette. She took another swallow of beer. "I don't know why she moved."

I ventured a guess. "Was she pregnant?"

"No," Schaefer said, giving me a look like I was stupid.

"But you knew her pretty well."

"Yes."

"And you identified the body."

"Yes."

"I'm sorry to ask this," I said, "but I read about the condition of the body. How did you even know it was Deborah?"

Jillian stopped the article there, even though there was a lot more that Schaefer had revealed to Jillian that night. It was all great material, but everything else that had been said was off the record, so it couldn't be used. What Jillian hadn't included was everything that Schaefer had said after Jillian's last question.

When Jillian said, "I'm sorry to ask this, but I read about the condition of the body. How did you even know it was Deborah?" Schaefer answered, "The tattoos she had on her—"

The words were barely out of her mouth when Schaefer lunged across the table, knocking empty bottles to the floor. "Fuck!" she said, "Fuck!" She grabbed the digital recorder, trying to turn it off, but she was too drunk and her hands weren't working well. "You can't write that. That's not been released yet. It could screw up the case. You can't, you can't write that!"

"Okay, okay, I won't!" Jillian took the recorder and turned it off. "It's off the record. You say off the record, it's—"

"Off the record!"

"Okay."

"Swear to God." Schaefer grabbed her arm. "Right now, swear to God."

"I swear to God."

She tightened her grip.

"Please, you're hurting me."

"Sorry," Schaefer said, releasing her. "Sorry. I didn't mean to." She looked to see if her brother was watching. "Just be smart about what you write. We want to catch this guy."

Jillian sat back down. "I won't print it."

Schaefer stared at the table for a moment. Her eyes glistened wet.

Jeannie came back from the bathroom. "You okay?" she asked Schaefer.

"Yeah, fine."

"We should get going soon, okay? I'll tell the boys."

"Sure."

Jeannie went over to the pool table. A little laughter and whistling welcomed her.

Schaefer spoke very quietly.

"I'd seen her tattoos before. When she crashed with us in Chicago once. We were getting changed together and she came out of the shower, and she showed me. She had lots of tattoos, in places where you usually can't see them. Birds and flowers, wings. Her dad didn't know about them, but I did, and uh . . . that's how I recognized her."

"Did you—"

Jeannie came over with the boys.

"All right, sis," Cal said, "you ready?"

"In a second," Schaefer said, chugging a last swallow of beer. "I gotta pee." She pushed herself up off the table and stumbled slightly.

Her brother caught her arm. "Whoa, a little drunk, are we?"

"Yes. And I'm going to get drunker. I'll arrest myself later."

Cal handed her off to Jeannie, who helped her to the bathroom. "Meet you out front," he called after them. He and his brother-in-law left. They did not say good-bye.

Jillian got up to leave. She checked her phone. Michael had texted her good night. Mara hadn't returned her call. It was late and she really had to get headed home. She was going to go to the bathroom too, when she kicked an empty beer bottle that had been knocked off the table. She reached beneath to pick it up and saw Schaefer's purse on the floor, its contents strewn about the filthy carpet. She gathered up her things quickly, shoving everything back in. As she did she noticed an official-looking document among the items. It was folded up, but she could clearly make out the heading.

A coroner's report.

Jillian glanced to the bathroom, then quickly unfolded the document.

Twenty-three-year-old female. 5′ 3″, 110 lbs. Caucasian. Thirty-two stab wounds to the neck and upper torso. Extensive incise and puncture wounds across anterior and left lateral neck. Blunt force trauma to the face and skull. Bruising on upper forearms and biceps. Left hand missing.

In the basement of the Chicago medical examiner's office, Detective Mangan met with Brian Rhys to discuss the forensic evidence sent by the Wisconsin medical examiner.

"Okay, Wonder Boy," Mangan said, "wonder me. Tell me something I don't know."

"That's a wide field of discussion."

"Blow me, Brad."

"Language, Jimmy, language."

"Don't call me Jimmy."

"Don't call me Brad."

Brian Rhys, early thirties, blond, handsome, and ridiculously intelligent, had aced forensic science at Michigan State, sailed through four years of internal medicine in Houston, and then enjoyed a sun-filled fellowship at the American University of the Caribbean School of Medicine before working his way up to the glory boy of Chicago crime analysis while simultaneously working his way through what seemed like every available woman in the downtown Chicago area. Mangan called him Brad because he looked a little like Brad Pitt. There was nothing particularly eccentric about Rhys, nothing like the morgue geeks or body doctors in crime novels and movies—always some weird quirk, or look, or habit—nothing like that. He liked his work, was good at it, liked his sports, was fascinated by things he couldn't figure out, and obsessed with work only during business hours. When the day was over he was gone, jogging up the steps from his basement office. He always seemed to be on his way to a Cubbies game or happy hour somewhere.

"It's nice and cool down here," Mangan said. "How come your AC's working?"

"It's not. I leave the doors to the body fridge open. Where's Coose?"

"He's following up at the Bank Street Diner, trying the find the girl Lachlan was with."

"Lachlan?"

"The guy with the hand. He's a magazine editor. *American Forum.* You know it?"

"No."

"A fake lit mag. Cross between the *Paris Review* and *People.*"

Rhys slid a photo of Deborah Ellison's battered face in front of Mangan. "Show and tell," he said. "This is the Wisconsin victim. Twenty-three-year-old female. Five foot three, a hundred and ten pounds, thirty-two stab wounds to the neck and upper torso, profound fracturing of the zygomatic and orbital—"

"Do I look like someone who uses big words? Slow down."

"You have a larger vocabulary than I do, James. I don't know why you pretend you don't. What's that get you, anyway? Power? Control?"

"Stop trying to analyze me and tell me what you're talking about."

"You know what I'm talking about, James, it's not brain surgery." Rhys took up the autopsy photo. "Well, actually, I guess it is." He pointed to a caved-in area around and below the victim's eye. "She was severely beaten. Her bones aren't just broken, they're crushed."

"I can see that," Mangan said, the words, *thy bones are marrowless, thy blood is cold*, running through his head.

Rhys exchanged photos, sliding another horrific picture across the table. Mangan winced at the image, the same area of the face, but the left eyelid was pried open wide with a stainless steel specula.

"Medical examiner in Wisconsin made a good catch," Rhys said. "Coroner overlooked it in the prelims. Easy to do with catastrophic injuries." He took a pencil and pointed to a spot on the victim's eye. "What do you see?"

"I don't have time to play games."

"Neither do I, I'm tailgating at Harry Caray's in an hour. What do you see?" Mangan tried to see what Rhys was alluding to. "Look at the sclera—sorry, James—*the big white part* of the eye. It's easy to miss." He touched the tip of his pencil to a fine threadlike line in a small patch of white in the eye. It was barely visible, a few strands of red spider webbing.

"Petechial."

"Look at you, using big words."

"So she was strangled."

"Yes." Rhys put another photo in front of Mangan, a wider shot of Debbie Ellison's massive facial wounds. "Blunt force trauma, predominantly on the left side. He used a rock or a piece of cement or something. The wound edges are ragged, and abrasion marks are scratched into some of the bone fragments. My guess is he sat on top of her, straddled her, keeping her arms down with his knees. There's bruising on her forearms and biceps." Rhys acted out the scene. "He strangles her, takes a rock to her face, and then gets to work with the knife."

"Was she alive? When he stabbed her?"

"I don't think so. There's not much vascular constriction or bleeding into the surrounding tissues."

Mangan picked up another photo, a mass of blackened flesh that was once the Ellison girl's torso and hip area. He studied the body, *upon whose dead corpse there was such misuse as may not be spoken of.* Despite the decomposition, he could make out numerous tattoos on her breasts and stomach, around her genitals down the inner thighs. Most were of birds, small colorful birds in flight, or clinging to leafy vines that wrapped around her limbs.

"There's a special providence in the fall of a sparrow," Mangan said quietly.

"What?"

"Nothing."

"Anyway," Rhys continued, "there were no clothes on the body when she was found and no jewelry. No earrings either, despite the fact that she had numerous piercings." He rifled through another stack of photos. "Here's a teaser. This little flap of skin on her neck. See that? Those dots." On a small section of the front neck there were about a dozen tiny bruise marks, cylindrical, and not much bigger than the typed letter *o* of a keyboard. "They're organized," Rhys said. "There's a pattern to them. Equal distance apart."

"What are they?"

"An impression mark of some kind."

"Are they anywhere else on her body?"

"No." Rhys checked his notes again. "Her stomach contents were partially undigested. She was found early Saturday morning, August eleventh, around twelve forty-five a.m. So, time of death, they're guessing, maybe four to six hours after her last meal, a little room either way. Sometime between five and ten o'clock the night before, Friday the tenth."

"You should be a detective."

"I am. Kind of."

Mangan considered what he knew so far: A young girl from a small town is killed. Most of the mutilation committed postmortem. *I am burned up with inflaming wrath; a rage that nothing can allay, nothing but blood.* "This is significant overkill," he said to Rhys, "this is rage."

"I'd assume so, but then again, somebody could want it to look like that."

Mangan mused aloud. "Why would he do that?"

"*Why* is your department, James. I do the *what* and *how*."

"I wasn't really asking you why, I'm just talking out loud. Don't you know that by now?"

"Sorry. Forgot." Rhys slid another Wisconsin file before Mangan. "They also report no signs of rape. And that's about all they have right now. Their chem analysis is still in the works." Rhys opened yet another file. "Now, as for *us*, and our little orphaned body part." He laid out photos of the severed hand. "Why are you so interested in this anyway?"

"What?"

"You've got plenty of actual bodies to keep you busy, what's with the hand?"

The phrase, *the bug which you would fright me with, I seek*, scurried through Mangan's thoughts. "I don't know, it's just bugging me," he told Rhys. He spied a copy of the letter that had been found with the severed hand. "Have you read that?"

"Yes. Pretty weird."

"That's what Coose said. What do you make of it?"

"You really asking or just talking out loud?"

"Really asking."

"Okay. Well, I'd say he feels justified in what he's doing. And he might do it again."

"Yeah, I'm thinking the same. You find any trace on the letter?"

"No."

"The envelope?"

"Nothing. No saliva, it wasn't sealed. We got a few latents, but they were all civilians' who'd handled the envelope. And the prints of the hand aren't in the system."

"What about the knife?"

"Hard to say." Rhys scanned the Wisconsin report. "But it's a different knife than the one used on the Wisconsin victim. There are indications of a serrated edge used on the severed hand. Not so on the Wisconsin victim. They approximate the knife used on Deborah Ellison at about eight inches. An inch wide at the hilt, single edged. A fillet knife maybe, a boning knife. Also the wound patterns are chaotic, wild, a frenzied kill. But the hand was severed very cleanly, no slicing or sawing motions, no preparatory cuts." Rhys started entering data into his computer. "Whoever did it knew what he was doing."

Mangan lost in thought, walked the room. "What's he, a doctor? A surgeon?"

"A vet, a butcher. Who knows? A chef."

"A forensic pathologist."

"Possible."

64

"Any trace on the hand itself?"

"No."

"No trace on the Wisconsin victim. He was wearing gloves."

"Yes."

"So, it's premeditated. He knew what he was going to do. He sought her out. Yes?"

"I would assume. Look, James, I actually have *Chicago* cases I have to—"

"She was living in Chicago, so she could've been killed here. Right?"

"Well, she could have—"

"Did they have a last known whereabouts on her?"

"I don't know."

"What was she doing in Winsome Bay? Or was she even there?"

"I don't know."

"No missing persons reports. Where's her family, the Ellison girl's family?"

"James, please, it's not even our case, so if you don't mind, I—"

"Why do you keep interrupting me? I'm thinking here."

"I'm sorry, I've got work to do."

"So do it already, go. Nobody's stopping you. Go."

"This is my office, James."

Detective Cusumano came in late the next day. "Friggin' traffic. Put a man on the moon, we still can't figure out how to merge." He tossed three copies of *American Forum* on the table.

Mangan took one up and flipped through it, looking for an article by Jillian McClay. "What did you get on that girl at the Bank Street Diner?"

"Not a whole lot." Coose tossed a paper bag on the sink counter and washed out a coffee mug. "Street name, Fenyana Petrakova. Real name, Petra Nadzenia. Where's the cream?"

"We're out."

He flipped Mangan a police mug shot and poured a cup of coffee. "That's her. Picked up a few times for the usual."

Mangan looked at the photo. "Jesus."

"Right?" Coose said. "She's beautiful. What's she doing on the street is what I'd like to know. She works a lot the northeast side. Lives in the Dearborn projects."

"You check it out?"

"Yeah. Nothing much. The landlord—who is a dick by the way—hasn't seen her for a while. And the guy who runs the Bank Street, whatever his name is . . ." Coose checked his notes. "Baratov. Savva *Baratov*. Sells a little more than coffee at his joint, but he's a nickel-'n'-dimer. Caters mostly to white-collar johns. Pretty straight up. Doesn't hurt his girls from what I could tell." He took a bagel out of the bag and tore it in half. "Want some?"

"No thanks. Where's the girl now?"

"Says he doesn't know, but he's lying. A girl like that? She's the money." Between bites of bagel and swallows of coffee Coose read through the rest of his notes. "One of my girls on the street says Baratov's in with the Russian mob. Says he's always shoving it in their faces. So I talked to Nazarkov to check him out."

"You talked to Nazarkov?"

Coose grinned. "I did."

"How the hell'd you get to him?"

"I know a guy. I made a call. You don't get any higher than Nazarkov, and he says this asshole ain't in the club, and if he keeps saying he is, he's gonna wind up in a fucking caviar can."

"All right, put Palmer on this," he said. "He knows the prostitutes on the Gold Coast and Boys Town. See if any of their friends have gone missing. Then get started on the Hicks case."

"You get started on it."

"I'm busy."

"So am I."

"I'm busier."

"I'll do it later."

"Do it now."

"Why are you being such a prick? What's your problem today?"

"It's just that I got a file full of dead bodies here and we're wasting our time on a friggin' appendage. Get someone else on it."

"Okay, I'll take care of it."

"Okay."

Coose, halfway out the door, said, "Hey, we're heading over to Dugan's tonight, bunch of us. Why don't you get out of your cave for a little while and come along?"

"I got plans."

"Female plans?"

"None of your business."

"C'mon, give me details."

"I'm discreet. You know what that means?"

"Yeah, but it's no fun."

"Go away."

As soon as Coose stepped out of the room, a rush of words slammed into Mangan's thoughts. They came at him like a gale. He grasped at them, trying to trammel up their meanings, but they flew by—too many, too fast—a wreckage of words hurled across his mind—and then they were gone.

Just as quickly, nothing. He quieted himself and concentrated harder, willing them to return, trying to force them into showing themselves again.

They wouldn't come.

So he ignored them.

He knew their game. Sometimes, to hear the words more clearly, Mangan needed to listen less closely. The words that circled behind his mind's eye sometimes behaved like diminutive stars that disappear when looked at too directly. But if one focuses on an area just slightly to the side of them, these shy stars will sometimes show themselves again. Murderers were like that, Mangan believed. In a case with a profound lack of evidence, if he focused on some larger thought, or on some seemingly innocuous piece of evidence, and not just on *who* committed the crime, sometimes a glimpse of the killer might appear.

You had to come at murderers sideways.

Mangan turned his thoughts to the Chicago case, the handless victim, wondering who she might be, wondering what her connection was to the Wisconsin murder. He had a hunch the Chicago victim was a prostitute. They frequently have no family to speak of and their bodies often go unclaimed. If there even *was* a body, that is. Coose could be right. It's possible that this was a kidnapping—no, no, Mangan knew the woman was dead, whoever she was. He took a sip of coffee, as cold as it was shitty. He dumped it in the sink, watching the rust-brown liquid swirl into the drain—

It will have blood, they say.
There they were . . .
Blood will have blood.
They were back.
See thy mangled daughter, sweet father.
See thy mangled daughter . . . and cease your tears.

The words came to him very clearly now. And he knew them. He'd just read them. "Thy mangled daughter" was a line was from *Titus Andronicus*. "Blood will have blood" was from *Macbeth*. Given his line of work, that play often spoke to him, or Shakespeare did, Mangan couldn't really say who was doing the speaking. Of course he knew it wasn't actually Shakespeare, he wasn't crazy, but when he wondered about this phenomenon of his brain, and the mental gymnastics that often played out there, he had to consider the possibility of whether something larger than himself was at work, something that was trying to contribute to his thinking or lead him in a particular direction.

Is it I, God, or who, that lifts this arm?

Or were these just the foolish musings of his mind? Was he merely assigning a meaning to these obsessive thoughts of his?

What is it, what nameless, inscrutable, unearthly thing is it?

Or perhaps the nature of the mind was inherently larger than one's own self, and if so, these thoughts might be part of a larger collective conscience, part of the *deeper, faraway things* in Mangan, *the occasional flashings forth of the intuitive truth*, as Melville said, for that author's words were now tacking through his mind also. Or, if he were really honest with himself, this could actually be some mild form of insanity, a fluttering of the wings of madness. He entertained the thought . . . then scuttled it.

There is a divinity that shapes our ends, rough hew them how we will.

Mangan knew these works of literature so well that he couldn't tell if it was merely his memory correlating poetry with evidence—a sort of involuntary associative leap—or if the poetry was actually guiding his thinking, helping him to draw conclusions from the evidence he'd gathered. He really didn't know. And he really didn't care, because it quite often worked. Like a placebo that cures: if it works, who cares? The words that came to James Mangan's mind sometimes led him to the truth of things, and that's all that mattered, *for in this world of lies, truth is forced to fly like a scared white doe in the woodlands; and only by cunning glimpses will she reveal herself.*

Mangan had memorized those words. They were Melville's personal musings on Shakespeare, whom he'd called the master of *the great art of telling the truth, even though it be covertly, and by snatches.* That's how Mangan most often discovered the truth about murderers, *covertly and by snatches.* Mangan loved Melville's writing, yes, but Melville never seemed to lead Mangan to any conclusions. Melville was all questioning, all observations and fruitless graspings at something deeply inscrutable, always gathering evidence, trying to figure out what it all meant, but never having it add up to anything, like a frustrated detective whose life's work turns out to be one massive unsolved case. Shakespeare, however, was a little more ballsy. He took a risk and actually posed some answers. He took a shot at the truth.

And Mangan liked that.

Whenever Mangan was teased about this literary eccentricity of his, which was quite often, his stock reply was always, "If anyone knows about murder, it's Shakespeare." And if anyone knew about Shakespeare, it was Mangan. He'd read all his plays, many of them a number of times, and had seen nearly all of them on the stage at one time or another. He'd traveled to Shakespeare festivals around the country, and also Ontario and London. He had a private goal to see all of the plays acted on the stage before he died. He'd seen thirty-three of Shakespeare's thirty-seven plays, if he didn't count *Two Noble Kinsmen* (questionable authorship). Mangan often told his water cooler hecklers about the fact that Shakespeare had written extensively about some of the most horrendous crimes imaginable: infanticide, patricide, mutilations, tortures, cannibalism, rapes, and beheadings, to name just a few. If people continued to razz him, he liked to rattle off the following stats, at which point they usually either shut their mouths or were left with them slightly agape: "In *Titus Andronicus* alone there are fourteen murders, six dismemberments, three rapes, and one live burial."

Mangan's world.

This somewhat unorthodox connection between Shakespeare and police work started back when Mangan was a student at Strayer University. One of his law professors, using *Othello* as a case study, ran a mock trial in class. An actor from a local theater played the role of

Iago, who was put on trial for the murder of another character in the play, Roderigo, and also for inciting the murder of yet another character, Desdemona. There was a preponderance of evidence against Iago, but as it turned out, it was all hearsay. The plaintiffs were all dead. Iago also couldn't be compelled to incriminate himself after he'd said, *"From this time forth, I never will speak word,"* which was undeniably his right. There had also been verbal commands, witnessed and recorded, ordering the torture of Iago. So any confessions obtained by such means would be inadmissible. The witnessed stabbing of Iago's wife, Emilia (Iago killed her too), could be presented to the jury in a sympathetic light as a crime of passion, an uncontrollable burst of rage brought on by her false accusations against him. In today's judicial system, Iago would have walked on at least the first two counts.

Later, Mangan found Shakespeare's plays a great way to study the psychology of evil: power, jealousy, insanity, revenge, the motives of thwarted ambition and sexual jealousy. He also discovered that they were a great way to get laid. Women seemed to like the contradiction, the no-shit tough guy cop, classical theatergoer. A Mickey Spillane–type character twisting the cuffs onto bad guys while quoting *Twelfth Night*: *"And thus the whirligig of time brings in his revenges."*

He would never admit it himself, but James Mangan was a closet artist. Not in the fruity I'm-so-special-because-I'm-an-artist sense. There wasn't an "artsy" bone of that kind in his body, or in his family's: four boys, Timmy and Eugene were marines—like his dad—and Johnny was a construction worker. Not big men, but bulls, short and thick. Scrappers. In the city Mangan grew up in, you had to be. He was the smallest of the boys, and as a kid he learned quickly that he had to fight—and fight *first*—with the biggest guys he could find. Most of the time he got the shit kicked out of him. Sometimes he didn't. It didn't matter; everyone thought he was crazy. And crazy goes a long way on the streets.

Much to his own surprise, Mangan became friends with some actors, like Lou Ciccione, who had played Iago in his law class. Lou lived in Rogers Park and worked in most of the Chicago theaters. Back in the day, Mangan was more likely to meet up with Lou for a drink after work than anyone else. The last thing he wanted was to go to a cop bar. No, with Lou's crowd it was a lot easier for Mangan to forget about work, forget about the horrible shit he dealt with every day, and besides, Lou loved Shakespeare. He and Mangan would talk nights away discussing the plays and arguing about what they meant. Some of the other actors were pretentious dicks of course—actually, *most* of them were—but Mangan just ignored them. A lot of the guys were gay, which Mangan took full advantage of because that meant a lot of rudderless women looking for direction come closing time.

After a while Mangan learned to tell the real artists from the bluffs. It was an easy tell: the laziest and least talented always talked the most about being *artists*. They were the angry ones, angry at the world for not having noticed them, for not having recognized their gifts. They were bitter and resentful and felt slighted and talked shit about everyone else and wanted everyone to know how great they were and to pay more attention to them.

Christ, Mangan thought, fucking serial killers think like that.

Emilio Flores was driving south on Sheridan Road, delivering his early run of bread to a long list of Chicago taverns and restaurants. A warm, foggy morning, the sun barely grayed the clouds blanketing Lake Michigan.

Traffic was already bad.

Emilio stopped for gas, bought a coffee and two packages of Ho Hos, hurried back to his truck, and pulled into the nearest alley to eat. A mist had rolled in off the lake, shrouding the Dumpsters and garbage cans in a soft milky haze. He rolled down his driver's side window and jerked suddenly, uncontrollably. He dropped his coffee and began muttering Hail Marys as he fumbled for his cell phone.

It was raining heavily when Detective Mangan arrived on the scene. The alley had been cordoned off with yellow police tape. Uniformed policemen stood guard, and a CSI team was hurriedly setting up a blue canopy of tarp above the body. Mangan and Coose got out of the car, neither bothering to grab an umbrella, and ducked under the tape. They joined the CSI team beneath the makeshift tenting, the rain smacking crazily on the plastic overhead.

"I'll see what they got," Coose said, heading over to the officers on scene.

Mangan nodded, staring down at the body, awash in rainwater. It lay in a twisted heap beside a Dumpster. Female. Naked from the waist up.

Left hand cut off at the wrist.

The body.

The one he'd known was out there.

Mangan crouched beside the ash gray corpse. *What stern ungentle hands have lopped and hewed and made thy body bare?* The victim's face, partially submerged in a shallow puddle, was nearly indistinguishable as a face. There were slash marks on both her shoulders and sternum, as well as on her arms. Crimped in its odd pose of death, it flashed images of the plaster casts of the victims of Pompey across Mangan's mind, something he'd seen as a boy in a magazine somewhere, charcoal-encrusted bodies cradled into each other, seared together in death.

"Thirty-eight," Coose said, coming up behind him.

"What?" Mangan asked, tugging on a pair of latex gloves.

"First officer on the scene found her purse and ran her license. She was thirty-eight. And get this, her name is Mara Davies. She worked for Kevin Lachlan."

"Lachlan?" Mangan said.

"She was a submissions editor for the *American Forum* magazine."

Mangan looked down at the body again. "What the hell is going on here?"

"I have no idea."

"Call Eagan and Palmer. Tell them to get eyes on Lachlan right away, bring him in again. Start interviewing his employees. Let's get ahold of anybody that's got anything to do with these articles being written about that Wisconsin murder. Call Wesley Faber in Winsome. Tell him what we got going on down here. Let's find this writer too, whoever's writing these articles."

Mangan leaned in closer and studied the corpse. Her face had been savagely beaten. There were contusions on the front of the neck and underside of the chin. The cheek, forehead, and left eye socket were crushed inward, giving the face a concaved look. *Let grief convert to anger; blunt not the heart, enrage it.* Superficial wounds could be seen on her wrists and chest, which Mangan thought at first to be defensive wounds, but on closer examination there was too much symmetry to them. No, he was wrong. He saw it then: her shirt and bra had been cut from her body, leaving shallow knife wounds on the flesh beneath. The wrist had been cut clean through. Mangan assumed that the hand from Kevin Lachlan's apartment most likely belonged to this victim.

When the CSI team gave the okay, Mangan called Coose over. They knelt beside the body and carefully rolled it onto its side, the limbs limp, dead long enough that rigor had come and gone.

Coose noticed it first. "Look," he said.

There was something in the corner of the victim's mouth. CSI moved in and photographed the facial area again. Mangan took a pair of tweezers and carefully removed a small balled up piece of paper.

There were words on it.

Another note.

Mangan carefully pried the wad of paper open. A single sentence:

STOP WRITING ABOUT HER
THE CHOOSER

He hadn't intended to cut off her hand.

She'd grabbed him that night and wouldn't let go, even after she was dead. She was the first. He thought that would be enough. It wasn't. The second one, he *had* meant to cut her hand off. It seemed the right thing to do. He had not been looking for her, though. No. He wanted the writer. He wanted to find the writer. He didn't want everyone reading about the other girl.

That was wrong.

He Googled the writer's name. Jillian McClay. He found her bio. Her résumé. He knew a lot about her. He could not find her address. He searched the magazine's website and found the staff directory. He found the editor's name. He wrote it down. He would remember that. Where he lived. He had a home. And an apartment. Jillian McClay wasn't listed with the staff. He was about to leave the website, when he saw a woman's picture. Mara Davies. Submissions editor. Mara Davies. It interested something in his brain. He fingered the computer mouse—*click*. The tab he tapped led him to the woman's résumé. Another tab—*double-click*—led him to a short bio.

Mara Davies graduated from William Ash High School and attended the Writer's Workshop at UNI. She is the proud daughter of Mrs. Rachel Davies, a retired music teacher, and Mr. Edward Davies, a parole officer in Elgin, IL.

And that's when it was revealed to him.

That's when the crack in his mind began to expand, and through the opening he now glimpsed the wide arch of the world before him, as if the horizon had suddenly extended outward a thousandfold, and he, rushing toward it, saw *the way*, the way was being shown to him. That's why he had been led to Mara Davies, that's why he had double-clicked the mouse that led to her bio. There was a reason behind all of it.

Something larger was at work.

He drove to the city. To the *American Forum* building. He had a plan for the editor and for Mara Davies. He waited for her. He had nothing else to do. He could not work, could not sleep, could not think about anything except the bad things. He got dressed up for the trip. He shaved. He combed his hair. He followed the Davies woman after work and took the "L" and sat far away from her, but close enough that he could watch her. He read a book while watching her, but he was not seeing words, he was seeing her face on the pages, her crushed dead face.

He followed her off the train. She went into a bar. He waited. He went in after her and sat in a far corner. Never looked at her. The music was loud. Very loud. She was with friends. And a man. Smiling. Happy. Touching the man—*drink, flirt, touch, drink, flirt, touch, drink, flirt*—she started walking his way, right toward him, and he heard her say, "Steven. Steven! I'm going out back for a cigarette. I'll be right back."

No you won't.

The heavy back door of the bar slammed shut when he walked out after her.

"Hi," she said, turning away to light a cigarette.

"Hi."

And he knew then that this was right. It was as if she had turned her back to him just to allow this moment to occur, *her* moment, as if she knew what was to come and had accepted it. Then the dark numby thing rose up in him, and he listened to it. It told him to put his arm around her neck. So he did. And then he just started to squeeze, and kept squeezing, harder and harder and harder and harder and he heard the sound of her cigarette lighter clink on the pavement and he felt her body begin to twist and squirm in a kind of bewilderment, and then in a panic, and then she started to make little-girl noises and spit and kick and squeak and he carried her away from the back door deeper into the darkened alley.

And then she stopped kicking.

And he let go.

He stared down at her. He dragged her behind a Dumpster and pulled on his powder-free exam gloves and took out his knife and cut off her shirt and cut the straps of her bra away and then he did things to her face and body with the heel of his boot. He stopped a moment to see what he had done. Then he cut off her hand. He let it drip-drip a little and put it in the pocket of his jacket. He took out the message he had written and placed it into what was left of her mouth.

Back in his truck, he took out the other note he'd written. He put it in the fat envelope he'd addressed to the editor. Then he put the hand in. Then he dropped it inside the lobby doors of his apartment building.

It was all so very easy.

He had done better this time. The first time was very sloppy. If he was too sloppy he would get caught and he would not be able to punish them and make them feel what he had felt, back when he could still feel, before he became the dark numby thing. He didn't care what happened to himself, no, he knew how that would end, that had been rehearsed a billion years before the oceans rolled.

But before then, he had much to do.

Jillian pushed her kitchen window up higher. The night was bright with moon and mist. She lit a cigarette and blew the smoke through the screen. A police car was stationed in front of her house. Michael was in his room packing. Mara Davies was dead.

Jesus God. Jesus God.

Wesley Faber had called and explained to her what had happened.

What have I done?

Nick McClay, tan and aging too well for fifty, walked into the kitchen. He'd flown in from Florida right away. She hadn't known who else to call. He had less hair than the last time Jillian had seen him, but he kept it groomed and full of product so that it seemed stylish. He looked out of place in Wisconsin, too bright and thin, like his shirt.

"Hey," he said. "How you doing?"

Jillian tossed her cigarette out the back door. "I just—I keep seeing her, sitting out here. Just a few days ago she was in my backyard."

"Jill, I really don't think you should stay here. You should come with us."

"No."

"Just till they catch this guy. I've got plenty of room."

"I can't, I . . ." The only thought on Jillian's mind was keeping Michael safe, and for Jillian that meant getting him as far away from her as possible. "The police need to talk to me, and Mara's funeral is this week. After that I'll come down. Okay? I'll book the flight tonight."

"All right. Well, call your dad, at least. He can get out here in a day."

"Yeah, I, I hadn't even thought about that. It's just—everything's happening so fast."

"Let me do it, I can call him right now."

"No, I'll do it. I should be the one to tell him what's going on."

Michael came walking down the hallway toward the kitchen. He'd been very quiet since Jillian told him what had happened. He seemed unsure of what to say or do, or even where to look.

"Hey, honey," Jillian said to him. "Did you pack shorts?"

"What?"

"Did you take shorts? It's really hot down there."

"Yeah, um . . . I got the blue ones."

"You need more than one pair."

"I couldn't find any more."

Michael looked to the floor and Jillian could tell that he was hiding whatever it was he was feeling. He always looked away or stared at the floor when he was upset, not wanting to make any kind of eye contact. She walked over and as soon as she touched him, the tears came, the inconsolable kind, like a child's. She held him tightly. It had been so long since she'd held him like that, so long since he'd let her into his private fourteen-year-old life. Despite the horrible thing that had happened, she couldn't help cherishing a brief moment of feeling like a mom again.

"It's okay," she said. "Everything's going to be okay." She looked over Michael's shoulder to Nick. "You're going to stay with your dad and I'll be down as soon as I can. Just a couple of days. I'm going to call Grandpa and have him come and stay with me. Okay?" She gently broke the embrace and held him at arm's length. "I need your help with this, buddy."

Michael nodded.

"All right. Go find your other shorts."

He walked away.

Nick checked the time. "We should hit the road if we're going to make our flight." He touched Jillian's arm, as if asking permission for something. "I'll put the bags in the car."

Jillian nodded, distracted. "Yeah. Yeah. Go ahead."

He walked away and Jillian couldn't help feeling a tug of longing for him. She remembered his laugh. There hadn't been much laughter in her house over the last few years. She remembered his body and the long weight of him on top of her, the pressure, what it felt like to be covered by him and feel safe, pinned beneath and protected.

She opened the back door and lit another cigarette. Sat on the step. The moon was so bright that the yard seemed to float in the vapory haze that had settled low across the ground. In the far corner of the yard, through a veil of mist, Jillian could just about make out four skinny giraffe-leg-like shadows: Michael's swing set, from an eon ago, when he'd played on them for hours and hours and hours. She gazed up at the old carriage house on the edge of her property, where her writing studio was. The window on the second floor glowed golden. She'd left her office light on. She wanted to be in there, writing. She always felt better when she was writing.

Nick called from the front room. "Jill, we have to get going."

Jillian stubbed her cigarette out on the steps and hurried in. Michael was standing at the front door, his suitcase in his hand. He looked lost. Like a lost little boy. The one who used to wake smiling and carry bad breakfasts out to her office.

She wanted to say something to him, something profound and reassuring, but all she could think to say was, "Make sure you wear sunscreen, okay?"

Michael nodded.

"I'll be down in a couple of days."

"Okay."

"I love you."

She kissed him good-bye and watched them leave. She waved to them when they got in the car. She waved to them as they pulled away. She waved until they were out of sight. She stared out her front door for a long time. She saw the police car parked in front of her house, and began to feel restless, a simmering anger rising in her, angry at herself for feeling so afraid, angry for having to send her son away, angry that she had ever started this whole goddamn thing.

She slammed the door shut and locked it and went into her bedroom.

Rummaging through the closet, she found her black enameled safe box, punched in the code, opened it, and pulled out a Beretta M1934 .380-caliber pistol. Her father had given it to her when she'd moved away from home. It was a stubby little thing, lighter than she'd remembered. It felt good in her hands, the rough notched grip, the way her thumb rested neatly on the grooved safety, the oily smell of steel. She reached in and took out the box of 9-millimeter cartridges. The pistol's magazine was empty, and she'd forgotten how to load it. She fumbled with the bullets, dropping them on the floor as she tried to thumb them into the mouth of the magazine.

"Damn it . . ."

She grabbed her laptop, first Googled, then YouTubed, and in two clicks she was watching a dentally challenged man with a mullet and tattooed forearms instruct her how to load seven rounds into a Beretta. She followed his instructions, smacked the magazine into place, and thumbed off the safety. To the kitchen next and out the back door, hurrying to her writing studio. She ran up the stairs, pushed open the office door, and sat herself in front of the computer. She was going to write. The police had told her about the note the killer had written, warning her to stop. Well, fuck him, Jillian thought.

I am the writer.

She put the gun on the desk and took the digital recorder out of her drawer. She hit the Play button and heard her own voice whispering "massive blunt force trauma to the face and skull." She threw the recorder against the wall. No. No! That's not what she wanted to write. Not that.

What then?

She looked at the quote she kept taped to her wall.

Do not worry.

You have always written.

You will write again.

Just write one true sentence.

She couldn't think of a single true sentence.

"Shit. Shit. Shit."

Was this even really happening? It was an actual nightmare, she felt, she was living in a nightmare and needed to wake up. It had all sounded so easy at first. She'd thought it was going to be fun and she'd make some money. She would write something really shocking and try to make it controversial, and maybe if it were gruesome and raunchy enough people might even buy it. She would put a hot sex scene in it and violence, and use words like *fuck* and *Jesus* and *cunt*, and if she got really lucky, maybe the church would ban it—and oh, God, if she could only get the pope to denounce it, she just might make a fortune. And why not? Other writers did it all the time, laughing all the way to the bank.

Jillian wasn't laughing now.

She wiped her eyes, wishing she'd never had the idea to write about Deborah Ellison. She tried to stop thinking about the murders, but she couldn't. Horrid, horrid images kept running through her head, like a movie reel looping the same gruesome shots over and over again— hacked and mutilated bodies, shattered skulls oozing brain matter and—

So she stopped.

She changed her mind and just stopped.

And decided to start over.

Jillian grabbed all the research books stacked around her desk and her notebooks, and she threw them in the garbage. She opened the files on her computer and deleted everything that had anything to do with Deborah Ellison's murder, every draft, every piece of research, every saved image. She deleted all of it and emptied the trash folder—*click*— gone. She never had to look at another word of it again. Ever. She opened a new document. It snapped up fresh and clean and white.

She stared at the blank screen.

She waited.

She waited longer.

Nothing.

She read the quote on her wall again.

Just write one true sentence.

She wrote, "I don't know what to write."

And that was true . . .

And that truth led to another.

And that led to another, and the ideas began to come to her, and she started writing about the fact that she wished she'd never written about this poor girl's murder, and that she wanted to be writing children's books again where the bad guys always got caught, and children always survived, and she wrote and wrote and wrote, and she couldn't stop, no, no, she couldn't stop, because she knew what she had to do now. She had to write herself out of this horror.

She would write herself clean again.

Detective Mangan and Detective Eagan watched Lachlan through the two-way mirror. He was sitting in the interrogation room. Eagan had interviewed him at the *American Forum* building, asking about Mara Davies and how well he'd known her. Lachlan had seemed completely forthcoming, but then Eagan stumbled across something while interviewing the other employees, information that Lachlan had failed to disclose. He'd had an affair with the murder victim, Mara Davies.

They let Lachlan squirm another five minutes.

"You ready?" Mangan asked Eagan.

"Let's do it."

"I'll take the lead."

"I'll listen."

He and Mickey Eagan walked into the room.

"Well, we meet again," Mangan said, coming through the door. "Mr. Lachlan, this is Detective Eagan."

Eagan nodded at him.

"How long are we going to do this?" Lachlan asked. "I've done everything you've asked. I canceled the series in the magazine. I've told no one about the note. I've told you everything I know. I've been—"

"Well, now, now, you didn't quite tell us everything, Mr. Lachlan," Mangan said. "I've come to realize that you have a habit of doing that. First the prostitute in your apartment, then this little thing about Ms. Davies."

"Yes, I—all right, you're right, I didn't. Okay, you're right, I didn't tell you. I'm sorry. I didn't think it pertinent."

"Didn't think it pertinent?" Mangan said. "Having an affair with a woman who winds up murdered would be the *definition* of pertinent."

Mangan sat at the table and read through Lachlan's statements again. He took his time. He looked up afterward and studied the man a moment, as the phrase *an infinite and endless liar,* came to him, *an hourly promise-breaker, the owner of not one good quality.* There was still something Lachlan wasn't saying. He was hiding something.

"So," Mangan said to him, "one more time. Why didn't you tell us about this affair?"

"It wasn't an affair. It was one time. I was drunk and we wound up at my apartment."

Mangan turned to Eagan, "It's always the boyfriend."

"I'm not her boyfriend."

"Then what are you?"

"Nothing. I wasn't anything to her. It was one time."

Eagan searched through the employees' statements, picked one out, and slid it in front of Mangan. He studied it for a moment, shook his head, and looked up at Lachlan. "You've got some very unhappy employees. This one here says that Mara Davies was promoted very soon after her arrival at the magazine. Seems you passed over a number of people who were in line for the job, who had more experience and were more qualified."

"I can explain that."

"Oh. Well. Please do."

"She—"

"Did you promise her a position in exchange for sex, Mr. Lachlan?"

"I did not."

"That's illegal, you know."

"Of course I know. I would never do that."

"That's not what your employees think."

"I don't care what they think."

"Well, you should, because we've got a number of statements here that say—"

"Mara's the one who forced me to—!" Lachlan stopped short.

"What? What'd she force you to do? To have sex with her?"

"No. She—all right, look, I can explain."

"Yes, you were saying that earlier."

"I was with her one night. A couple of days later she walks into my office and *suggests* to me that she'd make a really good submissions editor, a position that had just opened up, and, uh . . . I felt, I was pretty sure, that it was more than a suggestion. I have a family. I didn't want to take any chances. So I gave her the job."

"So she was blackmailing you?" Mangan asked.

"I'm not saying that. It's just—one could certainly interpret it like that."

"Yes, one certainly could."

"None of this would even have happened if she hadn't pushed her friend's story about the murder on me. That's what started the—"

"Whoa, whoa," Mangan said. "What friend?"

"The writer. Jillian McClay."

"Mara Davies knew the woman who wrote those articles?"

"They were best friends."

Mangan leaned back in his chair, thinking *at length, the truth will out.*

"Well, now," he said to Lachlan, "this is a whole other kettle of whatever. Mara Davies threatens to expose your affair with her if you don't promote her. Then she forces you to hire a friend of hers. So you're not actually *interpreting* this as a possible blackmailing situation, you're actually saying that that's what was going on. Yes?"

"Um . . ."

"She was blackmailing you."

"If you want to call it that, yes."

"Well, yes, I think I *do* want to call it that."

"Well, then, yes, she was."

"Well, now that's very interesting," Mangan said. "A woman who was blackmailing you winds up murdered. That, Mr. Lachlan, is not only *pertinent*, but it's what, in police parlance, we call *motive*." Mangan gathered up some of his papers. "A little reminder, you have the right to remain silent. Anything you—"

"I swear to God, I had nothing to do with this!"

"A dead woman's severed hand was found in your apartment. How'd it get there?"

"I have no idea. I get dozens of submissions every week. I'm a publisher! I have a slush box filled with submissions dropped off in the lobby of my apartment every day. Anyone could have left it there."

"Anyone? Including you?"

"What the—? No."

"Did you use Deborah Ellison's murder to cover your own?"

"My own what?"

"Did you try to make it look like Mara Davies was killed by the same person who killed Deborah Ellison?"

"What are you talking about? No!"

"Did you kill Mara Davies?"

"*No!*"

"Did you—"

Lachlan suddenly reached inside his jacket. Eagan leaped across the table and grabbed his arm. Mangan was on him just as fast, wrestling Lachlan into a headlock. Eagan wrenched Lachlan's hand out of his jacket and pried open his fingers. He was clutching a cell phone.

"What the hell are you guys doing?" Lachlan yelled. "I was calling my lawyer."

Mangan and Eagan backed off.

"Well, why didn't you say so?" Mangan said. "Don't bother calling him. I'm done with you for now." Mangan knew he had nothing to hold him on.

Lachlan stood up and straightened himself out. "I had nothing to do with this," he said, and left the room.

Mangan waited a moment and then asked Eagan, "You believe him?"

"Yeah," Eagan said. "It's a stretch, what you're saying."

"I was just trying to think outside the box a bit."

"You succeeded."

"Keep an eye on him anyway," Mangan said. "I still don't like the guy. Run another check on his alibis."

Eagan walked out and Mangan tried to sort through the new information. Mara Davies was apparently murdered by the same person who killed Deborah Ellison. Davies was also friends with Jillian McClay, the woman writing a story about the Ellison murder. The killer leaves a note to stop writing about it, but if he wanted to stop the writing, why kill Mara Davies? Why didn't he kill the writer? Or the publisher? And why were the murders so horrific? So much bodily damage inflicted postmortem, as if their deaths were not enough.

Oft have I heard that grief softens the mind,
And makes it fearful and degenerate.

Grief, Mangan considered, *the poison of deep grief.* It would make sense, but grief over what? Mara Davies's murder was in direct response to the articles being written, a reprisal killing. But why the first murder victim in Wisconsin? Why was she killed? What had she done?

Who was Deborah Ellison?

Mangan took out his cell phone and called the Winsome Bay police station.

"Wesley Faber, please," he said. "No, I'll hold."

Officer Tom Ellison, father of the Wisconsin murder victim, grasped the back of the oaken pew and knelt, easing his knees into the cushioned, soft-leather kneelers of Saint Francis church. They reminded him of his daughter, the kneelers did. The church had originally been built without them, a modern design for its day, and Saint Francis had functioned that way for almost fifteen years until the new bishop, who listed heavily to starboard, ordered the town to kneel once again. Saint Francis parishioners had to raise fourteen thousand dollars to do so, in the same year in which the town was trying to raise money for Melissa Becker, a young girl from Winsome Bay who had lost her leg to cancer. Deborah had asked Father Ryan if the church might be able to donate the fourteen thousand dollars to help buy a prosthetic for Melissa. But Father Ryan said it was impossible to divert the funds: the bishop wanted kneelers. So Deborah wrote to the bishop herself, respectfully asking for help. There was no reply. She wrote again. No reply. Disillusioned, and more than a little angry at the absurdity of it, she and her mother decided to take on the project themselves. They organized "A Day for Melissa," a fund-raiser held in the local park. There was a 5K Run, raffle tickets, silent auctions, the Lion's Club and the KC's worked side by side selling beer and burgers, bands played for free, people came from other towns and other churches, and everyone gave what they could.

They raised thirty-eight thousand dollars.

The bishop failed to make an appearance.

Or a donation.

Shame, shame on him, Tom thought, remembering what a sweet girl Melissa Becker was. She had been Deborah's friend. No, no, they'd been more than friends. Tom knew that. They had been so close, so happy when they were with each other. That was the last time he could remember seeing his daughter as his daughter, unpierced, undrugged, unhesitatingly her own self.

Undamaged.

And now they were gone. They were both gone.

Tom sat back in the pew and looked around at the church, cavernous and hollow. He placed his hand on the seat to the right of him, remembering when his daughter had sat there, wiggly during long homilies. He would place his hand on her leg, and that would be enough to still her. Sometimes they sat with Melissa and her family. Those were good memories, before Melissa had gotten sick, before they had found out what was going on between the girls.

He had acted so horribly, and he knew it. Why, why had he done it? It racked his thoughts. That's where it all started, he thought. It never would have happened if he hadn't pushed Deborah away in the beginning—and for what? He'd handled everything so badly. He wanted it back, wanted time back, he wanted his daughter back, so he could do it all over, and do it differently. He would be better, he knew he would. He would be a better man.

But it was too late now.

His daughter was gone.

That thought was still unthinkable.

Tom slid forward on the pew, kneeled again, and clasped his hands together, but he would not pray. He could not. The ever-widening gap between him and what he once believed was now a gulf unnavigable.

It was quiet in the church. Immeasurably quiet. A quiet so full, so absolute and pure that it was deafening. The world had never known such silence.

Never, never, never, never, never.

Wesley Faber got the call about four o'clock in the morning. He'd been having coffee with Vern Stenghal at the all-night Stop 'n' Shop out on the highway. The 911 call came over as "man with a gun" at Saint Francis church. Officer Michele Schaefer called him seconds later on his cell phone to tell him that Tom Ellison had broken into the church. He had locked the doors behind him. And he had a gun. Faber jumped into his cruiser and floored it, red lights and sirens. He called Father Ryan on the way and told him to get his keys and meet him at the church. He called the county for backup and got the fire chief on his walkie-talkie and told him to station himself at a safe distance.

Wesley Faber prayed as he sped back to town.

He pulled up behind the fire and rescue trucks that were just arriving, training their powerful spotlights on the building. He was radioing the county to report that he was on the scene when he saw someone running toward the church.

He flung open the door of his cruiser, screaming to know who the hell it was.

Inside Saint Francis church, Tom Ellison stopped to breathe a moment in the same spot where he'd stood so many times before, a lifetime ago, as an altar boy. His hands were bleeding. He couldn't feel them. He raised the heavy pry bar again and slammed it down over and over and over into the church altar, a flurry of blows, mindless, blurred, uncountable, knocking the great granite table off its pedestal. He straddled it, swinging the pry bar maniacally, clubbing off large chunks of stone and disintegrating others into clouds of dust. He swung at it till he couldn't swing anymore, picked up a large slab of the shattered altar and heaved it, spinning, through the window of the sacristy. He followed after, pry bar in hand, pushing over the lectern on his way, and knocked away whatever glass and leaden strips still dangled in the panes. He stepped through and smashed at the collection of sacred vessels, pulling over the tiny golden temple, in which, as a boy, he had believed God slept, and spilled the hosts across the floor. He kicked at them with his boots and trampled on them. There was nothing in his mind. Nothing coherent at all. Only a vague sense of heat. His thoughts felt like heat.

He ran along the walls, clubbing, tearing down the gilt-framed icons that hung there. Sounds were coming out of his body, sounds he had never made before, wolfish, otherworldly sounds, like those his wife had made when she was giving birth, sounds perhaps like those his daughter had made as she was being murdered. His mind screamed at the thought. He ran between the pews, striking at them, gouging out large splinterings of oak. He ran to the other side of the church and raked the wall, punching at it, clawing at the icons mounted there.

It was inconceivable. This could not be.

The world was awry, tilted. Gravity was gone.

There was just sound and heat, his own sounds, which did not seem as if they were coming from him; they were someone else's, some other being's, not his. And yet they *were* his, and he knew this, and he also knew, in some excruciating piece of his brain, that everything was true, that what had happened to his daughter had actually happened.

The Earth no longer existed. There was no God. No wife, no daughter, no son. No Winsome, no world. He clicked the safety off on his .45 automatic and stood at the top of aisle looking down at the wreckage where the altar had been, the rescue lights outside illuminating the stained glass in a confusion of colors. The dust in the air gave the shafts of light a solid look, as if massive I-beams, crayon colored, had smashed through the windows.

The crucifix, large and indifferent, hung squarely and serenely above it all.

Tom Ellison stared at it and felt nothing. He believed nothing. He was nothing. He raised his gun and fired ten shots, fast, into the figure on the cross, into its chest and stomach and neck, pieces flying in spinning chips through the streams of tinted light. He reloaded and took the figure at the neck, firing until the head and crown collapsed and dropped to the rubble beneath, then he fired mindlessly, unfeelingly, until nothing remained affixed to the crucifix but a single crumble of pierced palm.

He reloaded again and walked up to the lobby where he had soaked the carpet with gasoline, the new carpet that he'd helped raise the money for last summer at the Saint Francis Fun Fest by sitting in the Dunk-A-Deputy machine all weekend. He tossed a match to the floor and watched as a ripple of low flames slowly crawled across the lobby, much slower than he thought it would. A movement caught his eye and he swung his gun to the left. Father Ryan was at the front of the building. Tom walked over to the glass doors. He knelt before the priest and put the barrel of the gun into his own mouth and pulled the trigger.

Traffic was almost stopped.

"Move!" Coose yelled. "Move it!" He and Mangan had been trying to get out of Chicago for almost an hour and had barely made it to O'Hare. "People in Chicago don't know how to drive in the rain. It drizzles and it slows to a friggin' crawl."

They were on their way to Winsome. The news of officer Tom Ellison's suicide traveled quickly, and Mangan had called Wesley Faber right away. They'd already had a meeting set up and decided to keep it. Mangan was anxious to get some more details about the Wisconsin case and wanted to see the dump site of Deborah Ellison's body. He also wanted to interview Jillian McClay, the writer, who lived in the neighboring town of Enfield.

The traffic finally opened up a bit, and Coose stopped yelling.

The security tapes at the *American Forum* building showed Mara Davies leaving work at 9:07 p.m. on Sunday night. She never made it home. Her body was discovered by a delivery man a few days later behind a bar called the Nite Cap. Forensics was still doing a workup on some fiber and hair trace found on the victim. Dr. Rhys confirmed that Davies had been strangled, her larynx crushed. It appeared that the blunt trauma to the facial area had been inflicted by the bottom of the assailant's shoe. There were remnant heel marks on portions of the victim's face. A search of the area—Dumpster, the alley, garbage cans— turned up nothing. Any trace evidence that might have been on the pavement around her had been destroyed by the heavy rains. Rhys also confirmed that the severed hand delivered to Lachlan's apartment did indeed belong to Mara Davies.

She had last been seen inside the Nite Cap with a group of friends. The bartender there knew her. She frequented the place with her boyfriend, he'd said. He had been working the night she was killed. Mickey

Eagan was interviewing the friends and the boyfriend. He was also going to look at the bar's surveillance tapes.

It was nearly three hours before Coose made a left at a sign that said Welcome to Winsome Bay, Home of the Wildcats. The speed limit dropped quickly to twenty-five miles an hour. They drove down what seemed an endless green corridor—acres of cornfields spilled out to either side of the road. Mangan, lost in thought, watched the long, leafy, stalks flicker by.

It was a lover and his lass,
That o'er the green corn-field did pass.

Farther down the road, the farmland ended, and they passed a few houses. Then the small downtown began to appear and Mangan could see that a chaos of reporters and TV crews had converged on the little town. The Davies-Ellison murders were big news in the Midwest now. Enough information had leaked out for reporters to connect the Winsome Bay killing to the Chicago murder. And now, with the suicide of Tom Ellison, the town looked like halftime at the Super Bowl.

They drove slowly past a long, ranch-style funeral home where uniformed officers and state police were milling about the parking lot. Reporters and news crews were crowded behind lines of police barricades, fighting for position and jostling into each other, jabbing microphones and cameras out at anyone who happened by. The murders had created a frenzy of newscasts. Mangan knew this was coming, for *men, like ravenous fishes, will feed on one another.* There had been a sufficient amount of gruesomeness to warrant a grand media response, accompanied by the witty wordplay of the sick and shameless. Soon the TV experts, whose qualifications went no further than perky tits or loud mouths, began theorizing around large oak tables ringed with failed novelists and hack copywriters. The tabloids were in heaven. Sell all, sell merrily.

Few organisms disgusted Mangan more than those in the media.

Except for politicians.

Coose drove past the blackened remains of Saint Francis church. A good two-thirds of the building had collapsed into a crushed skeleton of charred timber. Fire hoses were propped up on tripods, spraying fine mists of water over the still smoldering ruins. The parking lot was littered with debris, plastic cups, food wrappers, empty water bottles. Three firemen sat on a curb staring at the rubble, bewildered looks on their faces. Coose drove farther into the town. The business area was tiny. Almost no cars were on the street, an odd sight for a city dweller like Mangan, who spent nearly a third of his life looking for places to park, a very pissed-off third.

They pulled up in front of the Dew Drop Inn, where they'd agreed to meet the chief of police, Wesley Faber. As Mangan stepped out of the car, he was struck by the smell of early fall already mustering in the clouds and a reeking of wet ash drifting over from what was left of the church. The steel door of the Dew Drop Inn had a horseshoe welded to it for a handle, and it took Mangan two heavy tugs and a yank to get it open. Inside, dark in the daytime, Chief Faber sat alone at the bar. A big guy, a face like Vince Lombardi. He got up and extended his hand to Mangan.

"You look like a city cop," Faber said.

Mangan shook his hand. "You don't."

Faber smiled. "No, guess I don't."

"My partner," Mangan said, "Frank Cusumano."

"Nice to meet you." Faber leaned in and shook Coose's hand, grabbed a fat file folder off the bar, and walked to a table at the back of the room. "You find the place okay?"

"The GPS did," Coose said, "kind of. They don't work so good out here."

Faber gestured for them to sit down. "You fellas want some coffee or something?"

"Please," Mangan said.

"Lou," Faber called out to the bartender. "Couple of coffees."

Mangan took off his jacket and sat. "Looks like you got a bit of a circus out there."

"Yes, I do. Never anything like this in these parts, least not in my time."

"I'm very sorry about your officer Tom Ellison."

"Thank you." Faber nodded slightly. "He was a good man." The bartender came up to the table and set down mugs and a carafe of coffee. Faber poured for everyone. "So, how can I help you gentlemen?"

Mangan sugared his coffee. "I think we start by sharing information. I'd like to see where Deborah Ellison's body was found and talk to this Jillian McClay. I understand she lives around here?"

"Yeah, not far at all."

"Well, she hasn't been very forthcoming over the phone. I tried to get her in for an interview, but she declined. So I thought we'd come to her."

"She lives over in Enfield," Faber said. "I know the chief there. He's got someone over at her place watching her twenty-four-seven. First, I'll take you out to where the body was found. It's on the way. Then we can head over to Enfield."

Faber and Mangan discussed Jillian McClay's connection to Mara Davies. Then they talked about the Ellison murder.

"You like anyone for it yet?" Mangan asked Faber.

"No. We called the state in for help. We're not set up so well for this type of thing around here. Forensics hasn't turned up much yet. Looks like she was killed somewhere else. They think whoever killed her cleaned up the body and then dumped it here."

Faber handed Mangan the latest forensic reports. The Wisconsin lab had found traces of an alkali-based cleaning solution on the Ellison girl's body, Mangan read, as the words *the wide sea hath drops too few to wash her clean again* drifted through his head. "This cleaning solution, anything on that?" he asked Faber.

"Nothing very special about it," Faber said, "except that it's not petroleum based, no hydrocarbons or phosphates."

"What are you, a chemist?"

"No. Any farmer around here knows what that means. It's organic. Biodegradable."

"Farmers use it?"

"Organic farms do. Environmental folks. Marinas and boat owners have to use it on the inland lakes here."

"Is it easy to get?"

"You can buy it just about anywhere. Farmers buy it in bulk, but you can get it in a hardware store, marinas—hell, you can get in the grocery store now. It's not distinct enough to get any kind of match on. Same with the soil sample."

Mangan read on. Some gritty sand-like soil had been found under one of the victim's eyelids.

"It's a kind of sand," Faber said. "Forensics is still working on it. It's probably from where she was killed. This is all old river bottom around here. Dig a foot down just about anywheres and you hit sand."

"But she was living in Chicago, wasn't she?"

"That's right."

"What makes you think she was killed around here?"

"Well, I don't necessarily. I'm just saying, if she was, it could have been anywhere."

"Had you seen her around here at all?"

"No. She'd been gone for a long time. Nobody knew where she was."

"Not even her family? They didn't know where she was living?"

"No. They got only one letter sent home, to her brother. Postmarked Chicago. No return address. I can get you a copy. We tried just about everything we could think of to get a last known whereabouts on her. Nothing. Can't find a friend, an employer, credit card with her name on it, nothing."

"And the letter? Anything in it?"

"Not much. She said that she'd found a job and was living with a woman named . . . hold on . . ." Faber sorted through the file papers and pulled out a copy of the letter. "A strange name, something foreign. Here it is. *Fenyana*. That's the only—"

"Hold on, hold on," Mangan said, turning to Coose. "Get Palmer on this right away."

"Got it," Coose said, already taking out his cell phone.

"Tell him I don't care what he has to do," Mangan said, "find this girl and bring her in. She lives in the projects, right? Tell him to get a warrant for her apartment if he can."

Coose walked away from the table to make the call.

"You know this woman?" Faber asked. "This foreign girl?"

"Yes," Mangan said, mulling over the link between the two women. "She's a prostitute in Chicago." He read the copy of the letter. "And Deborah Ellison was living with her? They were roommates?"

"Well, more than that, probably . . ."

Faber went on then to explain about Deborah Ellison's sexual orientation, about the relationship she'd had with Melissa Becker and her estrangement from her parents and the town.

"People found out in high school," he continued. "A lot of ugly stuff went on. She didn't have many friends here."

Coose came back to the table. "I got Palmer on it. He'll call as soon as he has anything."

Mangan wondered what the hell the connection was between Kevin Lachlan, Fenyana Petrakova, and Deborah Ellison. He ran the absurd scenario in his head: Lachlan has sex with a prostitute who is potentially a lover of Deborah Ellison. His magazine also just happens to be doing a series of articles about Ellison's murder?

O God, that one might read the book of fate.

Mangan turned to Faber. "Let's try Ms. McClay."

Faber took out his cell phone and called the woman. He got her voice mail. Mangan poured another cup of coffee and brought up the subject of jurisdiction. He and Faber discussed it briefly. If the Ellison girl had been alive when she was brought to Wisconsin it might involve interstate kidnapping, and then the feds would come in. The FBI would be involved anyway as they worked closely with VCTF in Chicago. Regardless, Mangan and Faber quickly agreed to share all evidence and start a mutual investigation. Faber, a trained sharpshooter and hunter all his life, was smart enough to know that he'd never tracked down anything that might actually shoot him first.

"To be honest with you," Faber said, "I just want the son of a bitch caught or dead, and I don't give a care much how we do it. Let's take a ride."

Wesley Faber swung by the police station and picked up another officer, Michele Schaefer. It was still raining, and she stooped slightly as she ran past the front of the cruiser. She hunched into the back seat, wet, and apologetic for being so. She smelled of cigarette smoke. Introductions were made all around. Mangan turned in his seat, talking through the safety cage.

"I'm sorry about your partner," he said. "Your boss tells me he was a good cop."

"Thank you. He was."

Faber pulled away, heading out of town.

"I read your interview," Mangan told Schaefer. "The one Jillian McClay wrote."

"I was off duty and drunk," Schaefer said, rubbing rain out of her hair. "I didn't know half of what I was saying. It's my own fault."

"Don't trust writers. You're better off walking away."

Schaefer nodded and looked out the window.

On the edge of town the cruiser slowed to an abrupt crawl behind a slow-moving John Deere combine that took up more than half the road. The driver pulled over as far to the right as he could and waved as Faber passed him. They turned into a new subdivision. A large green-and-white PeterSons Construction sign came into view, followed by another sign announcing the coming of the Deer Park Apartments.

"This is where the body was found," Faber said.

The car fell silent but for the dull thudding of the windshield wipers. They drove on, past a few half-built homes, piles of construction materials stacked beside them. Faber pulled over at a spot where no homes had been built yet. There were still crops of some kind growing in the fields. The leafy greens of the short plants had yellowed, their thin sickled pods dangling, rusty colored and furry.

"That's all soybean out there," Faber said, driving slowly. "Coming up here, to the right," he continued, "that's all hay. They're just about done cutting it."

The hayfield had been pretty much shorn clean to the ground.

New-reaped, Mangan thought, *like a stubble-land at harvest home.*

There was only one small spot where hay still grew, a small area just off the curb, a single, well-defined square of pale straw. It was about ten by ten, and the grasses there, tall and seed laden, bent heavily under their own weight. Torn pieces of yellow police tape flagged loosely from wooden stakes at each corner of the square. In the rain, which was falling heavier now, the bouquets and cards strewn around the area looked like garbage, sodden and limp.

Mangan stepped out of the cruiser. Faber followed, opening an umbrella. He handed it to Mangan and told Cusumano, "I've only got one."

Coose shrugged and flipped up his collar.

Mangan stood in the road. The air smelled of warm dirt, steamy and wet.

He could feel him. He'd been here. The killer.

Odd, Mangan thought. He felt closer to him here than he had in the alley where Mara Davies's body had been found. Why was that? Mangan opened himself up to what was around him and took everything in: the odors, the light, the colors of the field, the sounds, air, his feelings.

He stared at the barren fields beyond and the grassy ground where the body had been dumped. "*Here never shines the sun*," he said out loud.

"What's that?" Faber asked.

Mangan didn't hear him, the words continuing in his thoughts, *here nothing breeds*.

"Don't mind him," Coose said, stepping in. "He does that a lot, talks to himself."

Mangan walked to the edge of the curb and stepped up.

Faber stood off a ways, hands on his sides, watching. Schaefer stayed in the cruiser, staring out the window. Mangan studied the area where the body had been found. *Like to a slaughtered lamb, in this detested, dark, blood-drinking pit*. He walked back and stepped off the curb and knocked the mud off his shoes. He crouched and scanned the fields to either side, rain dripping heavily off his umbrella. He looked left, right. No streetlights anywhere. The killer knew it would be pitch black at night. He knew the area. A local maybe? *I must talk of acts of black night, abominable deeds*. The words were coming faster now. Like the beeps of a Geiger counter, when he was closer to a killer, or a killer's energy, or whatever it was, the words seemed to sound more often.

A crimson river of warm blood . . .

He walked back to the car and told Faber, "Let's go see this McClay woman."

His memory of the first one was nearly gone. It was no more than a blurry vagueness now, spider webbed and packed away deep within the crawl spaces of his mind. He remembered . . . birds, bird tattoos, tiny, like her, and how slippery the brick had been.

He had wanted to feel something after he had done it. But there was nothing. There had been nothing but blood and dirt and, afterward, quiet. She had been very quiet at the end, almost peaceful, like she was actually seeing something very pleasing behind him as he sat on her chest and crushed her throat. He'd almost turned around to look over his shoulder, to see what she was looking at. But he hadn't. He just pushed down harder and made her eyes go gray. But there had been no relief in it.

He felt as dead as her.

He thought of this, and wrote.
It took a long time for the words to come to him.

IT'S AS IF THERE IS A THING INSIDE ME
THAT IS VERY DARK AND VERY HEAVY.
LIKE A DEAD CHILD INSIDE MY CHEST.
THIS BLACK THING OF DEADNESS
PUSHES DOWN, CRUSHES, NUMBS.
BUT WHEN I WRITE OF THIS — OF THAT
WHICH CANNOT BE EXPRESSED — WHEN I FIND
THE RIGHT WORDS . . .

I FEEL.

THE DEAD THING INSIDE ME MOVES,
IT BLUSHES WARM AND KICKS.

AND I KNOW NOW WHAT I AM.
I AM NOT THE CHOOSER.

I AM THE RIGHTER
OF WRONGS.

It never ceased to amaze Mangan just how much blood was actually in the human body. Five quarts or so in the average male. Women, a little less. One has to actually see it spilled outside of the body to truly appreciate its volume. Imagine slowly pouring an entire gallon of milk on your kitchen floor and letting it run and pool everywhere. Now picture the milk as very thick, syrupy, like olive oil, and red, a deeply rust-ridden red. Now imagine a chair in the middle of this blood pool and a body sitting in it, its throat slit open, because that's what Detective Mangan and Chief Faber found when they entered Jillian McClay's writing studio.

"Oh my God," Faber said under his breath.

"Seal it off," Mangan said, thinking, *Who would have thought the old man to have had so much blood in him?*

Everyone backed away. Schaefer looked slightly sick. Faber, shaken. He called for backup, local EMS, and a CSI team from the City of Madison. From the open doorway of the office, Mangan stared at the body. Three. Three dead women now. They officially had a serial killer on their hands. They stepped outside when the CSI team arrived. Mangan saw Faber talking to a cop who was sitting in a cruiser. The officer looked distraught. Mangan walked over and listened. It was the man who had been assigned to protect Ms. McClay. He thought she'd been in the house the whole time. Apparently she'd snuck out the back door and gone into her office sometime during the night. The officer had been parked in the front of the house when she'd been murdered.

The CSI squad gave Mangan and Coose protective gear. They pulled thin covers over their shoes, stepped into loose, papery jumpsuits, and tugged on latex gloves.

Carefully, and behind the CSI techs, they entered the room again.

In her chair, poised in front of her computer—*posed* actually—was the body of Jillian McClay. Her hands, propped up on the keyboard. Her head hung uneasily to the side, eyes open. Blood was everywhere, beneath the chair, splashed across the desk and flooded between the crevices of her keyboard. Dappled arcs of arterial splatters had sprayed across the computer screen like a crimson Pollock painting. The deep gash across the victim's throat had severed both carotid arteries, leaving the white sheen of her trachea clearly visible. A merciful kill, Mangan thought; she would have been unconscious quickly.

On the desk beside the computer, Mangan saw a handgun.

"Behind you," one of the CSI techs said, stepping in and carefully photographing and then bagging it.

A local sheriff stepped in and said, "We'll run a check on it."

Another technician, kneeling beneath the desk, was retrieving a digital recorder that lay in a viscous puddle of blood. The rest of the forensic team wandered noiselessly about the room collecting, photographing, cataloging. Mangan stood back as they did their work and took in the rest of the office. He spied a small wastebasket under the desk, filled with books that appeared to be in good condition. Odd, he thought. After it had been photographed, Mangan removed one of the books and read the title off the spine: *Crime Writing for Rookies.* He flipped through it, stopping at a paragraph highlighted in yellow.

> *Mystery Story:* umbrella term for a type of fiction with several sub-genres, such as the detective story, including the police procedural. These types of fiction often deal with crime—frequently murder—and its successful solution. Suspense arises in the course of seeking that solution, which places the detective, others in pursuit of the villain, or innocent victims, in jeopardy.

Mangan couldn't help a wry shake of his head. He wasn't a big fan of tragic irony, but sometimes he just couldn't help acknowledging it.

From the blood spatters it appeared that Ms. McClay had been killed at her computer, perhaps while she was writing. Most likely she'd been grabbed from behind, her head pulled back and her neck slashed. One cut, deep, till the blade stopped at the bones of the spinal column. A large knife had been used, a very large and very sharp knife. There were no indications of any sawing motion around the wound site. It appeared to have been one powerful, swift cut.

On the blood-smeared computer screen there appeared to be something that had been finger painted into the once-wet blood, presumably by the killer. Mangan took a pencil and gently tapped the corner of the space bar on the keyboard. The computer brightened to life, backlighting the words etched across the blood-glazed screen.

I am the Righter.

"He's changed his name," Mangan said, the line *turning your books to graves, your ink to blood* coming to him. Coose peered over his shoulder.

A document was also up on the screen. Mangan could just make out some of the words through the film of dried blood, words presumably written by the victim. The first sentence was: "I don't know what to write." Below it was another paragraph, and from what Mangan could read, Ms. McClay seemed to have been writing about the trouble she was having writing about the Ellison murder case. The rest was too hard to read through the dried blood.

"Excuse me," a CSI tech said, stepping between Mangan and the computer.

"Sorry," Mangan said.

He and Coose looked around the small office, crowded with people. Nothing particularly noteworthy jumped out at him. It looked just about how he thought a writer's office would look: shelves jammed end to end with books, more books piled on top of them. Sloppy, though, not ordered or catalogued like Mangan's books. Not much light for a writing studio: one window, western exposure.

Chief Faber came up to Mangan and said, "We're going to go door to door."

It was another three hours before the CSI crew finished up their work. The keyboard, light switches, doorknobs, drawer handles, and areas near and around the computer were photographed and examined for trace evidence. Mangan was pretty sure they wouldn't find anything. He'd been on enough cases to know when a team was scratching cold, like watching a baseball player run out a short pop to center: they know they're out and they're just going through the motions, because, well, you never know. But they know. If the killer had been careful enough not to leave any physical evidence at the Ellison and Davies crime scenes, he wouldn't be leaving anything here. The CSI techs tagged, bagged, and ziplocked Jillian McClay, and local EMS carried out her body.

Mangan stood in the middle of the office and peeled off his rubber gloves as the CSI unit packed up and left the room. They made a racket tromping down the wooden stairs. He waited for the quiet he knew would follow. This was the time when he would think the clearest. The time he always took. After everyone had left.

When the words might come.

Mangan took into account not only the facts and physical evidence, but also the suppositions, the what-ifs, the horrible imaginings of his mind, because those thoughts had to come from somewhere, he reasoned, from some informed place. There were always larger things at work, Mangan was sure of that. After nearly thirty years on the force, one of the only things he was sure of was that some of his biggest successes had had very little to do with him. He was a part of it, yes, of course, he was in the mix, but something else was at play too, something that worked in his head, on its own, when he was asleep. Whatever this thing was, it was smarter than he was. He'd learned to listen to it, for it often led him to places where murderers slept.

"Could I have a minute?" Mangan asked the local sheriff in charge.

"Sure," the man said, and started away.

"Excuse me," Mangan called after him, "any word on that gun yet?"

"Not yet. They're still running the serial number." The sheriff checked his notes. "The victim's got a kid too. He's with her ex-husband right now. Nicholas McClay. We're trying to track him down. He's in Fort Lauderdale."

"Ex-husband, huh?"

"We'll question him as soon as we find him. I'll let you know what we get."

"Thanks," Mangan said, jotting down Nicholas McClay's name.

Coose said, "I'll be outside," and left the room.

Mangan was alone now. He listened.

A human being who had killed another human being had stood right where he was standing. He closed his eyes. He breathed. *Who are you?* he thought, his first and sometimes last question to a killer, *Who are you?*

The theory of trace evidence contends that every contact a living being makes with another object, no matter how slight, leaves some mark on it. There are many kinds of trace evidence, some that can never be seen, and that's the kind that Mangan was searching for, the unseen evidence, the evidence that had to be sensed or felt. He knelt and touched the carpet. There was nothing there to the eye, but he felt it anyway. The killer had walked on it. Mangan felt a little closer to him now. Not much, but closer. He stayed there for a long while, crouched, hand flat on the floor. He wanted to absorb him. *Show me something*, he thought. This kind of killer should leave a greater mark, something should be left behind, some dark energy, some unseen shimmer of evil. Mangan wanted to feel it, to absorb whatever it might be.

"Who are you?" he asked out loud, and this time an answer came to his mind.

I am Revenge, sent from the infernal kingdom
To ease the gnawing vulture of my mind.

. . . Revenge?

Revenge for what? What had these women done to deserve this? How were the other two victims connected to the first? Or was it just the Ellison girl that the killer had taken revenge on? But why the others? Had they all done something to him? Do they represent something for him? It had to be more than just anger about the *American Forum* articles. Or *was* that enough? But they'd canceled the series, so why wasn't the killer satisfied?

If I digged up thy forefathers' graves
And hung their rotten coffins up in chains,
It could not slake mine ire, nor ease my heart.
Till I root out their accursed line,
And leave not one alive, I live in hell.

What could Deborah Ellison have done that was so horrible?

Going to the door, Mangan retraced what he thought might have been the killer's steps. Deadbolt on the door, unlocked. No sign of forced entry. Everything pointed to the victim being at work at her computer and the killer coming up behind her. Why didn't she see or hear him? If she had, surely there would have been some signs of struggle. How had the killer known she'd even be here?

I will find them out,
And in their ears tell them my dreadful name . . .
Revenge.

Fenyana gripped the armrest of her seat and prayed. She didn't really believe in a God anymore, but still, when she was scared, she prayed. She hated flying, but she'd learned at a very young age, in Kujzistinau, that when you are in trouble, you don't run *to* the police, you run *from* them.

"We should be out of this turbulence shortly," the pilot announced. "If you look out the right side of the plane, you can see the Pacific coastline."

Fenyana glanced out. Sheeted gusts of rain raked the wings of the plane, the clouds were slate gray, and, for a moment, surprisingly, a pleasant thought came to her: At the beach, as a little girl, a rainy day, playing in the sand, a trip to the river Nistru. It had rained and rained and she had stayed and played in the sand, happy, with her mother, and her little sisters, Alyona and Anitsa. What might they look like now? she wondered. It seemed impossible to know, for so long had she not seen them. She tried to remember more. Small memories remained, unnamed graspy memories, fragments of a time before things had happened, bathing suits and sandy feet, flowers, she often remembered flowers, but those rememberings, the good ones, did not last. No. Thoughts of home, if she allowed them in, always turned to hunger and hurt. Home was not a home but only a place she had survived. The little girl, the happy one she once was, had been left on the rainy banks of the Nistru many years ago.

She was fourteen when they took her.

She'd screamed that her father would come for her, but he was dead, and she knew that, long dead, only a boy himself, killed in Afghanistan. She never knew him. After they beat her enough, she stopped screaming. The woman from Chisinau paid off the local police. She told her to stop fighting it and not to be afraid. There was work for girls like her in America, so many jobs, waitressing, housekeeping, dancing—but *she*, the woman had told her, *she* was so pretty, such eyes, so tall, she could be a model. Two thousand dollars a month, maybe more. They would even pay for her plane fare. She could pay them back after she got work and then send money back home to her mother, as the other village girls did, and she could live in America. Her village was so poor and polluted, the land contaminated by the waste of abandoned military sites after the wall went down. Trees festered, fish died, birds fell from branches. But Fenyana, *she* was so pretty, such eyes, so tall, she could be a model and live in America.

And Fenyana went.

But they did not take her to America. They went to Mexico. It was cheaper that way, they told her, to get to America. And there she met many other girls, each one a pretty could-be-model just like herself, only some even younger. And in Mexico they took away their passports and their shoes and their luggage, and they told them that they had to pay for their plane fares, and their food and housing, and when one tried to question anything, one was beaten. And Fenyana herself was warned, and remembers still the small man's mouth, wet and gray, as he told her that if she ran away he would find her mother and her sisters and do things to them, and if still she ran, he would, back home, slit slowly her little sister's throat from ear to ear, sweet little Anitsa.

He knew her name.

And Fenyana never ran.

Across the border into Texas. Every few weeks, it seemed, moving from house to house as they taught her the things they wanted her to do. She'd had a boyfriend once, Dimi, funny Dimi, and they had done some things together under the beech tree by Mr. Veselov's pond, but still she did not know how to do the things they wanted her to do. They did not believe her, and they beat her on her head and legs and kept her awake and gave her drugs and starved her and taught her the things to do.

And Fenyana learned.

For the younger ones, they put honey on the man to teach them how to do it, and beat them until they learned not to gag, and pushed things into them to help them learn to open up better. They taught them how to sound sexy in their talk or scared or hurt. Most of the men who bought them wanted them to sound scared and hurt. That was not hard to do. Later, after Fenyana had learned herself, she taught the younger ones how to float away so things wouldn't hurt as much.

She'd been floating ever since.

From Texas to San Francisco to Phoenix to Detroit to Chicago, where Fenyana first saw Deborah at a dance club. So small she looked, and light, that night, like sweet Anitsa might have looked now. A little girl's body but not. But there was something else about her too, something wild. She danced so hard, a rage of dancing it seemed, angry at the air around her. And she danced alone. And Fenyana stepped into her aloneness and looked into her eyes and they danced together, and raged together, and then, that night, late and hot and loose, Fenyana whispered, between their sweat-soaked kisses, of easy money. Work with me, she said, be safe with me. And Deborah listened. And they left that night together, and they worked together, and they lived together, and, Fenyana thought, sometimes, a little, they loved together, and Fenyana also got 10 percent from Savva for her. Savva liked little Deborah. He had customers that would like her very much.

With the extra money they rented a new apartment as clean and white inside as they were not, but, as Grandmother told her, the nadezhda bush grows best in blackest dirt, and Fenyana knew that her work had nothing to do with real life. Work was forgotten hours, floating hours. When it was over, she and Deborah had each other, and, together, they were a little happy.

But they should never have met, Fenyana thought, as the plane yawed slowly to the left. She looked out the window. He was only supposed to scare her. Beat her, maybe, but not badly. Maybe break her hands or a leg. Something like that had happened to all of them at one time or another. But something had gone horribly wrong. She had warned Deborah about trying to get out. There is no out once you are in. There may be better buyers or worse, more money or less, beatings or no beatings, but there is no out. Deborah would not believe her. Things like that don't happen here, she'd say, maybe in Russia but not in America, like it was all the stuff of Hollywood movies. Deborah was not afraid of anything.

She should have been.

Coose and Mangan stayed in Wisconsin the night that Jillian McClay's body had been discovered. They grabbed some food at a Culver's out on the highway, and some necessities at the local Stop 'n' Shop. Enfield had no hotels, so they drove to the neighboring town of Acushnet and pulled into a motel called the Barn, which, indeed, looked like a barn. The parking lot was filled with an assortment of pickup trucks and motor homes.

Mangan and Coose grabbed their laptops and headed in.

A small congress of teenage girls with tiny asses and babies cocked on their hips hovered outside the lobby, smoking. "Excuse me," Mangan said to a pubescent mom who looked at him like he'd just asked to buy her child. Inside they waited for a foreign-looking front desk clerk to stop talking on his cell phone and acknowledge their existence. Check-in was an ordeal that took nearly forty minutes. From the way the man typed, he appeared to have a phobia of computer keyboards. He also spoke very little English. Learn the fucking language if you're going to live in this country, Mangan thought. He couldn't help it. He was tired. And, anyway, he meant it. The lazy-ass clerk finally got them checked in, without once making eye contact, and Coose and Mangan headed to their rooms.

The carpeted hallway had the antiseptic smell of recently cleaned mold, and whoever was in charge of maintenance must have thought that any kind of repair in the building could be easily accomplished with a generous application of caulk. A heavy woman with tattoos and a twelve-pack of Busch Light passed Mangan in the hallway as he found his room and opened the door.

He turned back to Coose, "What time you want to leave tomorrow?"

"We should get on the road around eight. We go too early, we're going to hit traffic."

Mangan agreed and closed the door.

God, he'd been in so many rooms like this so many times throughout his career. No matter where he went, they all looked the same. Squalor had no originality. He checked that the sheets were clean and thought to call his daughter. It was getting late though, so he decided not to. He took off his jacket, put his gun and holster on the nightstand, and cranked the AC. He opened the fifth of gin he'd bought, grabbed a glass from the bathroom, and poured a drink.

He sipped and thought.

Lachlan.

There was something slippery about the guy, something Mangan couldn't hold onto, but he didn't like him for the murder. Eagan had been keeping him under surveillance, and Lachlan had been in Chicago at the time of McClay's murder. He was a misogynistic dick, yes, but not a killer.

Mangan recalled the words he'd heard at the McClay murder scene, *I am Revenge, sent from the infernal kingdom.* Those words had been from *Titus Andronicus*. He'd recognized them right away, but couldn't remember where the other lines were from: *If I digged up thy forefathers' graves and hung their rotten coffins up in chains.* He sat at the tiny motel desk and tried to Google it on his laptop, but there was no Internet service. He opened his file of the collected works of Shakespeare and searched the phrase.

It was from *Henry VI, part 3*.

The character of Clifford, seeking revenge on the House of York for his own father's death, says those words before he kills a child:

Had I thy brethren here, their lives and thine
Were not revenge sufficient for me;

And till I root out their accursed line
And leave not one alive, I live in hell.
The child, at knife's point, then pleads with his murderer.
RUTLAND: *Be thou revenged on men, and let me live!*
CLIFFORD: *In vain thou speak'st.*
RUTLAND: *I never did thee harm; why wilt thou slay me?*
Then Clifford stabs the child to death.

Mangan took another sip of his drink . . . *Why wilt thou slay me?* What could Deborah Ellison possibly have done to deserve such a horrific death? Somehow she was deeply connected to her killer, maybe intimately, Mangan felt sure of it. And if he could find out what that connection was, it could be the key to the other murders. But what was it? Deborah Ellison had been living with a prostitute. Had she been working the streets also? Had the killer been a customer? Had she humiliated him somehow? Sexually? But why murder the other women?

These wrongs, unspeakable, past patience,
Are more than any living man could bear.

Mangan finished his drink and got undressed. He needed a shower. He ran the water in the closet-sized bathroom and stepped into the tub. There was hardly any water pressure. He angled the cracked showerhead and let the water dribble over his head for a long time. His mind wouldn't quiet. Had the first murder been an act of vengeance, and then the killer developed a taste for it?

Past cure I am; now reason is past care.

Is he killing as it occurs to him? Is there a next victim?

My thoughts and my discourse as madmen's are.

Does he have a plan or is he mad?

O, full of scorpions is my mind.

Nothing, no answers were coming to Mangan. It was all questions now, all unknown—all Melvillian. Something was hovering nearby, though, some connection just beyond the reach of his grasp. There's always a connection. No matter how sick a motive, there was always a connection between victim and killer, some pattern, some horrific logic. Even the lack of pattern was a pattern.

Mangan got out of the shower and toweled off. He headed back into the room, a cloud of steam following at his heels. He poured another drink and sat on the edge of the bed.

Confusion now hath made his masterpiece.
He didn't need Shakespeare to tell him that.

Mangan and Coose got back to Chicago around eleven thirty the next morning. Willie Palmer was waiting for them in Room 70. Born and raised in the projects, Willie knew the streets better than just about anyone in the VCTF. At six foot three, he towered over Mangan and Coose and made it a point to stand as close to them as possible whenever he could. He dressed as if he were continually auditioning for *Miami Vice* and was confident that he was going to get the part. The hookers loved him. He was also annoyingly chipper. All the time.

"Morning, boys," he said, eyeing them both. "Well, don't *you* look like shit today."

"I always look like shit," Mangan said.

"I look like shit because I'm starving," said Coose. "He wouldn't stop to eat."

"They had bagels at the motel," Mangan said.

"They weren't bagels, they were Wonder Bread made round with holes in them."

"Can we stop talking about food, guys?" Willie said. "We got things to do."

"What have you got on this Fenyana girl?" Mangan asked.

Willie opened a file folder and placed it on the table. "Well, she's probably somewhere in California right now. I ran her real name, Petra Nadzenia. Even call girls got credit cards. She bought a ticket two days ago to San Francisco. Her card hasn't been used since, and her bank account is empty. Withdrew everything the day before she left. Almost four grand."

Mangan looked at the file. "She's running from something."

"The guy that killed her girlfriend maybe?" Coose said.

Mangan asked Willie, "We got anyone on the coast to reach out to?"

"Working on it now."

Mangan paged through Willie's file. "I hope this isn't more of that Russian shit."

"Sex trade?" Coose asked. "Baratov comes up clean on that end. His girls are all volunteers."

"Word on the street," Willie said, "is that Fenyana was trafficked. She was brought over from—I don't know, something Baltic. I forget the name of the place."

"Whatever," Mangan said. "What do you have on her?"

"She was a kid when they took her. She paid her way out though. Almost never happens, but she did. Then she freelanced awhile, doing the same thing, you know, the computer escort thing, till it got dicey. She got beat up a few times. Two trips to Cook County. Decided she needed protection, and that's how she got hooked up with Baratov."

"If Fenyana had protection from Baratov," Coose asked, "why is she on the run?"

Nobody answered.

"All right, what about her apartment?"

"We got the warrant," Palmer said. "You're good to go."

"And where's Eagan?" Mangan asked. "He find anything on the tapes from the Nite Cap?"

"I don't know." Willie checked a few more notes. "What else? . . . Mara Davies's boyfriend comes up clean. He never left the bar. Plenty of witnesses. She never came back from having a cigarette, so he and her friends went looking for her. They were together all night. That's all I got."

"All right." Mangan said. "See what Eagan's doing with those tapes."

"I'm starving," Coose said.

"We'll eat after we search this apartment."

"Why don't we eat first?"

"Why don't you—" Mangan was too tired to argue. "Fine," he said, "where do you want to go?"

The narrow hallway, barely lit, was littered with food wrappers, plastic pop bottles, beer cans, and the occasional hypodermic needle. The moist walls, moss green and peeling, were streaked brown with slim rivulets of rust.

"Police!" Coose yelled, banging on the door. "Open up!"

Nothing.

"Police!" Coose said, banging again. "We have a warrant! Open up!"

Mangan motioned to the landlord, a crusty gnome of a man who'd been bitching and moaning since they'd arrived.

"You see?" he said, brandishing his key. "You think I'm lying? I told you, didn't I? I said she's not here. Nobody believes me when I—"

"All right, all right," Mangan said. "Just open it up."

The man kept mumbling as he unlocked the apartment door. "If she's not coming back, I want her stuff out."

Mangan turned to a uniformed officer with him. "Would you mind getting this asshole out of here?"

"Yes, sir."

"What?" the landlord said to Mangan. "What did I do?"

"Please, sir," the officer said, "just step away."

Mangan and Coose entered the apartment carefully. It was empty. They holstered their weapons and moved about the room. A small apartment, one bedroom, the kitchen an extension of the living room. Mangan had expected it to be dark and filthy inside, but to his surprise it was clean and white. Mostly white, actually. The woodwork, ceiling and walls, all painted the same color.

Mangan took a quick glance around and followed Coose into the bedroom. Coose searched the closet, which was mostly empty except for a few blouses on hangers. The walls were bare but for a large mirror across from the end of the bed and a red picture frame on another wall, framing nothing, just a frame. The bed, small and blue pillowed, a nightstand next to it, its drawer empty, a snow globe on top of it. Mangan leaned in and took a closer look at the globe. A winter scene: snowman, penguin.

"Two different sizes of clothes," Coose said from the closet. He rummaged around the floor. "Shoes too." He held up a small black combat boot in one hand, and a much larger-sized high-heeled shoe in the other. "Ellison girl was small, right?"

"Yes," Mangan said.

They searched the rest of the room, which looked as if it had been ransacked already, and found nothing of great interest. "She got out in a hurry," Mangan said, opening the dresser drawers, empty mostly except for what he assumed were Deborah Ellison's clothes. A shoebox filled with assorted condoms was on top of the dresser.

The living room was spare: a couch and coffee table, a small TV, and one shelf on the wall. On the shelf was a butterfly figurine, a scented candle, and a matryoshka—one of those wooden Russian dolls that have smaller and smaller dolls inside the biggest one. Two ashtrays on the coffee table were stuffed full with cigarette butts.

From under the couch, Coose pulled a Junior Scrabble board, a Chicago White Pages, and a photo album. The album was a large binder, the cover of which looked as if someone had hand colored it blue with crayons. Across it, in large black letters was written "Deb's Mems." Coose tossed the album on the coffee table.

Mangan sat and opened it.

On the inside cover, written in a wobbly cursive: "This is the property of Deborah Anne Ellison of Winsome Bay, Wisconsin. If found please return." There were no photographs on the first page. On the second page were a series of photos of the two young women: Fenyana, long haired, dark and tall, and Deborah Ellison, alabaster skinned and slight. In one photo Deborah wore a black T-shirt, the fabric sliced through in places so that you saw mostly skin through it and a lacy bra. Mangan could make out tattoos starting about midthigh, just visible beneath her short black skirt. She looked happy in the picture, smiling ridiculously, as if she'd just said or done something outrageous. Fenyana was at her side, smiling too, not quite as wildly. The next page had similar photos of them around the Chicago area in bars, night spots, restaurants, down by Navy Pier.

The next page had only one photo on it, a five-by-seven of Deborah with another young girl. They couldn't have been more than sixteen, seventeen, Mangan thought. The photograph had been torn into pieces and taped back together. This was a different Deborah, calm and clear eyed, looking much the way any Midwest high school girl might look, wearing what appeared to be some kind of a sports uniform. The other girl wore one too. They were posing for the picture in a gymnasium, in front of a volleyball net, their arms flopped over each other's shoulders goofily, smiling. Under the photo, handwritten in blue ink, was "M. B. & D. E. 4-Ever."

"The Becker girl," Mangan said to Coose. "Melissa Becker. Wesley Faber told us about her. The girl Deborah Ellison had a relationship with."

Coose nodded and Mangan turned the page. There was an envelope with a few more photos in it. They were of Deborah and a different woman. One photo was of the backs of the two of them, the woman quite a bit taller than Deborah. It was night. They were outside on a street, facing a bar, and they were both pointing to a neon sign that read the Wicked Cherry. Mangan knew the place, a gay dance club over on West Belmont. Two years ago Internal Affairs had set up an operation there and nailed three dirty cops who were on the payroll. It had been a hot spot for dealing meth and heroin. The city had cracked down on the club after a rash of heroin deaths from bad batches of the stuff.

Another photo was of Deborah Ellison and the same woman leaning against a building. Their arms around each other. From what Mangan could see the woman was attractive. She had shoulder-length blond hair and was tall. He couldn't see her face very well, but something about her looked familiar. He fanned out the photos till he found one where he could see the woman more clearly.

"Holy shit," he said, picking up the picture. "That's Michele Schaefer." He handed it to Coose. "It's Schaefer, the cop from Winsome Bay."

Coose was silent.

Mangan studied the photo a little longer. "You think they were a couple?" he asked.

"If they were, why didn't she tell us? Why wouldn't she offer that up?"

"And what's she doing at the Wicked Cherry? Not a smart place for a cop to be."

"Why, you think she's dirty?"

"Anyone can be dirty." Mangan looked through some of the other photos. "You think Schaefer knew about this other woman, Fenyana? Were Ellison and Schaefer just a onetime thing? A couple of small-town girls out in the city for a night. Or did they have a relationship? They break up, and then Deborah Ellison moves in with this Fenyana girl?"

"Where you going with this? Jealous cop murders ex-girlfriend?"

"Just thinking out loud."

"It would work for the Ellison murder, maybe, but what about the others?"

"I don't know. People snap."

"Schaefer didn't strike me as a psychopath."

"They never do." Mangan put the photo of Schaefer and Ellison in his jacket pocket. "We need to have us a little talk with Ms. Schaefer. Looks like we're heading back to Wisconsin." He flipped the photo album closed. "Let's finish up here and get going. I'll get the kitchen, you take the bathroom."

"Why do I get the bathroom?"

"What's the difference?"

"I'll take the kitchen."

Mangan searched the bathroom. The medicine chest was pretty much cleaned out. He looked in the garbage can beneath the sink. Nothing—a few tampon wrappers, dental floss. The shower curtain, closed, was lilac colored with tropical fish on it. He smacked it open. Something was in the tub covered by a large green fabric. Shit, Mangan thought, palming his Glock and backing away out of habit. He thumbed off the safety and cautiously stepped in again. He pulled off the green cloth.

A birdcage was beneath it. In it, a small, sickly looking bird struggling to hold onto its perch, a canary or something, greenish. Parakeet? It had barely fluttered when Mangan pulled off the cover. Old rips of newspaper mixed with chalky bird shit and mincey pieces of feathers covered the bottom of the cage.

"What do you got there?" Coose asked from the doorway.

"I got a fucking bird, is what I got. It's a bird." Mangan lifted the cage out of the tub. "What do we do with it?"

"I don't know. Give it to the landlord."

"That asshole?"

"Then leave it."

"Can't leave it, the thing's dying. I think it's sick."

"Animal Control?"

"You got a number?"

"No."

"What good are you, anyway?"

"What good are *you*? You don't have the numbers either."

"All right, all right. We'll take it with and give it to someone. Okay?"

"Sure, whatever."

Mangan lifted the birdcage out of the tub and carried it to the living room. Chirpless. Coose sat on the couch and spread scraps of paper over the coffee table.

"What are you doing?" Mangan asked. "C'mon, we gotta go."

"I found some receipts," he said, sorting through them, "in the garbage."

"Well, don't do that now. Give 'em to Eagan or someone. Let's go"

"All right," Coose said, gathering them up again. "I didn't know we were in a rush."

"I don't want this thing dying on me. C'mon, let's get out of here."

"I'm coming."

"Take the album, I got the canary."

He knew where she lived.

The next one.

He was on his way there. Driving, driving. Peaceful, for the most part, while driving. It gave him something to focus on—the steering wheel, the road—instead of always thinking on the other thing. He played with the small metal hoops that lay on the seat beside him, smooth and shiny. He put them on his fingers. They reminded him of what he needed to do.

He could see the next one's house. In his mind.

On the map, on the Internet, he'd studied it. Watched it for hours. All he'd had to do was type in her address and the computer map told him how to find her. Then he selected the little orange-man symbol in the corner of the map and dragged him over by his neck, feet flailing, and plopped him down in front of her address, and in a moment there was a picture of her house. He could see everything. Just like being there. Her lawn, the car in her driveway, the tree in front, the cyclone fence of her backyard. He could even zoom in on her front door, behind which she and her daughter and her husband were maybe having a lovely day. Or maybe they were in the backyard. Playing. Or maybe the baby was asleep, and they were on the couch, the couch that was probably right on the other side of the curtained window that the little orange man had photographed.

I'll bet they're very happy, he thought.

Have a happy day.
I am coming.

Looks like you keep the taxidermist pretty busy around here," Mangan said, stepping into Wesley Faber's office. He was admiring the two mounted deer heads on the wall.

Faber, looking a bit surprised, half stood and held out his hand. "I wasn't told you were coming, Detective."

"Just passing through," Mangan said. "Thought I'd drop in, ask a few questions."

"Passing through?"

"Yes."

"Well." Faber sat down again. "How can I help you?"

Mangan kept studying the deer heads. "My partner's across the street at the Dew Drop asking a few questions. We don't have much to go on with our case in Chicago, and, well, things keep kind of pointing back this way." Mangan stepped behind Faber's desk, examining a series of broad-feathered tail mountings arranged on the wall. Faber swiveled around in his chair to see what he was doing.

"What are these?" Mangan asked. "Pheasant?"

"Turkey."

"Turkey, of course, turkey. You eat them?"

"We eat everything we kill."

"That's comforting to know." Mangan put on his glasses and leaned in to read some of the award plaques on the wall. American Patriot Sharpshooter, Wisconsin Long Range Rifle Champion, Midwest Classic Skeet Champion, NRA Marksmanship. "Impressive," Mangan said. "I'm glad you're on our team." He pointed to the deer heads. "You eat them too? The deer?"

"Yes."

"You butcher them yourself? The deer?"

"How can I help you, Detective? You said you had some questions."

"Yes, I do." Mangan walked from behind the desk and sat in a chair opposite Faber. "You know, I've always liked the outdoors, hunting, fishing, but being a city kid I never got out much—from the city, I mean. I watched nature things on TV, though. I still do."

"Detective, I don't mean to be rude, but—"

"Oh, sorry. You're busy. I'll get out of here in a minute."

Faber smiled. "That's okay."

"Thank you," Mangan said, taking out the photos of Deborah Ellison and Michele Schaefer. He placed them on the desk.

Faber's Midwest smile went the way of the glaciers. After a chilly moment, he asked, "Where did you get these?"

"Did you know these women were in a relationship?"

"Where did you hear that?"

"Did you know that Officer Schaefer had a relationship with the murder victim?"

"Yes." Faber picked up the picture. "Where was this taken?"

"Chicago."

He placed it back on the desk and pushed it toward Mangan. "Schaefer's a good cop."

"I'm not asking that, but I'd like to know why you didn't share this information?"

"I didn't find it pertinent."

"There's that word again—what is this? Of course it's pertinent."

"To *my* investigation, yes. I didn't think you needed to know. We followed up on it."

"Who did? *You* did? You've got you and Schaefer here. Is she investigating herself?"

"We have three other officers, and the City of Madison is helping out. We've asked all the questions we need to ask her, and I'm satisfied that she—"

"Have you ruled her out as a suspect?"

"She never was a suspect."

"Everyone's a suspect till they're not."

"Well then, she's not."

"So you've exhausted every line of questioning with her? You've—"

"Don't tell me how to do my job, sir. This—"

"I'm not trying to—"

"I am speaking, sir!" Faber yelled, slamming his hand on the desk and standing. His face flushed instantly red. "This ain't Mayberry and I'm no goddamned Barney Fife! I've got enough things going on out here without you poking your nose in business that's no concern of yours, stirring things up that don't need stirring. And I'd appreciate it if you'd keep your patronizing leading questions for all your educated city suspects, and let me do my job!" He sat again. Calmer now. "I will help you when I can, if it doesn't compromise my investigation. And if that's not enough for you, well, you can just march yourself on out of here."

The door to Faber's office opened and a gangly young cop poked his head in.

"Is everything—sorry to interrupt—is everything all right, sir?"

"Yes, Dan. Thank you. Everything's fine."

The officer backed out and closed the door. He lingered a moment, looking confused, and then walked away.

Faber stared at Mangan. "I do not appreciate your manner, Detective."

Mangan let the silence sit a minute.

"I apologize," he said. "You're right, bad habit of mine. I can be antagonistic, I know. I don't make a lot of friends that way, but I do learn things. Inadvertently. Like, what don't you want me *stirring* up around here? Was Schaefer's relationship with the murder victim a secret in this town?"

"What?"

"Is it a secret that Officer Schaefer is gay?"

"Schaefer? What are you talking about? She's not gay."

Mangan pointed to the photo again. "That's a gay club in Chicago, the Wicked Cherry. Schaefer has her arm around—"

"I believe you're starting to see lesbians everywhere, Detective." He tossed the photo back to Mangan. "A woman can have her arm around another woman, doesn't means she's gay."

"That isn't the issue. The issue is an undisclosed relationship with a murder victim."

"It wasn't undisclosed." Faber opened a bottom drawer in his desk and searched through it. "I've known Michele Schaefer since she was a kid. She went to school with my daughter. I know her father. I worked with him twenty years on the force before he retired. Believe me, I questioned Michele thoroughly as soon as we started this investigation." He pulled a large file from the drawer and dropped it on the desk. "That's her statement. She used to give Debbie rides to Chicago whenever she and her boyfriend were heading out that way. That's all. They found her hitchhiking once out on the highway, and so she started giving her rides. They'd drop her off wherever she wanted to go and sometimes bring her back home. Schaefer knew Debbie was gay—well, the whole town knew it, and most of them made that poor girl's life hell. You don't come out in a small town like this. You do, they'll make your life miserable. It ain't fair and I don't agree with it, but it's the way things are here, and I don't see it changing anytime soon. Schaefer was a friend, a good friend, trying to help out a kid that was pretty damn lost." He tapped the thick file. "It's all in there."

Mangan read through some of the statement. *You are deceived, for what you see is but the smallest part of humanity.* His hunch was wrong. He'd been too eager to make a connection. He looked up. "Well, I would have liked to have seen this report before."

"Well, you might try asking next time."

Mangan had no desire to get into a pissing contest with Faber. "Can I talk to Schaefer?"

"Sure, but she ain't here today. She's out on the farm helping her dad."

"Can you tell me how to get there?"

"Not much to tell." Faber led Mangan out of the office. They passed the young officer who had come into the room earlier. "Dan," Faber said to him, "this is Detective Mangan, from Chicago."

"Dan Ehrlich, sir," the officer said, shaking Mangan's hand. "Pleased to meet you. Oh, shoot—I got, I got a message for you. Just a sec." He ran back to his desk, rummaging through some papers. "I got it right here. The chief called, from over in Enfield." Ehrlich found a notepad on his desk and hurriedly thumbed through it. "Here we go . . . uh . . . they didn't find any fingerprints or trace evidence in Jillian McClay's office. Didn't find a murder weapon. The carpets were clean, no impressions or staining. The gun in her office was legally registered to her father, a cop in Philadelphia. The door to door turned up nothing, and the ex-husband is arranging a flight back from Florida right now. He should get in sometime tomorrow morning."

"Thanks," Mangan said.

Faber stepped in, "Thank you, Dan," and gestured for Mangan to follow him.

Mangan jotted down some of the information Ehrlich had relayed as Faber led him out the front doors of the station and into the street.

"Right up there," he said, showing him the way to the Schaefer farm. "Take a left and it's about ten minutes down. Can't miss it."

"Thank you," Mangan said, shaking Faber's hand.

"Yup."

Mangan glanced up and down the block. "Place to eat around here?"

"Right behind you." Faber was talking about the Dew Drop Inn, where Coose was. "Next restaurant's about thirty miles north."

"Not a whole lot of choices around here, are there?"

"No, sir, there are not."

Mangan grabbed the handle on the front door of the Dew Drop Inn and yanked it open. Coose was at a table talking to an older couple. Mangan nodded to him, and Coose continued talking. A few people were at the bar, some with plates of food before them, some with cans of beer, their gazes transfixed on a large TV screen hanging behind the bar.

"Hi, ya," the bartender said to Mangan. "We met awhile back. I'm Lou."

"Yes," Mangan said, sitting at the bar, "I remember. Got a menu?"

"I do." Lou grabbed one and flipped it down in front of Mangan. "Something to drink?"

"Club soda, please," Mangan said, trying to find something on the menu that wasn't deep fried.

"Fish fry is pretty good here," Lou said. "If you like fish."

"I'll have a cheeseburger."

"Fries or chips?"

"Chips."

Mangan scanned the length of the bar. At the far end, three men were eyeing him. Late twenties, early thirties. From their dress Mangan assumed they were laborers, maybe farmers, construction. They all had beer cans and empty shot glasses in front of them.

"Hey," Coose said, pulling up a stool next to Mangan. "How'd it go with Faber?"

"Good," he said. "We had a misread on Schaefer. I'll tell you about it later. We're going to take a ride and talk to her. She's just down the road at her father's place. You want to eat something?"

"I already did."

Mangan referenced the older couple Coose had been talking to. "What did you get from them?"

"Not much," he said. "But I talked to a woman earlier." Coose checked his notes. "Judith Meyers. She said that Deborah Ellison, before she moved away, was pretty messed up, you know, drugs, drinking, big flirt, all over the guys at the bar come closing time. This bar in particular. She wasn't very popular with the wives around town. Rumor is, she went home with a husband or two in her time. One guy in particular."

"You got a name?"

"Leo Peterson. I guess he's big time around here—as big as you can get in a town this size. He runs a construction company. And the development where Ellison's body was found is being built by PeterSons Construction."

The bartender put a club soda down in front of Mangan. "There you go."

"Thanks," Mangan said. "Hey, Lou?"

"Yeah?"

"You know Leo Peterson?"

Lou took a slight pause. "Everybody knows Leo."

"What do you know about him and Deborah Ellison?"

Lou took a longer pause this time. He glanced down at the three locals at the end of the bar. He looked back to Mangan. "You know, Detective, a bartender's sort of like a lawyer or a priest. There's some discretion a customer can expect when they come in here. I don't talk about things that happen in here. If I did, I wouldn't have much of a business left."

"I understand that, Lou," Mangan said. "You're a nice guy. I could tell right away. Unfortunately, though, unlike a priest or a lawyer, a bartender is not protected by law. And obstruction of justice in a murder investigation is a pretty serious offense. I'm not going to pull that though, I'm not here to get you in any trouble. I'm just trying to help Chief Faber out with his investigation."

Lou nodded.

"I see you've got a surveillance camera," Mangan said, "and it looks pretty up-to-date. I imagine it's all digitized? How many years do you keep the hard drives?"

"Hey," someone said from behind Mangan.

In the mirrored wall behind the tiered shelves of liquor bottles Mangan saw three men standing behind him. The trio from the end of the bar. He could also see Coose, very still. Coose always got very quiet and still at times like this.

The bartender took a half step back from the bar.

Mangan felt that thing in him rise, the tingly feeling in his gut and balls. Muscles tightened, thoughts and sight focused. He turned to the three men. Two were quite big, the third, slighter, but meaner looking. Mangan had spied a baseball bat behind the bar earlier, just to the left of the cash register, but he didn't think the bartender was that kind of a guy. In the split-second thoughts firing across his synapses, Mangan assessed that, if anything happened, the bartender would stay out of it. He also knew that this was a concealed carry state and any one of these bozos might be armed.

"Gentlemen," Mangan said. "How can I help you?"

The scrawnier one stepped forward, "You can help us by getting the fuck out of here."

The bartender said, "Gary, don't."

"Shut up, Lou." The man glared at Mangan. "You're not welcome around here."

"I'm beginning to get that impression."

"Gary," Lou said, "if you don't stop, I'm going to call the chief."

"Call the goddamned chief."

One of the bigger men made a sudden move and Coose was between him and Mangan in a flash, his barstool knocked backward.

"Whoa, whoa," Mangan said, raising his hands. "No need for this. You've made your point, boys. We're leaving."

"Then go on already," Gary said, "or we'll help you out."

"That's okay," Mangan said, turning to Coose. "I think we're just going to go, Coose. Okay?"

One of the bigger men said, "Coose? What kind of name is that?"

Gary chimed in, "Coose like a coon."

Mangan said, "It's Cusumano."

"What's that? Eye-talian?" Gary said. "Well, we don't serve wetbacks in here."

Mangan eyed Coose to see if he was okay. He was. It took more than a few insults from an IQ-less piece of trailer trash to flip Coose.

The mangy one with the big mouth said, "This is your last chance. Get the fuck out of here."

Mangan took a step toward him. "Now, uh . . . Gary, isn't it?" There was no answer. "Now, Gary, it's not illegal to curse at a police officer. It's pretty stupid, but not illegal. However, threatening an officer is a very different story. So, if I were you, I might want to be careful of whatever I was thinking of saying next. If you're capable of that, I mean—of *thinking*."

"What, are you going to arrest me?"

"Well, yes, there's a very high probability of that. Either that, or me and my partner will go old-time on you—since you guys seem to be about fifty years behind the rest of the world out here—and throw you a good beating." Mangan turned to Coose. "This is Frank Cusumano. He's of Italian descent, by the way, not *Eye*-talian. It also might interest you to know that the term *wetback* is a racial slur used against people of Mexican descent, originating in the 1920s when Mexican laborers crossed into the United States illegally by swimming across the Rio Grande—that's the really big river between the U.S. and Mexico. So, just to support your quite bewildering ignorance, for future reference, when insulting an Italian you might want to call him a Guido, or a guinea or a dago, a goombah or greaseball—what else, Coose?" Coose didn't say anything. Mangan continued. "Oh, *wop*. That's right. That's like the best one. Wop."

Gary attempted to speak, but Mangan cut him off.

"So—I'm almost done—so, as I was saying earlier, my partner and I would be more than happy to kick the living shit out of all three of you. I'd actually *prefer* to do that. But I'm an officer of the law and I've worked very hard to be able to rise above these feelings of aggression. I actually took classes on it. They're very good. You should try them. They're classes on how to rise above these feelings of anger that I experience when I'm forced to deal with moronic, lowlife assholes, like yourselves. And, I must say, I think I'm doing a pretty good job right now. Don't you think so, Coose?" Coose still said nothing. "He doesn't like to talk at times like this. That should worry you."

There was a pause.

Mangan was quite sure that the men before him hadn't understood a good two-thirds of the vocabulary he had just used, nor had they at all appreciated his Rostand-like riff on Italian racial slurs, which he thought he had performed rather well. *There is no darkness but ignorance; in which thou art more puzzled than the Egyptians in their fog.* He shook his head slightly in dismay.

"Anyway," Mangan said, "we're going to walk away now, and you're all going to keep your mouths shut. How does that sound?"

No one spoke.

"Coose?" Mangan said. "Let's not do this, okay? It's not worth it."

God, it was hard to do what he'd just done, Mangan thought, so hard. His fingers more than itched. The only consistently reliable truth that he'd learned in more than half a lifetime of police work was that, at times, some people just needed the shit kicked out of them.

Mangan went to pay his tab. Lou told him not to worry about it.

"Thank you," Mangan said, and started out.

As he did, Gary whispered to Coose, "Fucking guinea. Is that better?"

All that Detective Mangan could really tell Wesley Faber later that day, after the ambulance arrived, was that it was reflex. He wasn't lying. In an instant the current that continuously ran just beneath Mangan's skin clicked and triggered, and a breathing second after the man had let slip the word *guinea*, his nose exploded in a mash of blood and cartilage as Mangan slammed his fist into the front of the man's face, fracturing his nasal bone and snapping away his left lateral incisor. Gary fell to the floor and never moved. Coose stepped in front of the other two men at the same time and readied himself, but neither made a move. They were too busy staring down at their friend, who, waking fairly quickly, sat up, clutching at his nose and whimpering. They're all babies when they're beaten. Unfortunately for Gary, real punches aren't like the ones you see in the movies or read about in detective novels. Most fights last only a few seconds. A well-thrown punch quite often breaks whatever it hits. The nose in particular. It bleeds a lot and hurts like hell.

Coose helped Gary into a chair, whispering to Mangan, "Didn't have to do that."

"I know," Mangan said, kind of regretting what he'd done, but not really. He paced the bar, trying to calm himself and his breathing. Once the switch flipped in Mangan, it wasn't always easy to turn off.

"Sorry about that, bud," Coose said to Gary. "I should have warned you that he failed that class, you know, that anger management class he was telling you about." He asked the bartender to call for an ambulance and then grabbed some ice from behind the bar and wrapped it in a towel. He handed the ice-wrap to Mangan and whispered, "Help out a little. It'll look good in the report."

Gary flinched when Mangan approached him. "Here," he said to Gary, placing the ice-wrap in his hands. "It'll keep the swelling down. You're okay, it's just your nose. It bleeds a lot."

The local EMTs loaded Gary into the ambulance and headed to the hospital, accompanied by a state patrol officer who showed up. Mangan learned then that Gary's last name was Peterson. One of the other men was a Peterson too—Neal was his first name—both sons of the man that Mangan had been asking about, Leo Peterson.

"I thought he might have had a concealed weapon," Mangan explained to Faber as the ambulance rolled away. "He said something to my partner, and then made a sudden move, I wasn't sure, so . . ."

Faber stared at Mangan for a moment. "You mind if we go back to the station and talk?"

"No. Not at all."

Wesley Faber didn't look very happy.

They all have alibis," Faber said. "Leo Peterson and his sons." He closed the door to his office as Coose and Mangan stepped in. "They were in Hawaii for two weeks."

"Hawaii?" Coose asked.

"The whole family goes on business conventions every year. All a tax write-off. Vegas, Aruba, the Caribbean, cruise ships, you name it. They're the money around here, like their grandpa was. In this town you don't get a liquor license or a zoning permit, and your kid doesn't start on the varsity basketball team, unless you have the right name. And that means you better be related to the Petersons."

"That's illegal where I come from."

"It's illegal here too, just can't do a damned thing about it."

Mangan stared at the deer heads on the wall, thinking, *plate sin with gold and the strong lance of justice hurtless breaks.*

"Nobody likes the Petersons," Faber continued. "Half the town pretends they do, the other half ignores them. Those boys have had anything they wanted since the day they could walk. Pains in my ass. Privileged and stupid. But that doesn't mean they're guilty of anything."

Coose's cell phone buzzed. "Excuse me," he said, and left Faber's office to answer it.

"This thing with Leo Peterson and Debbie," Faber said, "happened more than two years ago, if it even did happen. Debbie was very messed up at that time, drinking and drugs. Half the boys in town took her home at some time. Just dropped her off or messed around with her in the car."

"How do you know all this?"

"We follow the drunks home here. We sit outside the Dew Drop at closing time and follow them, make sure that they get home okay. They usually drive a little safer if they know we're behind them. If they're really drunk we'll take them in, but we use a bit of discretion here."

Coose came back in the office. "That was Mickey Eagan. There was nothing on the security tapes from the Nite Cap, the bar where Mara Davies's body was found, but he got something else. Those receipts I got from the girls' apartment? Eagan found a credit card receipt with Fenyana's signature on it. O'Rourke's Pub and Grill on Ashland. Looks like three people had dinner. The date on the receipt's a Friday. August tenth. Deborah Ellison's body was found early a.m. on the eleventh. It's from the night she was killed."

"O'Rourke's have security cameras?" Mangan asked.

"Yeah. Eagan made a copy. He's sending us a link."

"Go get the laptop out of the car."

"You can use the computer here," Faber said.

Faber gave Coose the station's e-mail address and Coose called it in to Eagan. If Deborah Ellison was on the tapes, Mangan knew that he'd have a last known whereabouts for her. He also knew that Fenyana and whoever else had been at the restaurant that night might very well be the last people to have seen Deborah Ellison alive.

Faber led Mangan and Coose to a small media room behind a bank of windows. He called out to the front desk officer on the way. "Hey, Dan, come on over here. I got some computer stuff for you to do." Faber turned to Mangan. "I can do the computer, I just don't like it."

"He still has a flip phone," Ehrlich said, settling in behind the computer.

"And I'm going to keep it. Don't need all that other stuff."

"They're not going to make those phones anymore."

"Then I won't use one."

"What do you want me to do?" Ehrlich asked.

Coose told him about the receipt found at the apartment, "Chicago's sending you a video link. We just need you to upload it."

Dan opened the e-mail program and asked Faber, "You want to learn how to do this?"

"No."

Ehrlich smiled, shaking his head, and double-clicked the link. "It's going to take a little bit. It's a big file." Everyone watched the percentage bar color itself green as it uploaded. "Got it," Ehrlich said. He opened another program to play the file. "Here we go."

The quality of the tape was shit, a long master shot of the dining area rather than a close-up on any one table.

"This is a tape of the whole night," Ehrlich said. "You got a time on the receipt?"

"Give me a sec," Coose said. He gave Eagan a quick call, then told Ehrlich, "Start around six o'clock."

Ehrlich fast-forwarded until they saw two women enter the restaurant.

"There," Mangan said, "right there."

The men huddled closely around the computer screen. The two women were difficult to make out, but definitely recognizable: Fenyana's tall, lithe body, and Deborah Ellison, small and tight. The two women walked to a far corner table. Someone else, a male, was following them. Very closely.

"Who's that with them?" Faber asked.

Mangan whispered, "I don't know."

The man's face wasn't visible. He walked with them to a far corner booth and slid in first. Fenyana sat next to him. Deborah Ellison, clearly visible now, sat on the opposite side of the table, across from the unknown male and Fenyana.

"Damn it," Mangan said. "It's too dark."

The lighting was bad in the corner booth. They couldn't make out the male's face at all. He was tucked tightly into the corner and obscured by Fenyana, who was sitting on the outside of him. The camera angle didn't help. Fenyana was hard to see also, her long hair hanging loose across her eyes at times.

The men watched the tape.

Mangan studied Deborah Ellison. Always strange, he thought—seeing a murder victim alive, entirely unaware that she was soon going to be dead.

Thou art death's fool;
For him thou labour'st by thy flight to shun,
And yet runn'st toward him still.

The night at the restaurant was busy; waitresses and patrons passed back and forth in front of their table. There was no sound on the tapes. Mangan could tell, though, from the hand gestures and body language, that the conversation at the table was fairly unremarkable, except for the fact that Deborah and Fenyana seemed to be the only ones talking. The male stayed sitting back, his hands in his lap. A meal was served to him, but he didn't move. He didn't drink either, although a drink had been served to him. Mangan watched intently. Deborah Ellison looked distracted. She played with one of the large hoop earrings she was wearing, looking around often, as if she had to be somewhere else, or wanted to be somewhere else. At one point Fenyana reached across the table and touched Deborah's hand, but she pulled away.

"What was that?" Mangan asked.

Ehrlich played the moment back. They watched it again. Deborah looked scared at that moment, or was it anger? She'd pulled her hand away from Fenyana, then she got up and left the table. And didn't come back. Fenyana could then be seen waving to the waitress, who brought over a bill. She got up, took the bill from the waitress, and disappeared. The man then hurriedly scooched out of his seat and followed after them.

"Shit," Coose said, the man's face clearly visible now.

"What?" Mangan asked. "What, who is it?"

"That's Baratov," Coose said. "Savva Baratov. The guy that runs the Bank Street Diner."

"Change of plans," Mangan said. "Let's get out of here. Call Eagan. Tell him to bring Baratov in. Now."

Chicago.

Three thirty in the morning. Mangan drained his glass. He was sitting in his reading chair in the front room of his apartment, wide awake. Insomnia. It was happening again. It irritated the hell out of him—made him more irritated than usual, that is, for Mangan was well aware that he lived in a sort of perpetual state of irritability. Wakefulness didn't help matters. He'd had a bad relationship with sleep for most of his life. He couldn't remember the last time he'd slept eight hours. Sometime in his childhood, maybe.

Now o'er the one half-world nature seems dead,
And wicked dreams abuse the curtained sleep.

He never looked forward to the night.

He sleeps with clenched hands; and wakes with his own bloody nails in his palms.

"Oh, for Christ's sake, not Melville," Mangan muttered to himself, "not now." He squirmed in the chair. Melville had a way of sneaking into his thoughts at the most inopportune times, usually when he was exhausted and couldn't sleep, and that's not a good time to start contemplating Melville.

Mangan looked out the front window.

He'd been doing pretty well for the last few months. His wife hadn't been on his mind too much, but he'd been thinking of her a lot lately. The trips to Winsome, probably, to the countryside. She loved getting out of the city. *Whole oceans away,* he seemed to feel, *from that young girl-wife* he'd wedded once. They'd been quite happy for a long time, and then . . . they weren't. It just changed. The suddenness of it seemed improbable. But it had happened. They stopped liking each other. They'd lost themselves and were desperately trying to find each other again, and then there was the arguing, and the things said in anger, and the small daily cruelties, and the pettiness, and then the phone call that silenced the screaming and shamed them both.

The doctor, routine checkup, not so routine.

There's a great spirit gone. Thus did I desire it.
Would the hand could pluck her back that shoved her on.

Mangan got up and walked the long hallway of his empty apartment. Restless. Surveying the fortifications of his book-walled citadel. *When I think of this life I have led; the desolation of solitude it has been; the masoned, walled-town of a Captain's exclusiveness*—god, he had to get Melville out of his head. He grabbed the new book he'd bought and went back to the front room.

How to Gain Your Parakeet's Trust

He'd picked it up at the Windy City Parakeet Boutique on the way home from Winsome Bay. Coose thought he was insane. The day that Mangan had found the bird in Fenyana Petrakova's apartment he hadn't known what to do with it, so he brought it home with him. He didn't know why. He didn't like animals. And now he had to take care of the thing.

He flipped the book open to a random page.

"*When you first take your new parakeet home, expect him to be terrified. This anxiety and stress may make him bite.*"

Mangan looked at the sullen parakeet in the cage. "You bite me, and you're out of here. You understand me?"

The bird cocked its head slightly.

"*Reassure your parakeet in a calm voice and with slow movements.*"

"Reassure your*self*," he told the bird. "Life's tough, get used to it."

"*Whistle to your parakeet.*"

"Not a chance."

He read on, skimming through chapters.

"*Parakeets are extremely social birds and they must be kept in pairs to avoid harmful behavior problems.*"

"Well, that's not going to happen. We're bachelors here. Or you're a—whatever—a bachelorette, a bird bachelorette."

The bird was most likely a female, if Mangan understood the book correctly. Something about the color around its beak. Anyway, he decided it was a girl whether it was right or not.

"Phoebe," said to the bird. "That's your name now."

The book had said that parakeets make a lot of noise, but Mangan hadn't heard a chirp since he'd found her in the bathtub of the apartment. He leaned back into the armchair and watched the bird for a long moment. She watched him too. Gloomy little thing, he thought, probably traumatized somehow. A line of poetry came to him—*Bare ruined choirs, where late the sweet birds sang.* Mangan leaned forward and tapped the cage.

"Hey. You okay in there?"

Phoebe scooted sideways on her perch.

"Relax, I'm not going to hurt you."

She backed farther away, pressing up against the side of the cage.

Mangan tried a calmer voice and then realized he was talking to a bird.

"Jesus."

He put the cage on a table near the bay window, then went into the kitchen to make another drink. He cracked some ice into a glass, gave himself a two-finger pour of gin, hesitated a moment, and made it three. He splashed in a little soda and joined Phoebe in the front room. She skittered away as he flopped into the chair next to her. He took a long, deep breath and thought of nothing for exactly two seconds. He looked out the window.

"In the morning," he told Phoebe, "you'll see sparrows."

Mangan checked the time. Mickey Eagan would be bringing Savva Baratov in for questioning in about five or six hours. He drank deep and ran the scenario in his head. Baratov, Ellison, and Fenyana at dinner together. Coose said that Baratov definitely was not mob affiliated, but he might still be trafficking women. Most of the lowlifes involved in the sex trade in Chicago weren't associated with organized crime syndicates. They were most often part of the plague of entrepreneurs that had spread like pond scum around the world after the breakup of the Soviet Union.

A sort of vagabonds, rascals, and runaways,
A scum of base lackey peasants,
Whom their o'er-cloyed country vomits forth.

Their disregard for human life was unfathomable.

Mangan could imagine Deborah Ellison getting mixed up in the sex trade when she'd moved to Chicago; that wasn't such a stretch. Now, whether she was being trafficked against her will was another question. It wasn't uncommon to see trafficked women beaten or killed if they resisted. Maybe Fenyana wasn't her lover. Maybe she'd been assigned to watch Ellison, to keep her in line. Some of the more senior prostitutes sometimes did that. Mangan considered if he should be looking at the Fenyana woman more closely. She was on the run.

Had Ellison been made an example of? For some offense?

But why had Ellison's body been dumped in her hometown if somebody wanted to make an example of her in Chicago? If she was being trafficked, the killer, or killers, would want the other girls to see her, to scare them. Or maybe Winsome Bay was merely where they finally caught up to her, maybe she knew she was in trouble and was trying to get home.

Whither should I fly? I have done no harm.

But this still didn't shed any light on the motives for the brutal slayings of Mara Davies and Jillian McClay. Ellison's murder could certainly have been some form of retribution or punishment, but it didn't make sense with regard to the other victims. If it was a sex ring, why kill the other women?

Unless someone was afraid that the *American Forum* articles might bring attention to their operation. Unless the men running the ring wanted the police to *think* there was a serial killer murdering these women. All they'd have to do was to write a few weird notes and leave them for the police to find, try to make everyone think it was personal, some lone figure wronged by these women. That was a stretch, though, and Mangan knew it. The sleazebags who ran these operations weren't that smart. They preyed upon the innocent and the vulnerable, the immigrants, the drug addicted, the poor and abused, children.

Mangan checked his watch again. Shit. He knew he had to sleep. He turned to Phoebe. She was staring at him and had inched the littlest bit closer.

"What do you think?" he asked her.

She scooched away again, looking slightly panicked.

"You're no help," he said, and stared up at the ceiling.

Why? Why were these women murdered?

If he could figure out the why, he could maybe figure out the *who.*

The man sat in his truck, in the parking lot, the engine running. The radio playing, quietly. Country music. The sun just up. The lake so crispy blue, so different from his lake, the one to which he would lead them later. This lake was much bigger, much wider.

A sea-lake.

He could make out a dock to his left. The boats there, bobbing. Fishermen waiting on the dock, in small huddles, coffee cups in their prayerful hands, steaming. Their mouths moving mutely.

He rolled down his window and dropped the note out. It clinked on the pavement. It was too windy, though, he thought. It might blow away. He got out and picked it up. He placed it under the wiper blade of another car.

The cottony clouds, puffy white and low, scuttled across the sky from north to south. He marked the wind. Its speed. He breathed in deeply and stilled himself, steadied his mind. Checked his watch. Focused.

He got back in his truck.

She would be here soon.

She would be here very soon.

Savva Baratov looked half asleep when Mickey Eagan escorted him into the interview room.

"Why do you bring me here?" Baratov said. "I have nothing to do with this."

Eagan left and shut the door. Coose leaned against the far wall, arms crossed. Mangan pulled out a chair, spun it around, and sat across from Baratov, a stocky, crevice-faced man with a look of privilege smoldering about him. He had wide hands, fingers like fat sausages, and was too well dressed for the owner of a diner.

"I have done nothing," Baratov said again. He took off his black-rimmed glasses and cleaned them. "Why do you bring me here?"

"Actually," Mangan said, "I'm the one who gets to ask the questions."

"I am United States citizen. Eighteen years I am here now. I have rights."

"Yes, you do."

"My lawyer, he comes. Then you ask your questions."

Mangan ignored him and asked, "Where are you from anyway?"

"The Bank Street Diner."

"Very funny. I don't meet a lot of Russian comedians."

"There is no jokes in Russia."

"Not a fuck of a lot here either. I asked you where you were from."

". . . Constanta, Romania."

"Not familiar with it," Mangan lied, well aware that Romania was a global center for human trafficking, a leading exporter of human flesh. He opened a file and took out a photo of Deborah Ellison. He slid it across the table. "You know this girl?"

Baratov looked at it for a long moment. "I must wait for lawyer," he said. "I am United States citizen."

"Look, you can sing that song all the way to the state penitentiary. The place is filled with United States citizens." Mangan pointed to the photo. "I asked you if you know this girl."

Baratov folded his arms across his chest.

Mangan folded his.

A long silence passed. Mangan let it strain.

Finally, Baratov, smiling slightly, looked to the ceiling and said, "A policeman was just born."

Something clicked in Mangan's brain. Something about those words. He'd heard them before. "What? What'd you just say?"

"Nothing. It is a, how do you say, a *proverb* where I come from."

Mangan couldn't place where he'd heard the phrase before.

"And for each police baby that is born," Baratov added, "there is little lawyer baby born too. That is *my* proverb. And now, I am so sorry, but I must talk no more until my baby has arrived."

Mangan ignored Baratov and nodded to Coose, who walked over and loaded a DVD copy of the security tapes from O'Rourke's tavern into a laptop. He cued it up and turned the screen toward Baratov. "Where were you on the night of August tenth," Mangan asked, "between five o'clock and midnight?"

"Lawyer," was all Baratov said.

"Video," was all that Mangan said.

Coose pressed the Play button on the laptop.

Baratov's wall of a face fell slightly. "I did not—I have nothing to do with this."

"With what?" Mangan asked.

"With her, with what happened to Deborah. It is too horrible to think."

"So, you know her?"

"Who, Deborah?"

"Yes."

"Yes, of course I know her. I like her."

"Doesn't look like you were getting along too well on this tape."

"No, that was, that was business meeting."

"What kind of business?"

"Come now, my friend, you know my business," Baratov said, far too smugly for Mangan's patience. "My girls are clean. Yes? I keep them off the street. But sometimes I need to remind them of the rules, yes? Ask Sergeant Burke, my friend Mr. Burke, in vice, he will tell you. I am fair and safe."

The more Baratov talked the more Mangan wanted to punch him in the head. "First off," Mangan said, "I'm not your friend. And what I *do* know, is that this girl disappeared very shortly after you had an argument with her."

"What argument? We discuss business."

"The tape has you leaving the restaurant around seven forty-five, right after her. Where did you go?"

"I do not remember."

"This shows you with a girl a few hours before she was murdered. Where did you go?"

"Okay, okay, I go to the Bank Street!" Baratov said, his cockiness limply retreating. "I am open all night, and through weekend. The drunks they come late for food, yes? You can see, my receipts, my cameras. I have cameras too. I am on the tape if you look. I work all night. I give you tapes, yes? Come, we go now and get them, I don't care. No warrant. We go now."

Mangan looked to Coose and said, "Send Eagan over there."

Coose stepped out of the room.

"I do not lie, Detective," Baratov said. "I take care of my girls. You ask them."

"Why were you at a restaurant with two of your girls? I don't see a lot of hookers going out to dinner with their pimps."

"That word—pimp—it is terrible. I am like father to my girls."

"Yeah, I'm sure you're a regular bang-up dad."

"What is this *bang-up?*"

"Just—would you—just shut up, okay?"

"Okay."

"How do you know Deborah Ellison?"

"Fenyana bring her to me. For a job. I say yes. They work together sometimes. I take care of her."

"To the tune of 70 percent, right?"

Baratov gave a half nod.

Mangan asked, "Do you know anyone that might want to hurt her?"

"No."

"She have any trouble with your customers? Any violence or drugs?"

"No."

"No drugs?"

"No. No drugs. Fenyana tells me Deborah has quit the drugs."

"Deborah Ellison was on drugs?"

"Yes, you know, the meth."

Mangan noted this. "She owe anybody money that you know of?"

"I don't know."

"She owe you money?"

"No."

At that point the door opened and Coose walked in, followed by a thin, well-dressed man.

"Good morning," the man said. "I'm Marcus Grigory, Mr. Baratov's lawyer. You're charging my client with what, may I ask?"

Coose closed the door and said, "Violating the Clean Indoor Air Ordinance. Permitting smoking in the Bank Street Diner. Health department sent us."

"I'm sorry, Officer," Grigory said, "are you trying to be funny?" No one said anything. "If you have formal charges to make against my client, please do so. If not, we're finished here." He waited for an answer. "Very well." He gestured to Savva. "Come, Mr. Baratov." Baratov stood as Grigory opened the door for him. "By the way," Grigory said, "you'll be hearing from us. This frivolous and unwarranted harassment of my client by the Chicago police is just one more example of the continued ethnic stereotyping of—"

"Would you please stop talking," Mangan said.

"Excuse me?"

"Look, I don't care about your client's little titty business, but I promise you I will make his life absolutely miserable if he doesn't co-operate." The only people Mangan hated worse than guys like Baratov were lawyers for guys like Baratov. "I will have the Department of Health, the fire inspector, the building inspector, the IRS, the INS, and every other S-ending acronym I can think of, camping out on the sidewalk of his restaurant twenty-four-seven." Mangan wanted to hit something, he closed in on Baratov. "I will put you *under*, Mr. Savvy, Ali Baba—whatever the hell your name is! You are fucking with the wrong guy!"

"Hey, hey," Coose said, stepping between them. "Enough! James, back off. Back off!"

Baratov threw up his hands. "Why is this?"

"Asshole," Mangan yelled as Coose shoved him away.

"Everybody relax," Coose called out. "Just relax, James!"

Mangan mumbled, "Piece of shit," under his breath as he forced himself to keep distance. The switch had clicked in him again—*On*—and like an electric current it buzzed his legs and tingled his hands with rage. He removed himself to the other side of the room, breathing deeply, willing himself calmer.

"Why do you do this to me?" Baratov yelled. "I tell you all I know!"

Grigory stepped in. "Mr. Baratov, don't say anything. This is ridiculous, Detective, but nothing that I didn't expect. I do my homework. I know you. I know your history of violence, don't think I don't." They started out. "We'll be seeing you in court, Detective. Trust to it."

"You're damn right you will," Mangan said, catching Baratov's eye. "And by the way, I am personally going to be the one who tells Mr. Nazarkov how your client is going around telling everybody he's in the Russian mafia. Yuri *Nazarkov's* Russian mafia. I'm sure he'll be very pleased to hear that."

Baratov stopped two steps from the doorway.

"He's a friend of yours, isn't he?" Mangan asked. "Your buddy, Yuri? I'll give him a call as soon as you leave. Let him know where you live."

Baratov faltered. "Please do not do such a thing."

"Mr. Baratov," Grigory said, motioning to leave. "Don't say anything."

Mangan asked Baratov again. "Why were you meeting with the girls?"

"I, I talk to Deborah because—"

Grigory grabbed Baratov's arm and pulled him away. "Mr. Baratov, please."

"*Zatknis'!*" Baratov screamed at him, and shoved him off. "Go! You go now!"

Grigory backed slowly through the open doorway. "Very well, Mr. Baratov," he said, leaving. "I'll, I'll wait for you out in the hall."

Coose closed the door and Baratov sat back down.

"I will be honest here, Detective."

"I look forward to that."

"You will not talk to Mr. Nazarkov?"

Mangan pressed the question again. "Why were you at dinner with Deborah Ellison on the night that she was murdered?"

"I go because Fenyana, she tells me that Deborah wants to work on her own. She does not want to share so much the money with me. Yes? And she does not want Fenyana to work for me no more. She has a computer, the laptop, and the girls now, they do their own online escort service. All by themselves they want to do this, but I tell her this is not safe."

Coose sat on the edge of the table. "And that you'd be losing a shit-load of money, right?"

"Yes, I will not lie. Yes. I think, maybe she takes my customers. So I go with Fenyana to the restaurant, to talk. Fenyana does not want to leave me, she knows it is not safe. She has been by herself alone before, and beaten, one time very badly. So I tell Deborah, this is dangerous. You cannot be alone. You must stay with me."

"Did you threaten her?" Coose asked.

"No, I do not really threaten. I want to scare her, yes, but that is all. I tell to her what happens to these girls sometimes. She does not believe me."

"What did she say?" Mangan asked.

"Nothing. She is mad and says I go home now and she leaves. She is mad at Fenyana too, because Fenyana agrees with me."

"Where'd you go after she left the restaurant?"

"I follow her, she is not outside. So I send Fenyana to work, in the cab. And I tell her I will go to Deborah, I will find her and convince her."

"And did you?"

"No. I cannot find her. I go to her apartment, I bang the door. She is nowhere. And that is it. I do not see her again. Fenyana does not see her. She did not come home that night. And then, of course, so sad, later, we hear what has happened to her. It is so terrible. And that it should happen after I speak of such dangers."

Baratov appeared moved. Authentically. Mangan looked to Coose.

"Is it not strange?" Baratov continued. "And then Fenyana, she goes away too, and one of my girls, she tells me that Fenyana has run away because she thinks I am the cause for this, for what has happened to Deborah."

"What does she think?" Mangan asked.

"She thinks I am the person who has done this to Deborah! I am not. I would never." Baratov dropped his head. "Never. That is all I know. I do not lie."

"We think she's in California," Mangan said. "You know why she might have gone there?"

"San Francisco, maybe. Richmond. It is Russian—how you say?—Russian area. She worked there when she first come to America."

Mangan jotted the information down. He knew he had nothing to hold Baratov on, but what was worse, he believed him. "Okay," he told him. "You can go."

"Yes. I go."

Coose hopped off the table and showed him to the door and said, "I'll keep in touch."

"Yes. Yes. And, please," Baratov said, half in the hallway, "please, you will say nothing to Mr. Nazarkov?"

Coose tried to slam the door on him but didn't get a chance because Willie Palmer came barging through first. He shoved Baratov into the hall and closed the door.

"What?" Mangan asked. "You got something?"

"No, no—it's—Wesley Faber, from Wisconsin? The police chief?"

"Yeah?"

"His daughter was just shot. Just this morning, about an hour from here. They think it's the same guy."

"Jesus Christ."

When sorrows come, they come not single spies but in battalions.

"What the hell is going on here?"

Every morning at six thirty, five days a week, Jennifer jogged the breakwater that led to the Stony Point Marina in Waukegan, Illinois. On this morning, she had been pushing herself. She felt strong, her legs, her breathing. It had been almost a year and a half since having her first child, Kayla, and although she'd hit her goal weight she still didn't feel like she'd gotten her old body back yet, and she was becoming dimly aware that she might never get it back completely. Her mind drifted as she quickened her pace, wishing she could wear sports bras all the time, wondering whether or not she'd be able to stick to her diet once the holidays ambushed her.

The sun had risen just enough to begin taking the early chill out of the air as she jogged through the entrance of the marina. To her right, Lake Michigan, glittering, looked beautiful; to her left, a wide swath of grass was dotted with picnic tables and clusters of silver birch. Through the trees she could see the dock, crowded with sailboats and power boats of all shapes and sizes. Two charter boats were loading gear and customers on board. At one of the picnic tables in the grassy area sat a man sipping coffee from a Styrofoam cup. He watched her as she ran past in her very short shorts, her long legs and long arms bare, her damp skin sparkly in the morning sun.

At the end of the jogging path, which skirted the breakwater, was a cul-de-sac lined with various sand-boxed exercise stations: a pull-up bar, a place for step training, another for sit-ups. This was the halfway mark of the route Jennifer ran each morning. After some sit-ups and stretching, she would head back home.

A gently windy day. Jennifer sprinted the last few yards, aware that the man she'd passed at the picnic table was still staring at her. She ignored him. She wasn't concerned; the seven o'clock fishing boats hadn't sailed yet, and the concession stand was open, selling coffee and donuts. She did her sit-ups quickly, wanting to stop at one hundred, and almost did, but made herself do one hundred and ten. She stood and leaned over, fingers to toes, to the left, to the right, and then a slow roll up. She reached high above her head and looked out over the ruffled waters of Lake Michigan, a long stretch left, then right. She took in a deep breath, very deep, a yoga class breath, and let it out slowly—

When her head hit the pavement she felt violently nauseous and needed to vomit. A puddle of viscous liquid quickly pooled up around her mouth, thick and warm, and she gurgled in the tepid blood that caught in her throat and bubbled out her nose. Her limbs trembled uncontrollably, her bowels loosed themselves, and then all went still and quiet . . . and she wondered then, for some odd reason, whether her husband and her baby girl had eaten breakfast yet.

She died quickly.

The bullet, which entered her back a few inches below her left shoulder, had shattered her scapula and sixth rib, ripped through her lungs, and lacerated her pulmonary vein and aorta. A kill shot. A single .243-caliber bullet fired from a distance of perhaps seventy-five or a hundred yards had dropped her to the ground, as one witness would later describe, as if "her legs just went out from under."

Jennifer Faber Paulsen, daughter of police chief Wesley Faber of Winsome Bay, Wisconsin, was dead.

There would be more.

But first he would write.

He would write the story now, for all to see and read.

He spent a long time writing, and while he wrote, a thing like calmness closed in around him. Something about it, about the act of writing, eased the compulsion in him to keep doing more of what he had been doing. If he looked not left nor right, but kept on straight ahead, sailing into the illusionary white square of words before him, his mind settled into what seemed a smooth and glassy levelness.

But then his words ran out.

And he began to hear her.

She was coming.

Her thoughts . . . were coming . . .

They had found him again. They pressed at this mind, swelling the space around his brain and bulging his skull inward till her inexistence burst the weir of his mind. Her thoughts spilled everywhere, gushing out his eyes and fingers, leaking onto the keyboard and desk and puddling beneath his chair. These thoughts—the obscene conjectures of his mind—were the frantic rats that gnawed incessantly at his brain: on that unthinkable night, which she did not survive, in her last moments before she ceased to be, what had she been thinking?

A guttural cry escaped him at the thought. He clutched his head and slammed it down on the keyboard. A searing split ripped open deeper, yes, even deeper in his brain, and the rats burrowed in further, pushing, chewing—and so he cut himself, in the wound which had not yet healed. "Yes, yes . . ." He drew the blade up his forearm, ". . . yes," until the pain passed and the thick red warmth drowned her thoughts, it bubbled up and floated her out of the room and out of his brain.

She drifted off, a dead, rose-tinted phantom.

He could not bear it.

Could not bear it, could not bear it, could not bear it . . .

He knew who would be next.

Detective Sergeant Linda Brennan walked Mangan through the Stony Point Marina in Waukegan, where Wesley Faber's daughter had been murdered. A sunless day, and nightfall not far off, Lake Michigan looked leaden.

"A one-shot kill," Brennan said, pointing to a parking lot in the distance. "We think from over there."

The murder had happened in broad daylight. In a public area. There had been a note found at the scene, but other than that, there was nothing consistent in the killer's MO. Not even in the choice of victim, aside from being female. The other three murders were at least somehow connected. Why this woman? It made no sense.

Tell him Revenge is come to join with him,
And work confusion on his enemies.

Mangan and the sergeant ducked under a taped-off area near the pier and stood in the spot where Wesley Faber's daughter was last seen alive. "Witness says the victim was facing pretty much south, southeast. Angle of entry puts our shooter in the north corner of the parking lot somewhere. We found the note there also, stuck beneath the wiper blade of a car."

The shooter's note, with a large hoop earring taped to it, read "I am the Righter"—the same message etched into the blood-smeared screen of Jillian McClay's computer, which hadn't been made public knowledge yet. Four killings now. The earring belonged to Deborah Ellison, confirmed by her mother and corroborated by the surveillance tapes at O'Rourke's Pub and Grill. Deborah Ellison had been wearing it the night she was murdered.

"The parking lot was about a quarter full that morning," Brennan said, "ten, twelve cars. He might have been in a car or hiding behind one. No cameras in the parking lot. One witness thinks he remembers a light gray or silver pickup truck in the lot. Said it was parked oddly, away from the other cars. That's as specific as he got. We're checking everybody who was working here that day, and also the customers on the boats."

"Anybody hear the shot?"

"No. Plenty of people around too."

"Any other noise that day? Construction crews? Garbage pickup?"

"Not that we know of. Probably used a suppressor of some kind."

Mangan walked over to the picnic table where the witness had been sitting.

"Which side was he on?"

"That one."

"Here?"

"More center."

Mangan sat at the table. "What was he doing here?"

"He was going fishing, waiting for his charter boat to load."

He looked at the other two picnic tables. He looked at the position of the birch trees. "So this witness just happened to sit at the one table that had a clear view of the victim?"

"Not exactly. She was a pretty girl, sports bra, shorts. He sat here to get a better view. She was over there stretching when she got hit. He thought she fainted or something and ran over. Saw the blood, panicked, and ran to the concession stand for help."

"His story check out?"

"Yes. He was pretty shook up." She led Mangan over to the parking lot. "There were people around all morning." She pointed to her left. "An eight-person fishing charter right over there, loading at the time of the shooting. The concession stand was open. Nobody saw anything."

They strolled the lot, empty now but for Mangan's car and two police cruisers.

He looked back to the victim's last position. "Pretty clear shot from here."

"Yes."

"Shell casings?"

She shook her head. "Nothing. We swept it clean up to the—" A slur of static from Brennan's walkie-talkie interrupted their conversation. "Excuse me," she said, taking the call.

Mangan walked off by himself.

Something in the killer was changing, he thought, deepening. No passion this time. No rage. No mutilation. Not so much how he killed now, as long as he killed. Stabbing or strangulation is extremely intimate, personal. This killing showed indifference, detachment. The Beltway Sniper attacks crossed Mangan's mind, two killers working in tandem, a driver and a shooter. Could the killer be working with someone else? What the hell's the motive, though?

I have done a thousand dreadful things
As willingly as one would kill a fly,
And nothing grieves me heartily indeed
But that I cannot do ten thousand more.

He's starting to enjoy it, Mangan thought. He's believing he's untouchable, killing in public, changing his MO.

"Detective," Sergeant Brennan called across the parking lot. Mangan had wandered clear to the other side. They met in the middle. "That was ballistics I just talked to," she said. "It was .243-caliber. About a 140-yard shot."

A marksman, perhaps. This meant Mangan could start checking military records, hunting licenses, rifles, silencers. Ballistics would work up the rifling patterns from the bullet taken from the victim's body. Finally, a little more to go on. This was the sick way it worked, he thought: the more victims, the more chances the killer has of being caught. Each murder brings more data, more information, more evidence. More opportunities for the killer to make a mistake. He's mobile, Mangan considered, traveling to Enfield, Winsome, Chicago, Waukegan. What's he drive? Where's he from? What's he do for a living? Is he missing work? The killer had thought things through and chosen this spot. Had he known the victim's routine? Or had he just followed her that morning? An impulse kill? No, no, he must have known what he was going to do before he arrived that morning.

"Excuse me, Detective," Brennan said. "Anything else I can do for you?"

"No, no, just thinking."

"Well, you've got my number. Feel free. Anything comes up on my end, I'll give you a call."

"Thank you."

Brennan started toward her squad car. Mangan looked again to the position where the victim had been shot. A beautiful young woman. He thought of Wesley Faber, losing his daughter. He thought of his own daughter and could not envision the kind of a man he might be if anything ever happened to her.

Alack, alack, my child's dead,
My soul and not my child.

Where were those lines from? Mangan thought. It was hard to know. So many of Shakespeare's stories dealt with the loss of children, and sometimes the words intermingled in his mind, lines from one play merging with those of another, transposing themselves, paraphrasing. It didn't always make sense.

Dead art thou, alack my child is dead.

Shakespeare knew death well. He'd lost his own son, Hamnet, when the boy was only eleven.

The sweetest, dearest creature's dead.

The words were coming steadily now, easily. Mangan walked a tight circle, keeping his mind open, listening.

Her blood is settled, and her joints are stiff.
Life and these lips have long been separated.

He was close to something, he could feel it, hovering just out of reach. *'Tis here, but yet confused.* What was he missing? What was the connection between Faber's daughter and the other victims?

If ever you chance to have a child,
Look in her youth to have her so cut off.

He stopped.

The last line ran deeper to his heart, something about it . . . it kept repeating itself—*look in her youth to have her so cut off, look in her youth to have her*—and then suddenly Deborah Ellison's father loomed large in Mangan's mind. He remembered the other victims, Jillian McClay, Mara Davies, all of them, all the victims had—

"Shit!" Mangan said, fumbling for his notepad. "Sergeant! Sergeant!"

Linda Brennan hurried back as Mangan skimmed the histories of the other victims. Mara Davies: daughter of Edward Davies, *a parole officer.* He flipped to another page, to the gun found in Jillian McClay's office: registered to her father, *a cop in Philadelphia.*

"What is it?" Brennan asked. "What?"

"They're all cops."

"What?"

"The fathers of all four victims," Mangan said. "They're all cops."

That was the connection. It was right there the whole time—and then Mangan's heart dropped for a horrible moment.

His daughter, Katie.

"Jesus."

He fumbled for his cell phone, deep in his coat pocket. "Fuck!" He had the number on speed dial. He pressed the number. Answer, he prayed, please, God, please, God, let her answer. She did. "Katie it's Dad. Yeah, yeah—I'm sorry, no—hold on a second, just—*Kathleen, stop! Just listen!*"

The dad voice came out of him, the sound he'd made when Katie was six years old and almost walked in front of a car, the sound he'd made when she was eight and climbed the pine tree at her grandpa's house and was inches away from touching a power line, and he had yelled, "*Kathleen, stop!*"

That was the sound that had just come out of Mangan.

Katie silenced immediately on the other end. She knew the sound too. As fast as he could, Mangan explained the situation. He hadn't told her anything about the investigation yet—they usually didn't talk about each other's cases—but he got the gist of it across quickly and asked her to reach out for protection. She promised she would, and that she'd sleep somewhere else that night and keep her service revolver with her at all times. Mangan wanted more assurances, but just at that moment another thought struck him. He took off at a run for his car.

"What!" Sergeant Brennan asked, jogging close behind.

Mangan yanked open the car door and rifled through a number of *American Forum* magazines strewn across the back seat. He found the article he wanted: Jillian McClay's interview with officer Michele Schaefer. He scanned it quickly, hoping he was mistaken.

He wasn't.

"Schaefer's dad, *a cop for twenty years*, retired early to run an organic dairy farm."

Mangan flung aside the magazine, searching desperately through his cell phone for the number of the Winsome Bay police station.

Michele Schaefer sat behind the police chief's desk.

It was quiet in the station. Tom Ellison was dead and Wesley Faber had taken a leave of absence. He and his family were in Illinois for his daughter's funeral. The Winsome police force pretty much consisted of herself and Dan Ehrlich now.

Schaefer shuffled and stacked the paperwork she'd been trying to get through. She'd been sitting there for almost an hour and hadn't done much of anything. Her mind kept wandering: have to find a replacement for Tom Ellison, have to meet with the town council, have to go the DARE program at the high school, have to help Dad get the hay in, have to stop thinking, thinking all the time about these murders. She lost track of time. The room dimmed as evening slipped in the windows. She pulled the chain dangling from Faber's reading lamp. It illuminated the framed photo beneath it: Faber's wife and kids—his daughter.

Part of Schaefer wanted to scream right then. She wanted to tear through the police station and break things and pound the paneled walls. She saw herself doing it, heard her own screams, like a scripted action sequence in a movie: *"Suddenly Schaefer sweeps the desk clear— lamps, photos, papers flying everywhere. She's wild. Uncontrollable. She flips the desk over, letting out a wrenching howl of anguish. Jump-cut: Schaefer curled on the floor, fetal position, sobbing."*

But no. She did nothing like that.

Her rage had settled so deeply that she felt extremely, frighteningly, calm.

"Do something," she told herself. She took up the paperwork she'd been putting off. She read the first report: a chicken loose in town. She crumpled it and tossed it in the trash. She read the next—

There was a noise then.

Different from the noises she was used to hearing at the station. Footsteps down the hall, toward the office, running now. Schaefer stood and—

Dan Ehrlich burst into the room, a panicked look on his face.

"You're here!" he said from the doorway, breathing heavily, rambling. "You scared the hell out of me. I thought you were in your office, and I was trying find you, and I got worried 'cause I just got off the phone with the guy, the guy from Chicago who—what's his name—"

"Slow down!" Schaefer said.

"The detective. What's his name? The one that—"

"Mangan? You talking about Detective Mangan?"

"Yes! He . . . I . . ."

"Dan, stop! Dan, look at me!"

He stopped. Caught his breath.

"Now," Schaefer said, "what did he say?"

"All the victims so far . . . all of the victims' fathers were cops. The killer is targeting the daughters of cops. Mangan called here trying to find you 'cause he knew your dad was a cop, and he wanted to warn you. You gotta watch yourself and get some protection at—"

"Oh my god," Schaefer said.

"What?"

"My sister."

Jeannie Schaefer wiped her sleeve across her cheek and pulled her cap back on. Even though it was nearly dark and the wind was picking up, it was still stifling up in the barn. All she could think about was taking a shower. She and her brothers had been hauling and stacking hay all day.

Another bale came tumbling off the elevator. Jeannie sank her two red-handled hay hooks into it, squatted low, dragged it to the back of the mow, and then ran back for the next one. Her brothers were out in the field, hauling in a last load, and she and her father were trying to get this one in and stacked before the rains came. At sixty-seven her father could load fifty-pound bales faster than most men half his age.

"Dad!" she called down from the mow. He was loading the bales too close together, they were coming too fast. "Dad, slow it down!" He couldn't hear. The hay elevator was running rough this year and, ever the frugal farmer, he'd refused to get it fixed. Jeannie threw a water bottle down at him.

"What?" he yelled up.

"I can't—"

She had to stop as another bale fell off the conveyor belt and nearly knocked her over. She snagged it and pulled it sloppily to the side as another tumbled off. She gave up and let them pile crazily beneath the end of the conveyor. She sank the two hay hooks into a rogue bale and walked back to the opening beneath the roof peak.

"Dad, load 'em farther apart!" she said, hanging halfway out the mow. "I can't keep up!"

"Don't be a candy-ass," he yelled up, grinning. "The rain's coming, we gotta get 'em in! Don't worry about stacking 'em right, just—" The engine died then. "Christ all-Friday!" he cursed, trying to start it again.

Jeannie laughed as the engine sputtered and choked. "That's what you get for being so cheap!" she said. "Gonna give yourself a heart attack trying to save a buck."

Her father didn't hear her because at that moment the motor barked into a loud rumble and he started swinging bales onto the raised links of the conveyer belt again. They were coming at a decent pace now. Jeannie turned back, tugged her gloves tight, and reached for the red hay hooks she'd left stabbed into a bale. They weren't there. She stood there, puzzled for a moment, and had just enough time to register a sense of movement to her left. It was slow, and in her mind, for some reason, she thought then of a cow—a slow shadow, and she'd thought of a cow—and in that same fleeting instant she knew that she was on the second floor of the barn and it couldn't be a cow because—

That was all her synapses had a chance to flicker through because in the next instant there was a six-inch piece of sharp steel embedded in the back of her skull, flush to the curve in the hay hook handle. It felt to her, at first, as if someone had grabbed her by the back of her head. There was no pain for the merest of moments, and then there was, and then a hot pressure behind her eyeballs and blood clogging her throat and then suddenly she was yanked backward and spun around on her feet.

A man was facing her. He had one of her hay hooks in his hand.

She was going to say something to him, but didn't, or couldn't, because her brain went black as he raised high the second hook and wracked it deep into the side of her neck and ripped downward till the hook caught at her clavicle. He wrenched it out and let her fall. He crouched and held the hook before her eyes, slick and wet with her own blood. She didn't seem to be able to see it. Her eyes were empty now.

So he stabbed them out.

The man stared at the blank document on his computer screen a very long time.

She'll have her own chapter, he thought. Each of them will. And then he would mail them to the fathers. So they could have the details. Policemen like details. Testimonies. Statements. They had given him many details. They deserve the same.

He had watched the one in the barn for some time, waiting behind her on the ladder to the loft, her flannel shirt all covered in wispy bits of straw, like cat hairs only yellow, like she was a magnet, a straw magnet. He had read about her in one of the *American Forum* articles. The woman's sister, Michele Schaefer, had been interviewed for the magazine. In the article she talked about how big her family was, and how her father had been a police officer, and how she had five brothers.

And a sister.

Jeannie.

She was easy to find. They were all easy to find. Especially the first one, Deborah Ellison. She had been handed to him. In the beginning, he was only going to punish her and her father. They were the cause of all. He knew that killing Tom Ellison's daughter was the way, kill her horribly and let him ruin his mind with the thought of it, destroy his brain with the never ending, never ceasing, always waking, thought of it. That should have been enough, and it would have been, but then the others were shown to him and the dark thing in his depths rose into the back of his mind and spoke quietly, but fiercely, and it said,

Carry on.

Each time was easier. The last one easiest of all. Out in the country, no neighbors for miles, a clunky motor drowning out any sound of his approaching, the barn door wide open, nothing hindering him. The way lay open, as if all his actions were greased. He moved without sound, now, invisible.

For this was he ordained, for this was he set on this earth.

Mangan took off his glasses and rubbed his eyes.

He and Coose had driven to Winsome Bay as soon as they'd learned of Jeannie Schaefer's murder. The woman's sister, officer Michele Schaefer, had taken a leave of absence for the funeral and to be with her father. The police chief, Wesley Faber, was still in Waukegan with his family, and Dan Ehrlich, a young officer covering for them both, had no idea when they'd be back.

Mangan and Coose had been allowed to set themselves up in the chief's office. Strewn about Faber's desk were the arrest records of all the victims' fathers. Mangan, sitting in Faber's chair, was culling through the records of Tom Ellison, looking for something, anything, to stand out. Something that might drive a person to kill five women. Coose, on a small couch across the room, was sifting through Wesley Faber's records, and Dan Ehrlich, sitting next to him, was looking through the records of Michele Schaefer's father.

Mangan glanced at a wood-framed photograph on Faber's desk as he picked up another arrest record. He couldn't help looking at it every so often. It was the first thing he'd seen when he sat in Faber's chair. He wanted to move it, or put it face down, but he couldn't do either. It was a picture of Faber's wife and three boys, his daughter and his grandchild, a fall scene, pumpkins and puffy coats.

The man had lost his only daughter.

Grief fills the room up of my absent child.

Mangan chased the thought away.

"You guys want anything?" Dan asked from the couch, stretching. "Food or something?"

Mangan shook his head. Coose said, "Yeah. I'm hungry."

"I'll call the Dew Drop, we can get a pizza or something. Is that okay with you guys?"

"Sure," Coose said.

Ehrlich had been doing his best to help Mangan and Coose get access to whatever files they needed. Before the day had started, over coffee, he had told Mangan the details of Jeannie Schaefer's murder.

After getting the call from Mangan, Dan had hurried to find Michele Schaefer and tell her about the break in the case. That's when she remembered her sister was out at the farm. They jumped in the cruiser, speeding, lights and sirens. As they approached the farm Michele could see her brothers still on their tractors in a far corner of the field. She knew where Jeannie would be, up in the old barn, where she'd been for the last two days, baling. The cruiser spun out sideways as they skidded to a stop on the dirt driveway. Michele flung open her door, grabbed the shotgun, and was sprinting up the rutted dirt path before Dan had his seat belt off. The barn was perched on a steep rise behind the main farmhouse.

When he caught up to Schaefer, they could hear the sound of an engine running in the near distance. Reaching the barn, they edged their way around the side of the building. They reached the corner and peered around. The hay elevator was running clunkily, but no one was tending it. Michele called out for her father. There was no reply. She called out for her sister. Nothing. Dan drew his weapon and they continued around the building and entered the barn. That's where they found Mr. Schaefer sitting in the dirt at the bottom of a ladder that led to the hayloft, legs straight out in front of him, hands in his lap. He stared up at them as they entered, his eyes adrift and childlike. He said nothing. His overalls were darkened wet with blood. His hands were covered in blood too, as were the bottoms of his work boots. Michele and Dan didn't speak. They both knew where to look next. The rungs of the loft ladder were stained with blood. Michele went up the ladder first, and then Dan. And then they saw.

It was horrendous. Too, too horrible.

Dan had gone a little pale at that moment in his story. His lips blued, and Mangan thought the young man was going to be sick. Ehrlich searched his pockets for a moment and handed Mangan a letter.

"You can read the rest yourself."

It was the coroner's report.

The three men had spent most of the day in Faber's office, each in their own little worlds, studying their respective files. The last hour or so had been very quiet, and Dan had finally broken the silence and ordered some food.

"Pizza," he said, carrying it in. He put the box on the coffee table and flopped open the cardboard cover. "I got jalapeños on half of it. I hope you guys don't mind."

"I can pick 'em off," Coose said, already eating.

"I got some pop too, diet and regular. In the bag there."

Coose grabbed something to drink and continued reading arrest reports. "I've got a shitload of DWIs here."

"Yup," Dan said, "we get a lot of that around here."

"Concentrate on the women," Mangan said. "Under thirty."

Dan held a slice of pizza out to him.

"No, thanks."

Mangan continued searching through Tom Ellison's arrest records. Most of his perps had been males, and mostly picked up for minor crimes: public intoxication, DWIs, a few bicycle thefts, cars broken into, CDs stolen. There were a few drug arrests, also. Nothing too major, some marijuana, OxyContin at the high school, a meth lab that was—

The last record caught Mangan's eye. "What's this?" he asked, holding it up.

Dan got up from the couch and joined Mangan at the desk. "Oh, that," he said. "Yeah, that was pretty wild. I'd just started. Hazmat and Dane County SWAT came in. They busted up a meth lab out on one of the old farms, Vern Stenghal's old place. Some Chicago guys were cooking crystal meth out there. They were selling it too, before moving it back to the city. They were dealing right behind the high school." Mangan took the report back and studied it. Dan kept talking. "Meth, heroin. It's huge out here, you guys know that? It's all over the place. When I was a kid, all we did was—"

"Deborah Ellison's name is in here," Mangan said.

"What?" Coose asked.

"Her name is here. She was picked up that day. Suspicion of narcotic trafficking."

"Yeah," Dan said, "she was at Vern's farm when they raided it, she and another girl. Everyone knew she was using. She was pretty messed up for a while back then, but she had nothing on her when they picked her up. They brought her in for questioning."

"Who did? Who questioned her? Her father? He was leading the investigation."

"No, the chief did. He took over once they got back to the station."

"So they just let her go?"

"Yes. There was nothing to hold her on."

"There were three other arrests that day." Mangan read more of the report. "Two men and another woman, but Deborah was the only one released?"

"Yes. The others all had priors. They were cooking the meth here and then selling it out of some bar in Chicago."

Mangan searched the report for Deborah's statements. It appeared that she had given up information in return for her release. She gave up the name of the bar where she used to buy her drugs, the Wicked Cherry. She stated that that's where she'd met the two men who had been arrested with her. One of them had mentioned needing to find a place to cook meth outside of the city. She had told them about Winsome Bay and about Vern Stenghal's old farm that was up for sale.

Mangan shook his head. "So, Deborah Ellison helped to get a meth lab set up. Then she turns informer when she gets caught, and the police let her go?"

"Well, I, I guess it was something like that," Dan said.

"You guess?" Mangan said, things not quite falling into place for him. Some of it had a kind of logic to it. A retribution killing? Because Deborah Ellison had given up information? Maybe. But why the other killings? Why target the daughters of policemen?

"What about the other woman arrested that day?" Mangan pointed to a name in the arrest report. "Lynnette Anderson, nineteen years old. Tom Ellison arrested her."

"Uh-huh," Dan said, reading the details. "Uh, I think she was . . . let me see . . . yeah, here it is. She was from Rockford. Deborah Ellison knew her from Chicago, a friend of hers, she said. She was out here trying to buy. She had fifteen grams on her when she was arrested. It was a second offense so she got third-degree possession."

"Coose," Mangan said, "get on this. Find this girl."

"She'd be in Davis County," Dan said. "That's our max security prison for women. About five hours from here."

"You got a number for the warden there?" Mangan asked.

Dan took out his phone. "I will in a second."

"Good. Get us an interview with this girl," Mangan told him. "Coose, find out where her parents are."

Coose hustled out of the room and Ehrlich was already on the phone with the Davis County prison. Mangan combed through the details of the arrest report. It was a pretty large bust for such a small town, but he was well aware that a lot of meth cookers had moved their operations to the rural areas outside Chicago and Milwaukee.

Dan ended his phone call and looked at Mangan. "I got through to the prison."

"Good," Mangan said. "When can we talk to her?"

"We can't."

"Why not?"

"She's dead."

"Dead?" he repeated. "How?"

Dan hurried over to a computer and Googled a search of Lynnette Anderson. Mangan watched over his shoulder. An article in the Davis County *Lakeside News* appeared first.

Three deputy sheriffs were found not guilty in the death of Lynnette Anderson, 21, a prisoner forcibly restrained during a struggle in the medical unit of the Davis County Correctional Institution. Anderson, whose death was ruled a homicide, died of asphyxiation caused by the "combined effects of mechanical and physical restraint," an autopsy report said. The deputies, accused of using excessive force, have been absolved of all charges and ordered reinstated with back pay.

"Jesus." Mangan thought for a moment. "Did Tom Ellison know about this?"

"I, I don't think so."

"He was the arresting officer, how could he not?"

"I don't know."

"This never came up in the investigation of his own daughter's murder?"

"Tom checked his own records himself," Dan said. "We looked through them too, but we were only looking for men that he'd arrested."

"Nobody knew this girl had been killed in prison?"

"It was awhile ago. She'd been away almost two years."

"Find out when she died."

Dan scrolled to the top of the article. "July third, this year."

"That's about five weeks before the Ellison murder."

Coose hurried into the room. "Daniel Anderson," he said. "Forty-eight, a software analyst for the Middleton Credit Union. Married to Elizabeth Anderson, forty-two. Got a photo from his driver's license record, and car registration. Drives a silver pickup truck." He handed the suspect's picture to Mangan. "Last known address: 32 Woodland Court. Just outside of Rockford."

Mangan posed a possible scenario in his mind: a man's daughter is arrested and dies at the hands of police under suspicious circumstances.

Brought up on charges, the police are later acquitted. He's outraged. *I am a man more sinned against than sinning.* He goes on a killing spree. His first target: the policeman who arrested his daughter. *This one hand yet is left to cut your throats.* But he doesn't kill the man, he kills his daughter. He wants the father to feel what he feels. He wants to torture him, not kill him. *I would have thee live, for in my sense 'tis happiness to die.* Death would be too lenient. And then he can't stop. A psychotic break, perhaps? *My wits begin to turn.* Insatiable rage? Compelled to kill. He has a mission now—

> *There's not a hollow cave or lurking-place,*
> *Where bloody murder or detested rape*
> *Can couch for fear, but I will find them out.*

It all made a horrible kind of sense, to Mangan. These murders weren't the sex trade, or a love triangle, or drug-related retribution.

They were revenge.

He had not moved.

The room was very small, but he could not bring himself to move.

She was there again. Watching him. She was always watching.

He saw her broken reflection in the window, and in the mirror as he passed, and in the shimmery black surface of the coffee he sipped. Her eyes glimmered in the sheen of the dark enameled stove. She was everywhere and nowhere. Outside the window, within the trees, her thousand faces and eyes watched him from behind every thin wisp of shifting branch. She hid shallowly within the thick forests, that swayed as one, deep bending with the wind, on trunks that should have broken, as he had, but did not. Her voice was there too, in the wind, in his breaths, in his heartbeat, everywhere, like the ever-present and never quiet quick crick of a clock.

She was in the air today.

He could feel his mind going again to the place where he could not be, could not live for long. There was no breathing there. He wrenched his thoughts away and sent them elsewhere, to another place, yes, yes, to someplace else. He saw himself as a boy again. He was a boy, out in the woods, on the island, learning to shoot the deer and the turkey and the pheasant on the wing. He was a boy at the cabin that his father had built overlooking the lake, Crane Lake, where there are no more cranes.

He had seen them, though, in his youth, he had seen the cranes. Lynnette had too, when she was very little. She'd seen them before they flew away forever.

As she had.

His daughter's face wormed its way back into his thoughts, but this time it wasn't the frightening face that filled his reflections, it wasn't the battered face that had been locked inside the casket, no. He was seeing her other face now.

Her child-face.

And he let it in.

. . . she was playing in the water, her saggy diaper dripping heavy between chubby knees. Splashing. He sensed a warmth of some sort widening within him, a certain softening of a part of himself that was still human. He saw his daughter's birth and remembered the first moment that he had seen her miniature hands and enormous eyes. Like a magic trick, this small thing suddenly appearing. How many quadrillions of tiny, minuscule things, he'd wondered then, had to have gone perfectly right for her to have turned out so . . . perfect. And he had thought then, also, of how easy it was for one thing, one infinitesimally almost-not-noticeable thing, to turn all that perfectness to ruin. One misstep, one "in the wrong place at the wrong time" moment and it was all gone—*poof.*

Like magic.

Like Lynnette.

Like Deborah Ellison.

He remembered then the beginning of it all. When he had first found Deborah. The drive that he and his wife had taken up to the Davis County prison to escort their daughter's body home. A long drive. No sound in the car. No words spoken. Profound silence. "Stop thinking about it," his wife finally whispered. "There's nothing to do about it now." But that's all he could think about. Nothing else existed. There *must* be something to do. There must. The thought gripped his mind and turned manic, a fanatical urging ever pecking at the cracking shell of his brain. Driving toward his dead daughter, the urging grew to a riot in his mind—and that's when it started, when his brain began to fester. For hours he had been watching an unchanging highway disappear beneath the front of his car, but now the road began to warp before him, the asphalt softened and buckled, then liquefied and spilled sideways, blurring the road and his mind and his world into a measureless, roiling, ash-gray vagueness. For every mile driven closer to his daughter's body, something within his being rotted deeper and deeper.

This was the blighting of his mind.

By the time they arrived at the prison something in him had died, and some other thing had been born. He had changed. He could actually feel it, physically. He felt stronger, taller. He wondered if he looked different. His hands were thicker and felt heavier. Objects looked clearer, sharper. The barrage of thoughts had stopped, and something felt calmer now, because somehow he knew that he was about to do something. He did not know what it was yet, but still, there was comfort in the promise of it.

And then it was handed to him.

Literally.

After signing papers at the prison, an indifferent deputy slid a small box across his desk. It contained their daughter's personal effects. He took it and left the room. He and his wife sat on a steel bench in the hallway. He opened the box with his new hands. It felt clumsy in his grip. There were only a few things in the box: some money, two paperbacks, stamps, old letters, a magazine. He handed the letters to his wife and she shuffled through them, quietly, her face a featureless blank. Beneath the letters, he noticed envelopes addressed to other people that had never been mailed.

One of the envelopes was addressed to Deborah Ellison.

He opened it and saw his daughter's handwriting. It reminded him again that she was actually dead, and the festering in his mind swelled. His daughter had written about how terrible prison was, how withdrawal sucks, how she hoped to get her teeth fixed in the prison dental program, and that she was lonely and scared.

He could do nothing about that now.

But the thought came to him of what he would do.

He had Deborah Ellison's address.

In Chicago.

And that's when the circuit closed and his purpose became clear. His daughter had even put it down on paper for him and had it placed in his hands. Yes, he would do something now. For his daughter. And he felt now a kind of peace settle over him, a murdering peace.

She had been his all-the-world.

And now she was gone.

And now he was gone.

There was nothing left of whoever he had once been.

Coose kept up a steady eighty-five miles an hour down I-90 while Mangan called the Rockford SWAT team with the suspect's address. When they arrived at the entrance to Woodland Court, he saw that a perimeter had already been set up. They got out of the cruiser and buckled on their vests. An officer introduced himself and pointed out the incident commander who was at the back of an ambulance surrounded by a small group of EMTs. Coose and Mangan walked over and waited for the man to finish briefing the medical team.

"We've got a paramedic with us," the commander was telling the crew, "but if this goes bad, we're going to need your help. Rule number one: get the good guys out first. Rule number two? See rule number one. That's the only protocol you need to remember. Okay?"

The EMTs, all of whom looked young and nervous, nodded.

"All right," the commander said. He dismissed them and turned to Mangan and Coose. "Detective Mangan?" he asked.

"Yes."

"Captain John Pribyl." He snugged his vest tighter. "Little hot today, huh?"

"Yes."

"Follow me."

Pribyl led Mangan and Coose down a wide residential street lined with nearly identical looking SUVs, their glossy black fenders gleaming in the low afternoon sun. A long row of Tudor cottages and Chicago-style bungalows ran along either side of the road, nestled in among the proper allotment of maples and oaks. Manicured lawns ran uninterrupted between the lots, occasionally broken up by short runs of hedges or azalea bushes. Sprinklers spun out whispery water-circles across yards. From the columned porches, American flags hung in abundance. A blue-and-orange football lay on a driveway, a bike on a lawn. It was all clean and quiet and passive and American and not at all where you would expect to find a serial killer. Unfortunately, serial killers were never where Mangan expected them to be.

And thus I clothe my naked villainy
And seem a saint, when most I play the devil.

"We cleared this block and the one behind," Pribyl said. "Perimeter's secure, exits are covered."

They continued walking. As the road bent slightly to the left, Pribyl stopped and pointed out Daniel Anderson's house. An ordinary, slightly above-middle-class home, well kept, two stories, a large front porch, a dormer perched high on the front peak of the roof. No car in the driveway, which skirted the side of the house.

"Front, back, and side doors are covered," Pribyl said.

The three of them drew their weapons and took cover behind an SUV across the street. There was some glare off the upper windows of the house. It was late in the day, but the sun, at Mangan's back, was still bright. He thumbed off the safety of his Glock and leaned across the hood of the SUV. Pribyl whispered into his walkie-talkie. The SWAT units hidden across the road and around the yards were barely visible, their sniper rifles trained on the house.

Inside his room, Daniel Anderson made sure his police scanner was set to all channels, and then returned to his computer. He double-clicked the Internet icon and typed in the words "Detective James Mangan Chicago." He had just read about the man in the newspaper. He tapped the enter key. A lot of entries came up on the screen. Lots of awards. The Carter/Harrison Lambert Award for Distinguished Act of Bravery, the Cook County Medal of Honor, Cook County Distinguished Service Award, and the Unit Meritorious Performance Award.

Anderson clicked for images on the Google search and saw photos of the man at an awards ceremony, standing between other officers. He was stocky. Not very tall. He saw another photo where the man had his arm around a pretty woman in uniform. She was much younger than he was. He read the date above the photograph. It had been taken a few years earlier. He clicked the photo to enlarge it. In the teeny font of the credits below the picture he read the woman's name: Kathleen Mangan.

He considered this, and thought . . . how uncoincidental.

That this man should have a daughter.

This police man.

He wrote the name down, softly mouthing the word, "Kathleen . . . Kathleen . . ." He searched her name on the Internet. A few different Kathleen Mangans came up. One was a lawyer—no, no. He added *police officer* to her name and searched. There were a lot of Mangans, mostly men. He scrolled to the second page—*yes*—there she was.

Kathleen Mangan, 635 Stanwell Avenue, Milwaukee, WI.

He went to Google Maps and typed in his destination. The police scanner on the shelf above crackled static, then voices. It always made so much noise. He turned the volume down and glanced out the window. He saw nothing. He returned to his computer and studied the blue highlighted route to Milwaukee.

Road trip.

Daniel Anderson!" a megaphoned voice called out. "Daniel Anderson! This is the police! Come to the front door with your hands where we can see them!"

Mangan watched the house carefully from across the street.

"Daniel Anderson!" Pribyl said again. "This is the police! Come to the front door with your hands where we can see them!"

Nothing.

He lowered the megaphone and looked to Mangan. "Guess we're making a house call."

Mangan agreed, asking, "Who's doing the knocking?"

"Be my guest," Pribyl said. "On my go, okay?"

Mangan nodded.

Pribyl radioed the rest of his team and Mangan saw them adjust their stances and steady their aims. Pribyl looked to Mangan and Coose, "You good?"

They both nodded.

"We'll take the front door," Pribyl said. "One point of entry. SWAT covers the side and back from outside." Pribyl took one last glance around, and then said, "All right then. Let's go."

They sprinted across the yard and up the front steps, Coose and Mangan ducking to either side of their door. Pribyl and his men did the same, and when they were set, Coose reached up and smacked the screen door hard.

"Police! Open up!" he yelled, banging. "Police!"

He opened the screen door and tried the doorknob. Locked.

Pribyl signaled to a SWAT member across the road who started for the house at a full run—battering ram in hand—and slammed it into the door, splintering it open. "*Clear!*" Mangan yelled, following the man in and moving left. Coose, was next, moving to his right, "*Clear!*" Pribyl and his men poured in next, searching and clearing all the rooms—"*Police! Police! Down!*"—first floor, second, attic—"*Down! Down!*"—in the basement, the crawl space, the closets. "*Police! Police! Down!*"

The screaming and ransacking went on for a long time before the adrenaline settled. Pribyl, his face flushed and wet, yelled for everyone to gather in the living room. A tense silence followed. He holstered his weapon and shrugged.

"Nobody home."

Captain Pribyl went outside to brief the rest of the team and see if he could track down Daniel Anderson's wife. Mangan tugged on latex gloves and joined the CSI team flooding into the house. Coose and a few CSI techs headed up a steep set of stairs to the second floor. Mangan looked around the main area of the house. It was filthy. The living room had newspapers strewn about and dishes with half-eaten meals still on them. The TV was on, the sound muted. Half-filled drinking glasses with cigarette butts floating in them were scattered about the kitchen; the sink was filled with dirty dishes. The place looked abandoned, but there was a coffee pot on, still hot, and fresh milk in the fridge. "Hey, James," Coose called down from the second floor. "Come on up here."

Mangan hurried up the stairs, a bit winded when he reached the top.

Coose leaned out a doorway in the hallway. "In here."

"What do you got?" Mangan asked, joining him.

"I think I'd call it evidence."

The room was a small attic space which had been turned into a den, neatly kept compared with the rest of the house. A few books on the shelves, a file cabinet, a small couch, a coffee table with some magazines fanned out on it: *CHIP, PCWorld, Wired.* A desk was pushed up against the wall facing the street, beneath the dormer window. There was a computer on the desk, and Coose was hovering behind a CSI tech who was working on it.

"Where's this evidence you're talking about?" Mangan asked.

Coose, busy watching the CSI tech, nodded to a stack of magazines on the desk. "The *American Forum*," he said. "Every article by Jillian McClay."

Neatly piled beside the computer, the magazines had been folded open to the articles. Mangan looked through them. Sentences and names had been highlighted and underlined, Post-it notes attached to some the pages, all of them well worn and dog-eared.

"There's more," Coose said, stepping back. "Take a look."

The CSI tech was running through the search history on the computer. The dropdown file looked like a prosecutor's dream: Michele Schaefer's contact info, the address of the Schaefer family farm, map searches of Winsome, Wesley Faber's address and his daughter's wedding announcement, her address in Waukegan, searches of the *American Forum* website, Mara Davies's bio, Jillian McClay's author website, and a dozen other entries all related to the murder victims.

"I think it'll hold up," Coose said.

Mangan nodded. "We have to find him first."

A glimmer of light caught Mangan's eye, just a flicker, and it drew his gaze to the window. It must have been open slightly because its gauzy white curtain fluttered gently. Something was dangling behind it. Mangan stepped closer and pushed a corner of the curtain aside. A thin monofilament fishing line was tied to the window lock. On the end of it hung a circular piece of metal. It twirled lazily, flashing the tiniest glints of sun. It was a single, large hoop earring. Identical to the one found at the Waukegan murder site.

"Detective Mangan?" Pribyl called from the first floor.

"Yes," Mangan said, stepping out of the room.

Pribyl took two steps up the stairs and leaned on the banister, looking up. "It's the wife. I've got her in the kitchen."

Elizabeth Anderson was sitting at the kitchen table. A frail woman with a panicked look in her eyes, she sat sideways in the chair as if trying to hide within it. She was unkempt in body and clothes. Her gray roots had spread widely down the center of her once-dyed hair. No makeup. She was struggling to open a pack of cigarettes, her hands shaking. She had the appearance of a thing that had been broken.

"This is Mrs. Anderson," Captain Pribyl said. "She was at the store. We found her watching from the perimeter line. A neighbor pointed her out."

Mangan sat opposite her at the table. She flinched slightly and scooted a little farther back into the chair, reminding Mangan of his parakeet, Phoebe. The woman was still trying to get a cigarette out of her pack. Mangan reached out.

"Can I help you with that?" he asked.

"Why are you in my house?" Her voice was thin and weak, but pointed. "Why are you here?"

Pribyl said, "I tried to explain to her—"

"Haven't you done enough?" she said. "Haven't you?"

Mangan spoke easily, "Mrs. Anderson—"

"Get them out of my house," she said. "All of them. I want them out of my house."

"Please, Mrs. Anderson, if you'd just—"

"*Get them out of my house!*" she screamed. She stood, kicking the chair away, and crushed herself into the corner of the kitchen. "*Get out of my house! Get out! Get out!*"

"All right," Mangan said, getting up and backing away.

"*Get out! Get out!*"

"All right."

Quietly, calmly, she kept whispering, "Get out, get out, get out, get out, get out."

Mangan called Pribyl over as he stepped out of the kitchen. "Give me a little time with her, okay? Let's get everyone out for now, we'll bring them back in a bit."

Pribyl called for his team and the CSI unit to clear the house. Coose left too. The whole time there was a soft murmuring from the kitchen, "Get out, get out, get out, get out, get out."

Mangan knew the woman was in some other place. A place of madness. Not clinically mad, worse: Melvillian mad. *That wild madness that's only calm to comprehend itself.* If she were mad, she might perhaps forget what had happened to her family, her daughter, her life. But no,

Mangan could tell that she was vividly, outrageously, aware of her own life. The story of it was carved into her face.

He waited till the home was completely cleared. He waited a little longer and let some silence settle into the house. Then he ventured toward the kitchen again. Mrs. Anderson had managed to get her pack of cigarettes open. She still hovered in a corner of the room. She looked thinner standing up, as if her body had been drained of something and the skin now hung loose and resigned. His wife came into his mind. Those terrible last days. *My wife, my wife. What wife? I have no wife.*

The strike of a match focused Mangan again.

Elizabeth Anderson lit her cigarette, staring at Mangan, her eyes dilated with anger. Life had dealt her a shit hand, Mangan thought, and she had no idea how to play it. He peeled off his latex gloves and sat.

"Can I have one of those?" he asked, gesturing to her cigarettes.

She hesitated for a moment, guarded. Then threw the pack on the table. He took one out and looked at her. She tossed over the matches.

"Thanks," he said, and lit up. He hadn't had a cigarette in almost three years. My god, it felt good. It tasted like defiance. "Mrs. Anderson," he said, "I am so sorry. So sorry for what happened to your daughter. I have a daughter. I . . . I can't imagine."

Her lips tightened and she stood up a little straighter. "She was a good girl, you know. A good girl. For a long time."

Mangan nodded.

"It was the drugs," she said. "It wasn't her. It was the drugs." She seemed lost in thought for a moment. She ashed her cigarette on the tiled floor. "Why are you here?" she asked. "What is all this?"

"Mrs. Anderson," he said, "we're here about your husband."

"He's not here." She took a long, deep drag of her cigarette. "He's hardly ever here."

"Do you know where he might be?"

"Why?" she asked.

"We have reason to believe," Mangan said, "that your husband may have been involved in some very serious crimes."

Mrs. Anderson's face crooked slightly and she seemed to truly see Mangan for the first time. "Daniel? What are you talking about?"

"We just need to talk to him," Mangan said.

"What crimes? What do you mean?"

"Do you know where he might be?"

"What crimes?"

"There . . . there have been some crimes against women, young women."

"What kind of crimes?"

Mangan didn't want to say it. "Have you read about the recent murders in Chicago and Wisconsin?"

A second of silence, and then, "Daniel?" she said. "No. No, you're wrong." Her eyes were deeply confused and pained. "He would, he would never do anything like that. He couldn't. That's, that's crazy. He can't do anything. He can't work, he can't eat, he can't be around me—he can't even look at me. That's, that's why he's gone all the time, why he leaves."

"He's gone all the time?"

"Yes. He can't be here long, in the house. He has to leave after a while. He'll come home, mow the lawn, do some work on the computer, but then he starts wandering around the house and he has to leave again. He's away for days sometimes."

"Where does he go?"

"He just, he fishes, or hunts. It helps keep his mind off things."

"But where? Do you know where he fishes?"

"At the cabin."

"What cabin?"

"We have a cabin over in Lena. On the lake."

They pulled up quietly, no lights or sirens, some fifty yards from Daniel Anderson's cabin. A silver pickup truck was parked on the side, partially obscured in the trees. Captain Pribyl positioned his SWAT team and again sealed off a perimeter. Mangan and Coose surveyed the layout. A lake was behind the cabin, and a thin expanse of trees to either side.

Coose conferred with Mangan and Pribyl and asked, "How about no introductions this time?"

"Fine with me," Pribyl said.

Mangan agreed.

Coose nodded and took off at a run, not stopping until he'd cracked in the front door. Mangan entered behind him, sweeping the barrel of his Glock across the main room. Pribyl followed close, clearing the bedroom and kitchen. Mangan moved quickly along the living room wall and kicked open a bathroom door—left, right—nothing. He backed out, scanning the main room. There was a sliding door, half open, that led to a porch off the back of the cabin. He signaled to Coose to cover right and sidestepped through the open glass doors.

It was empty. The cabin was empty.

"Shit," Mangan said. "Get CSI in here."

One step behind, he thought, we're one step behind the guy.

He holstered his gun and looked around. The screened-in porch ran along the back side of the cabin, facing the lake. He walked the length of it, taking a moment to look out at the water. A few hundred yards from the shoreline was a small island that seemed overrun with trees, a floating forest nearly. The sun, beginning to dip low behind the island, skipped wooded shadows across the surface of the water, flat and calm and wide. Far out on the lake, he could make out the silhouette of a small boat puttering toward the tree-lined island, the sound of its outboard a soft, muted murmur. He watched it slip silently behind the island.

He did a quick search of the porch. Nothing. A window there looked into the cabin, into a bedroom. He glanced in. A CSI tech was at a table working on a laptop. Mangan started to go inside, but stopped to look out at the lake once more. He wasn't around this kind of nature all that often, away from the cement and stench and blood of the city. Lake Michigan wasn't anything like this lake; no, Lake Michigan was a city lake, cold and rough, like everything else in Chicago. He lingered a moment longer, enjoying the—

He heard something.

He gripped the handle of his Glock and felt the familiar rush of adrenaline through his body.

If of life you keep a care,
Shake off slumber, and beware.

Something was outside, making a sort of purring noise, a soft, elongated buzz. He eased off the safety of his gun. And then he saw it.

A bird.

Jesus. He put the gun away. It was a hummingbird, hovering head high, just on the other side of the screen. What is it with birds lately? he thought. It was just sort of floating there, eye level, its head and tail a glint of emerald, its wings a lavender blur—and then it was gone. So fast that it seemed not to fly but to melt into the air.

Mangan pressed close to the screen to see where it might have gone.

He was watching them.

From the island.

Watching all of them from his aerie high above, in his father's tree stand, nestled tightly among the limbs of the great white pine. He was very still, as still as the branch on which he nestled his .243-caliber Remington. He chambered a round—softly—nestled his cheek into the rifle stock, and centered the crosshairs of his scope on the policeman on his porch. The man had been walking back and forth, but now he was standing still and looking out the screen, looking straight at him.

Three hundred yards. No wind.

They must think I'm stupid, he thought, bracing his back against the padded crossbar of the tree stand. They must think I'm too stupid to buy a police scanner and listen to everything they're saying, or at least to hear enough of what they're up to before they switch to secure frequencies or use their cell phones. The SWAT team was smart, but the local police put out calls for their ambulances and firemen to be on standby and gave away everyone's positions.

They had come, just as he knew they would one day. That's why he had prepared. That's why he was ready. He adjusted his rifle scope minutely. His breathing was good, calm. The sun was at his back. The target, standing behind a dark screen on his porch. He'd made harder shots than this, much harder. Given the distance, he didn't really want to take a head shot, but the target was probably wearing a vest, so there wasn't much choice. He calibrated his boresighted 40-millimeter scope slightly, rifle zeroed in 2 inches high at 100, elevation good, dead on—and then the man walked back inside the cabin.

He lowered his rifle.

And waited.

He could outwait them all.

He pulled the safety back and folded his arms around the rifle. The lake shimmered a mottled gold. In the distance, he could hear the smallest slapping of waves against the shoreline, not really waves, more like gentle pushes of water, easing themselves up the sand and then falling back again, being pulled into the darker thing behind them. They tried to leave the lake, tried to break free, but the pull was too strong.

They would never be free.

Like Lynnette.

She could never break free.

She always got pulled back into the darker thing behind her.

A good home. A safe home. A normal home, he'd thought. Work, church, school. Sports. Proms. College visits. Homecoming. And then . . . He could not help her. She would not listen. She could only hear the other thing, the thing behind her that she could not resist. And then she began to change, a metamorphosing before his eyes, unstoppable, until, like some malformed butterfly, she emerged from her bedroom one day a still-breathing abortion of herself, a skeletonized shadow gorging on her own flesh. Her body, their beautiful daughter's body, ravaged and decayed by poison—oh god, oh god, oh . . .

His mind was doing it again.

He tried to stop his thoughts but he couldn't.

A lightning crack flashed through his skull, blistering his brain. He doubled over, gripping his rifle so hard his fingers hurt. His thoughts were dragged to the ruined part of his mind again, where the other world was, and he saw his still smoldering flesh there, the actual physical part of his brain that had been ripped open during the earthquake of his mind. He walked to the edge of it and peered down into the dark canyon and watched it fracture open even wider, and he saw—more vividly than ever before—he saw the gaping, milk-white chasm of his mind.

A movement in the cabin window freed him from his thoughts.

He raised his rifle.

What were you doing out there?" Coose asked when Mangan found him in the cabin.

"Bird watching."

"Yeah, well, come here. I got something to show you." Coose led him into the kitchen where CSI was snapping photos of the open freezer section of a refrigerator. Coose asked the techie, "You almost finished?" The man took two more photos and stepped away. Coose reached in and removed a plastic bag containing a small human hand.

"Christ," Mangan said. There were still rings on its fingers. "The Ellison girl?"

"Pretty good bet."

The cabin was a hush of activity, everyone engaged in their own jobs: bagging, dusting, boxing, photographing, cataloging, videotaping. Captain Pribyl came over, taking off his vest, his blues soaked through with sweat.

"Need anything else?" he asked Mangan. "I'm gonna get my guys back to Rockford."

"No. You've been great today. Thank your team for me."

Captain Pribyl turned to a young uniformed officer behind him. "This is Dean Gaffney, from Lena."

Gaffney, looking as if he'd just stepped out of the academy, came forward. "Sir."

"He cleared the other cabins around the lake for us," Pribyl told Mangan. "He knows the area well, grew up here. He'll do a search of the grounds, take a look around the lake."

"Good," Mangan said to Gaffney. "Take some guys with you."

"Yes, sir," the young officer said.

"What about the other cabins?" Mangan asked Pribyl.

"We evacuated everybody we could find."

"You talk to any of them?"

"No. They're still outside the perimeter. We'll open the roads soon and get them back in here. You can question them then."

"I talked to two guys," Gaffney said. "When we did the evac." He took out his notes. "A father and son from Chicago. Their cabin's a rental directly across from this one, on the other side of the lake. Said they haven't seen anything over this way, except the lights on at night sometimes. Said there hasn't been much traffic on or off the lake either. Deer season hasn't started, too early for walleye."

"What about the owner of the rental?" Mangan asked.

"I'll find out who it is," Gaffney said.

Mangan stripped off his vest and joined Coose in the bedroom, the room he had looked into from the porch. Against the wall was a small desk with a laptop on it. On the sill of a window just above the desk was a line of coffee cups and empty glasses. Scattered about the desk were stacks of paper, pencils, pens, a notepad, and a small razor knife with what appeared to be blood on it. A garbage pail on the floor was filled with bloodstained paper towels and ink cartridges. A CSI tech, kneeling beside it, was bagging samples. Another techie was at the desk working on the computer.

"Shit," Coose said.

"What?" Mangan asked.

Coose pointed to some writing on a small notepad beside the computer.

Kathleen Mangan, 635 Stanwell Avenue, Milwaukee, WI.

"Christ." A wintriness shot through Mangan's veins as he groped for his cell phone.

"I got something," said the CSI tech working on the computer. "A file. Looks like this guy wrote everything down. There's a title page . . . chapters."

Mangan leaned in and read as he pressed the speed dial for his daughter.

The Righter, by Daniel Alan Anderson.

The CSI tech scrolled through the document, pausing every few pages at the chapter headings, one for each victim. Mangan read them, waiting for his daughter to pick up.

DEBBIE ELLISON
MARA DAVIES
JILLIAN MCCLAY
JENNIFER FABER PAULSEN
JEANNIE SCHAEFER
POLICEMAN IN MY CABIN

—the crack of a gunshot smashed through the window pane at that moment and a piece of skull the size of a softball disappeared from the back of the CSI tech's head, misting the room and Mangan in blood and brain matter. Coose and Mangan dropped to the floor as the CSI tech rose from his chair for a bewildered moment. A second bullet slammed into his chest and thudded him dead to the floor. Pribyl came rushing into the room, gun drawn, and Mangan hit him hard, tackling him to the ground as a third shot splintered the pine doorway just above Pribyl's head. Out of the corner of his eye, as he was taking Pribyl to the floor, Mangan glimpsed a muzzle flash outside the window.

"The island!" he yelled. "He's on the goddamn island!"

Mangan crawled over to the CSI tech's body. He knew the man was dead, half his head was gone. He checked for a pulse anyway, then made his way out of the room at a crouch. They regrouped in the hallway. "Get SWAT back here," he told Pribyl. "We need a boat. Who's got a boat?"

"We do," Gaffney said, running up to them, his walkie-talkie out. "Fire department's got a water rescue team. There's a boat back at the station."

"Get it here fast as you can."

Mangan remembered seeing, when he was on the porch, a small boat disappear behind the far side of the island. It had to have been the shooter. The other cabins had been evacuated. Shit, he thought, *Where is my judgment fled, that censures falsely when I see aright?* Too busy looking at a friggin' bird.

"Get eyes on the lake," Mangan told Pribyl and the others. "Keep out of range. Take whatever guys you've got to the north side. Watch that island and—wait," he said. "Hey, Gaffney."

Gaffney yelled from down the hallway, "Yes, sir?"

"The guys in that other cabin, did they have a boat?"

"Uh, yes, yes, they did."

Mangan threw on his vest and found Coose. "Come on," he said. They jumped into their car.

It was getting darker outside, still enough light to see by, but fading fast. "Keep the lights off," Mangan told Coose, who floored it and headed toward the south end of the lake. A twisty dirt road skirted the perimeter of the lake and Coose took it at about sixty. Mangan held on to the dashboard and kept an eye on the lake as they sped toward the other cabin, the darkening island flitting in and out of view behind clumps of trees along the roadside. Neither man in the car said a word. They usually didn't at times like this. They knew what they had to do. They knew everything that could go wrong. They knew that they should wait for SWAT to arrive, but the shooter might be long gone by then. It wasn't that big of an island, though; a boat leaving would easily be seen.

Too easily, Mangan thought.

Coose took a hard curve, just missing a stump, as Mangan unlocked the 870 short barrel from its mount between the seats. The car fishtailed to the right and slid to a stop on the side of the Chicago man's cabin. Mangan hopped out, meeting Coose at the back of the car.

"He's waiting for us," Mangan said, handing Coose the shotgun. "You know that, right?"

Coose popped the trunk. "Yeah, I kinda figured that." They both grabbed flashlights. "Then again, maybe he's just stupid."

"He's not been stupid yet, why now?"

"I don't know," Coose said, pushing the cross-bolt safety on the shotgun. "Suicide-by-me?" Coose stopped what he was doing. "You want we should wait for the troops?"

Mangan thought for a moment. "He'd expect that, wouldn't he?"

"What?"

"If he wanted to draw us out there, he'd expect us to come with everyone."

They both looked out at the island.

"It's almost dark," Coose said. "We could use some more light."

"So could he."

Mangan wanted the guy. Badly. He knew he should wait for backup, but he also knew that every second he waited was another opportunity for the guy to get away. Plus, if the shooter was waiting for them, the fewer targets the better. Mangan glanced down at the dock by the water. There was a boat tied up to it. He looked back to Coose.

"Let's do this."

Coose took off at a run, Mangan following close behind. Coose jumped in the boat and untied the lines as Mangan lowered himself in. It was an outboard, two-seater, with a dashboard and small storage area below the bow.

"You know how to drive this thing?" he asked Coose.

"Anybody can drive a boat. Help me find the keys."

"They're right there."

"Where?"

"In the ignition."

Coose pushed the boat away from the dock. He turned the key and a muffled spit of smoke and water kicked up behind the engine. He grabbed the wheel and slammed the outboard into gear. The boat lurched forward, the bow rising out of the water for a moment before leveling off. They sped toward the island. Mangan, holding onto the side railing, made his way to the seat beside Coose and ducked below the windshield to keep from getting soaked. He radioed in to Pribyl.

"How far away are your guys?" he asked him.

"Ten minutes."

"You see anything on the island? Any movement at all?"

"Nothing," Pribyl said. "The water's like glass, no boats, no lights, nothing. I've got men all along the north side here. He comes this way, we'll see him."

"What about Gaffney's guys, with the boat?"

"He's not in my sights right now. I'll find him."

"Radio me when they get here. And don't send anyone out here without telling us. I don't want us stuck in a shooting gallery with each other."

Mangan held on to the side of the boat, watching the island loom larger as they neared it. The sun was going down quickly now. The island appeared before them as a low, broad, silhouette cut out of a deepening lavender sky. Coose slowed the boat to a stop, keeping well out of range. They could make out a dock on the island. A boat was tied to it.

"We pull up to that dock, he's got an easy shot," Coose said.

They studied the island's shoreline, the engine idling. The dock extended far out onto the water and had a small building on it, about the size of a tollbooth. Only the one boat was tied up to it, a small skiff with a thin outboard motor, a trolling motor. To the left side of the dock was a long stretch of sand and marsh grass.

Coose pointed to the sandy area. "What do you say I run us up over there? I'll run us right up onto the beach. We use the boat for cover."

Mangan nodded. Coose spun the wheel in the direction of the island and gunned it. Mangan stayed low and braced himself as the shoreline came rushing at them. The boat crashed the beach at an angle, running a good ten feet up onto the sand, engines screaming as the propellers hit the open air. Coose killed the motor and both men were out of the boat and taking cover before the props stopped spinning.

They waited. Nothing.

Coose slid over to Mangan. He gestured to the woods. "I think we—"

A barrage of gunfire exploded across the boat, obliterating most of its stern. Mangan and Coose hit the ground, rolling close against the keel, bullets striking the inside of the fiberglass boat and flying straight through it.

"Go!" Mangan yelled at Coose. "Go! Go!"

Coose ran for the trees as Mangan leaned out from behind the stern and let off five rounds from his Glock in the direction of the shooter.

Coose, in the tree line, yelled, "Come on!" and fired cover rounds for Mangan, who ran and joined him.

The firing stopped.

"He's in the branches," Coose whispered.

Mangan, catching his breath, said, "What?"

"Up in the trees! I saw the muzzle flash, it's high."

Mangan's radio crackled loudly and he heard Pribyl's voice. He tried to shut it off, but the sound brought an immediate hail of gunfire in their direction. Mangan dropped the radio and he and Coose took off deeper into the woods, a spit of gunfire trailing after them. They left their flashlights off, ducking under the low limbs and feeling their way among tree trunks, trying to flank the shooter. They heard more gunfire now, but the bullets weren't coming at them. The sound was farther away, and lower.

"Sounds like he's on the ground," Mangan said.

"What's he shooting at?"

"I don't know. The guys on shore maybe?"

Mangan knew this was the time to close distance. They made their way in the direction of the gunfire, which was intermittent now, as if the shooter were taking more time to aim between shots. They followed the sound until it stopped.

"What now?" Coose asked.

Mangan looked around. To his right, the trees thinned away into a small clearing. Past it, he could make out the lake again.

"Over there," Coose said, pointing to a shadowy outline near the shoreline. There was a small cabin in the distance, barely visible in the near dark. Attached to it was another dock, which led almost up to the building. A teeny glimmer of a light suddenly lit up a window of the cabin.

"What the hell's he doing?" Mangan asked.

"I don't know, he—"

Mangan heard the muffled *pfft* of a silencer and Coose's neck burst open in a flow of black liquid. "Fuck!" Mangan said, spinning in the direction of the shot and firing blindly. "Fuck!"

Coose went to his knees, clutching his throat.

"Coose!" Mangan yelled, firing his gun till it was empty. He smacked another magazine into the chamber, and crawled beside Coose. "Goddamnit! Coose!" No answer. There was blood everywhere. "Jesus Christ!" He tried putting pressure on the wound. "Jesus." The blood was hot and Mangan could feel the frantic throb of Coose's heart pushing against his hand. "Coose," he said, "Coose!"

Coose clutched the hole in his throat, his eyes looking everywhere but at Mangan, as if watching some curious scene play out around him. His lips were moving, trying to say something. Out of habit, Mangan reached for his radio to call for help, but it wasn't there.

Coose's eyes closed.

Mangan felt that thing in him rise, that darker thing. He grabbed the shotgun lying beside Coose and ran straight in the direction of the last shots, laying out his own cover fire as he ran. He made it to the side of the cabin, back against the outside wall. No sound now but his own breathing. Wait, he told himself, wait. Breathe. Listen. He thought of his daughter. Don't die, he told himself, don't fucking die.

He heard a metallic click of something inside the cabin and smashed the barrel of the shotgun through a window, firing off two rounds. He ran around to the front door and kicked it in, firing another blast, and dodging to his right and sweeping the room. No movement in his immediate line of view. He was intensively focused now, the room was vividly clear, every object seeming a magnified version of itself, everything brought to extraordinary clarity. The cabin was a single large space inside, industrial looking, empty except for a large stainless steel table in the middle of the room, faucets on either side of it, a drain in the middle, an assortment of knives lined up on one side. It looked like an autopsy room. A sign on the side of the steel table said No Scaling.

A fish-cleaning station.

Mangan heard a movement then, outside, and glimpsed a shape coming through the open door. He spun the barrel of the shotgun toward it and got off a single shot, wide, before being knocked hard into the table and slammed to the ground. Mangan threw punch after punch at the back and side of the man's head, but the blows didn't seem to faze him. He was a big man, his clothes camouflaged and thick with body armor. The man wrestled the shotgun away from Mangan and threw it across the room, giving Mangan just enough time to reach for his Glock, but before he could draw it, Daniel Anderson had a gun aimed at Mangan's forehead.

Anderson was out of breath.

So was Mangan.

"Daniel," Mangan said, trying to buy some time. "Daniel, I know what happened to your daughter."

Anderson leaned in slowly and took Mangan's gun from its holster and tossed it aside.

"We talked to your wife," Mangan continued. "You can stop this now, Daniel. Just stop."

Anderson looked at Mangan for a long quizzical moment. He lowered the barrel of his gun and fired into Mangan's knee.

Mangan screamed, crashing to the ground. He writhed on the floor, scouring his mind, and the room, for a way out. His Glock and shotgun were out of reach. His backup snub .38 was strapped to his ankle. The assailant was wearing body armor.

"You're not going to die," Anderson said, in an oddly detached voice. "No, you live. Live a long life. But Kathleen . . . your daughter—"

Mangan loosed a furious cry and rolled left, drawing his .38. Anderson fired, missing, as Mangan got off two shots—center chest—knocking the assailant backward, but not stopping him. Anderson came at him again, aiming and—

Two thunderous blasts deafened Mangan as the cabin window behind him shattered and Anderson went flying across the room, knocked against the far wall, his shirt and body armor smoldering. He dropped his weapon and fell to the floor, gasping for breath. Mangan, unable to stand, kept his weapon trained on Anderson, wondering what the hell had just happened. A moment later a flash of silver pushed through the doorway—the unmistakable barrel of a .44 Magnum, gripped by officer Michele Schaefer.

Schaefer advanced steadily, keeping a level aim on Anderson, kicking weapons out of the way as she approached. He was sitting on the floor, trying to breathe. Taking a .44-caliber shot wearing body armor is like getting hit by a sledgehammer, full swing, without wearing body armor. Anderson looked up at Schaefer, dazed. She stared back at him, expressionless. The long barrel of her gun, absolutely motionless. Her breathing, steady and calm.

There was a long silence.

Very long.

Then Schaefer, in a near whisper, said, as if only to herself, "A policeman was just born." Anderson moved and she fired again, snapping his head back in a vapory blur of red.

At Rockford Memorial Hospital, a level-one trauma center, Mangan waited to be prepped for surgery. His vitals were good, he'd lost some blood, but was stable. The gunshot had shattered part of his upper tibia and ripped through his patellar tendon, which is why his kneecap was no longer in the right place. The surgeon, who looked like he'd just graduated high school, came in after examining the MRI scan and said he'd know more after he opened Mangan up, whether he could repair the injury sufficiently or whether a total knee replacement might be a better option.

"Will I be able to dance after this, Doc?" Mangan asked him.

"Yes, you'll be able to dance."

"That's great, I never could before."

The doctor almost smiled. Coose was alive, that was the best news. Critical but stable, the bullet having just missed his carotid artery and spinal column. "Luck of the Irish," Mangan had called out to him when they wheeled him past. Coose had been unable to respond, although he did muster a nearly indiscernible smirk. Mangan thanked his God for Coose's life. He'd lost one partner in his career, he didn't think he could bear another.

Captain Pribyl dropped by. "You look awful," he told Mangan.

"Thanks."

He dropped a manuscript on the table. "This is for you," he said. "A copy of the document found on Anderson's computer."

Mangan ignored it. "Is Schaefer around?"

"She's out in the hall, talking to IA about the shooting."

"Anderson made a move."

"That's what she said."

They were silent for a moment. "She's okay," Mangan said.

"Yes, she is."

"How the hell did she find us anyway?"

"One of her officers told her. Dan. Dan something."

"Ehrlich."

"Yeah. Schaefer showed up around the time Gaffney's guys got there with the boat. We heard shooting coming from the island, so Schaefer and me, we got in the boat and tried to raise you on the walkie, but you didn't answer. As soon as we got to the island we heard more shots, so we headed into the woods to flank them. That's when we found Cusumano and saw the cabin. We heard more shots coming from there, so I went around the far side, and Schaefer took the front. She saw the guy through the window and fired." Pribyl pointed to the manuscript on the table. "The prelim CSI report is in there too. Thought you might like some reading material. You're probably gonna be here awhile."

Mangan picked up the report.

"I gotta get going," Pribyl said, heading toward the door. "Nice working with you."

"You too, John," Mangan said. "Thank you."

"I put a *Victoria's Secret* in there too. Found it in the cafeteria."

Mangan smiled as Pribyl left. He skimmed the CSI report. Of the evidence found in the cabin, a few things stood out: 1. Fillet gloves, the fingers and palms of which were dotted with tiny metal studs, the same shape as the impressions found on Deborah Ellison's neck. 2. Bottles of organic boat soap, similar to the cleaning solution found on Deborah Ellison's body.

Mangan took up the manuscript that Pribyl had left.

The Righter, by Daniel Alan Anderson.

He turned to the first chapter.

Mangan wasn't sure he wanted to read it.

I WATCHED HER. NIGHT AFTER NIGHT. BY HER
APARTMENT. IN THE CITY WHERE MY DAUGHTER
WAS ONCE ALIVE AND NOW WAS NOT. WHY SHOULD
SHE, OR THEY, OR ANYONE, HAVE LIFE, AND LYNNETTE
NO LIFE AT ALL?

I FOLLOWED HER ON THE NIGHT WHEN SHE STOPPED
BEING. ON THE CORNER, SHE STOOD AS IF SHE WERE
TELLING ME, YES, YES, NOW, NOW IS THE TIME FOR
ME TO PAY FOR THE SINS OF MY FATHER. I PULLED
UP NEAR HER AND ASKED HER HOW MUCH. SHE
LEANED INTO MY WINDOW AND I TOOK HER.

IT WAS SO EASY. IT WAS ALL SO—

Mangan tossed the manuscript back onto the table. He didn't want
to read it, didn't want to go there just yet.

I have supped full with horrors.

The door opened and Michele Schaefer walked in.

"Hey," she said.

She looked exhausted. "Hey, yourself," Mangan said. "How you
doing?"

"Okay. How about you?

"Oh, I'm fine. Never liked this knee anyway."

"They're asking me a lot of questions out there."

"You were justified. I was there. He moved."

"That's what I said."

"You said right. That's what happened."

"Well . . . thanks. Thanks for finding the guy." Schaefer looked to
the floor, hesitating, as if she were going to say something. "Anyway, I,
uh, I have to get headed back to Winsome. My dad."

"Michele," Mangan said, "I'm so sorry about your sister."

She nodded and eased out the door. "See you around."

"Bye."

Mangan watched through the window of the door until she disappeared down the hallway.

And down I laid, to list this sad-tuned tale;
A plaintful story from a sistering vale.

He thought of his wife and daughter. He picked up the phone and called Mickey Eagan in Chicago.

"Eagan, it's me," he said.

"Glad to hear you're breathing."

"Me too. Hey, I need a favor."

"What?"

"I got keys to my apartment in the top drawer of my desk."

"Yeah?"

"I need you to get something for me."

"Sure. What?"

"You know that parrot store over on Jefferson?"

"What?"

"The Windy City Parakeet Boutique, 58—write this down—5840 Jefferson."

"What the hell are you talking about?"

"I need you to get over there and get some bird food, take it over to my apartment."

"For what? You got a *bird*?"

"Yeah, I got a bird. You got a problem with that?"

"No, I—it's just—no."

"You got to feed it for me. She's going to starve. I want you to get the fruit blend, the supreme fruit blend. You got that?"

"I'm writing it down."

"It's got good stuff in it, nuts and things. You do that for me?"

"Yeah, sure."

"All right, there's a little cup in her cage, you fill it halfway. Not too much."

"Is it going to fly out at me, when I open the cage?"

"No, she'll hide in the corner. She's nervous. I got a nervous bird."

"All right, I'll take care of it. Don't worry."

"Thanks, Mickey."

"No problem."

"Hey."
"What?"
"Her name is Phoebe."

Acknowledgments

My deep thanks to Sara Young, for being a trusted and tireless reader of the various incarnations of this book. Her insightful criticisms, and encouragement, were, and always have been, a great help to me. Thank you, Sara. Thanks also to Raphael Kadushin of University of Wisconsin Press for championing the book and for his very helpful criticism; thanks to my editors; and to Noel Silverman, for his belief in me and my work for many years.

Much appreciation to my wife, Brenda, for slogging through some very early drafts of the book; to Ms. Sarah Day, for once mentioning something about an actor who wrote crime novels; to James Bohnen, for bringing the great authors of the world to my door, literally; to Morgan Henry Cafaro, for sparking my imagination many years ago when the book was just a vague idea drifting around her kitchen; to Dean Bakopoulos, for his generosity and support; to John Christianson, for his encouragement; to D. P. Lyle, M.D., for graciously sharing his knowledge of forensics; to Nils Richardson, for coaching me through my first experience of firearms; and a special note of thanks to Fred.

Appendix

I have freely and unabashedly plundered the works of *the divine William*, as Herman Melville referred to Shakespeare. Most of the excerpts have been quoted verbatim. Some, however, I paraphrased, changing the words, changing the punctuation, adding and/or cutting words. I made no attempt to remain textually precise with the quotes. The words come to Mangan through his particular veil of memory, and they adapt themselves freely in his own mind, mingling with whatever experience he is having at any given moment.

There are many different editions of Shakespeare's works, all of them with their own textual idiosyncrasies. They differ greatly in word choice, punctuation, meter, act breaks, line numbers, stage directions, etc., and I referred to a great variety of texts while working on the book. For those of you interested in seeing the quotes in the context of Shakespeare's plays, I have included the notes below. The notes include the name of the play, the character who speaks the lines, and the act and scene in which the lines can be found. I also noted whether or not I paraphrased the quote. For the really ambitious, read the Variorum editions of Shakespeare's plays and *all* the notes. (It's a bit like making your way through *Moby-Dick*—worth the effort.) You will occasionally find yourself laughing out loud at the subtle, and often not so subtle, disagreements between scholars.

28　And who has cut those pretty fingers off? *Titus Andronicus*, Marcus, Act 2, scene 4 (paraphrased).

28　Thou hast no hands to wipe away thy tears. *Titus Andronicus*, Titus, Act 3, scene 1.

28 What accursed hand hath made thee handless? *Titus Andronicus*, Titus, Act 3, scene 1.

35 and I . . . with tears . . . do wash . . . the blood away. *Henry VI, part 3*, York, Act 1, scene 4.

35 Vengeance is in my heart, death in my hand, / Blood and revenge are hammering in my head. *Titus Andronicus*, Aaron, Act 2, scene 3.

37 Habit, the great deadener. Samuel Beckett, *Waiting for Godot*, Vladimir, Act 2 (paraphrased).

37 I was not angry until this instant. *Henry V*, King Henry, Act 4, scene 7 (paraphrased).

38 This thing of darkness I acknowledge mine. *The Tempest*, Prospero, Act 5, scene 1.

39 This is a subtle whore, a closet lock and key of villainous secrets. *Othello*, Othello, Act 4, scene 2.

39 we have scotched the snake, not killed it. *Macbeth*, Macbeth, Act 3, scene 2.

50 They were his Yale and Harvard. Herman Melville, *Moby-Dick*, Chapter 54, "The Advocate" (paraphrased).

51 I'll find a day to massacre them all, / And raze their faction and their family, / The cruel father and his— *Titus Andronicus*, Tamora, Act 1, scene 1.

62 thy bones are marrowless, thy blood is cold. *Macbeth*, Macbeth, Act 3, scene 4.

62 upon whose dead corpse there was such misuse as may not be spoken of. *Henry VI, part 1*, Westmoreland, Act 1, scene 1 (paraphrased).

63 There's a special providence in the fall of a sparrow. *Hamlet*, Hamlet, Act 5, scene 2.

63 I am burned up with inflaming wrath; a rage that nothing can allay, nothing but blood. *King John*, King John, Act 3, scene 1 (paraphrased).

64 the bug which you would fright me with, I seek. *The Winter's Tale*, Hermione, Act 3, scene 2.

68 It will have blood, they say, / Blood will have blood. *Macbeth*, Macbeth, Act 3, scene 4.

68 See thy mangled daughter. *Titus Andronicus*, Marcus, Act 3, scene 1 (paraphrased).

68 Sweet father, . . . cease your tears. *Titus Andronicus*, Lucius, Act 3, scene 1. (paraphrased).

68 Is it I, God, or who, that lifts this arm? Herman Melville, *Moby-Dick*, Chapter 132, "The Symphony."

68 What is it, what nameless, inscrutable, unearthly thing is it? Herman Melville, *Moby-Dick*, Chapter 132, "The Symphony."

68 deeper, faraway things the occasional flashings forth of the intuitive truth. Herman Melville, "Hawthorne and His Moses."

68 There is a divinity that shapes our ends, rough hew them how we will. *Hamlet*, Hamlet, Act 5, scene 2.

68 for in this world of lies, truth is forced to fly like a scared white doe in the woodlands; and only by cunning glimpses will she reveal herself. Herman Melville, "Hawthorne and His Moses."

69 the great art of telling the truth, even though it be covertly, and by snatches. Herman Melville, "Hawthorne and His Moses."

70 From this time forth, I never will speak word. *Othello*, Iago, Act 5, scene 2.

70 And thus the whirligig of time brings in his revenges. *Twelfth Night*, Feste, Act 5, scene 1.

72 What stern ungentle hands have lopped and hewed and made thy body bare? *Titus Andronicus*, Marcus, Act 2, scene 4.

72 Let grief convert to anger; blunt not the heart, enrage it. *Macbeth*, Malcolm, Act 4, scene 3.

75 rehearsed a billion years before the oceans rolled. Herman Melville, *Moby-Dick*, Chapter 134, "The Chase—Second Day."

79 Do not worry. . . . Just write one true sentence. Ernest Hemingway, *A Moveable Feast* (paraphrased).

81 an infinite and endless liar, an hourly promise-breaker, the owner of not one good quality. *All's Well That Ends Well*, Second Lord, Act 3, scene 6.

82 at length, the truth will out. *Merchant of Venice*, Launcelot, Act 2, scene 2.

84 Oft have I heard that grief softens the mind, / And makes it fearful and degenerate. *Henry VI, part 2*, Queen Margaret, Act 4, scene 4.

84 the poison of deep grief. *Hamlet*, Claudius, Act 4, scene 5.

86 Never, never, never, never, never. *King Lear*, Lear, Act 5, scene 3.

89 It was a lover and his lass, / That o'er the green corn-field did pass. *As You Like It*, Second Page, Act 5, scene 3.

89 men, like ravenous fishes, will feed on one another. Various authors, *Sir Thomas More*, Sir Thomas More, Act 2, scene 4 (speech attributed to Shakespeare, paraphrased).

89 Sell all, sell merrily. *Henry IV, part 1*, Hotspur, Act 4, scene 1 (paraphrasing of "die all, die merrily").

90 mustering in the clouds. *Richard II*, King Richard, Act 3, scene 3 (paraphrased).

91 the wide sea hath drops too few to wash her clean again. *Much Ado About Nothing*, Leonato, Act 4, scene 1.

93 O God, that one might read the book of fate. *Henry IV, part 2*, King Henry, Act 3, scene 1.

94 New-reaped, like a stubble-land at harvest home. *Henry IV, part 1*, Hotspur, Act 1, scene 3.

95 Here never shines the sun; here nothing breeds. *Titus Andronicus*, Tamora, Act 2, scene 3.

95 Like to a slaughtered lamb, in this detested, dark, blood-drinking pit. *Titus Andronicus*, Martius, Act 2, scene 3.

95 I must talk of acts of black night, abominable deeds. *Titus Andronicus*, Aaron, Act 5, scene 1.

95 A crimson river of warm blood . . . *Titus Andronicus*, Marcus, Act 2, scene 4.

96 Who would have thought the old man to have had so much blood in him? *Macbeth*, Lady Macbeth, Act 5, scene 1.

98 turning your books to graves, your ink to blood. *Henry IV, part 2*, Westmoreland, Act 4, scene 1.

100 I am Revenge, sent from the infernal kingdom / To ease the gnawing vulture of my mind. *Titus Andronicus*, Tamora, Act 5, scene 2 (paraphrased).

101 If I digged up thy forefathers' graves . . . I live in hell. *Henry VI, part 3*, Clifford, Act 1, scene 3 (paraphrased).

101 I will find them out, / And in their ears tell them my dreadful name . . . / Revenge. *Titus Andronicus*, Tamora, Act 5, scene 2.

105 Had I thy brethren here . . . I live in hell. *Henry VI, part 3*, Clifford, Act 1, scene 3.

106 Be thou revenged on men, and let me live! . . . why wilt thou slay me? *Henry VI, part 3*, Rutland and Clifford, Act 1, scene 3.

106 These wrongs, unspeakable, past patience, / Are more than any living man could bear. *Titus Andronicus*, Marcus, Act 5, scene 3.

106 Past cure I am; now reason is past care. Shakespeare Sonnet 147.

106 My thoughts and my discourse as madmen's are. Shakespeare Sonnet 147.

106 O, full of scorpions is my mind. *Macbeth*, Macbeth, Act 3, scene 2.

107 Confusion now hath made his masterpiece. *Macbeth*, Macduff, Act 2, scene 3.

117 You are deceived, for what you see is but the smallest part of humanity. *Henry VI, part 1*, Talbot, Act 2, scene 3.

121 There is no darkness but ignorance; in which thou art more puzzled than the Egyptians in their fog. *Twelfth Night*, Feste, Act 4, scene 2.

123 plate sin with gold and the strong lance of justice hurtless breaks. *King Lear*, Lear, Act 4, scene 6.

126 Thou art death's fool; / For him thou labour'st by thy flight to shun, / And yet runn'st toward him still. *Measure for Measure*, Duke Vincentio, Act 3, scene 1.

127 Now o'er the one half-world nature seems dead, / And wicked dreams abuse the curtained sleep. *Macbeth*, Macbeth, Act 2, scene 1.

127 He sleeps with clenched hands; and wakes with his own bloody nails in his palms. Herman Melville, *Moby-Dick*, Chapter 44, "The Chart."

127 Whole oceans away, from that young girl-wife. Herman Melville, *Moby-Dick*, Chapter 132, "The Symphony."

127 There's a great spirit gone. Thus did I desire it. / Would the hand could pluck her back that shoved her on. *Antony and Cleopatra*, Antony, Act 1, scene 2.

127 When I think of this life I have led; the desolation of solitude it has been; the masoned, walled-town of a Captain's exclusiveness. Herman Melville, *Moby-Dick*, Chapter 132, "The Symphony."

128 Bare ruined choirs, where late the sweet birds sang. Shakespeare Sonnet 73.

129 A sort of vagabonds, rascals, and runaways, / A scum of base lackey peasants, / Whom their o'er-cloyed country vomits forth. *Richard III*, King Richard, Act 5, scene 3.

130 Whither should I fly? I have done no harm. *Macbeth*, Lady MacDuff, Act 4, scene 2.

137 When sorrows come, they come not single spies but in battalions. *Hamlet*, Claudius, Act 4, scene 5.

140 Tell him Revenge is come to join with him, / And work confusion on his enemies. *Titus Andronicus*, Tamora, Act 5, scene 2.

142 I have done a thousand dreadful things / As willingly as one would kill a fly, / And nothing grieves me heartily indeed / But that I cannot do ten thousand more. *Titus Andronicus*, Aaron, Act 5, scene 1.

143 Alack, alack, my child's dead, / My soul and not my child. *Romeo and Juliet*, Capulet, Act 4, scene 5 (paraphrased).

143 Dead art thou, alack my child is dead. *Romeo and Juliet*, Capulet, Act 4, scene 5.

143 The sweetest, dearest creature's dead. *The Winter's Tale*, Paulina, Act 3, scene 2.

143 Her blood is settled, and her joints are stiff. / Life and these lips have long been separated. *Romeo and Juliet*, Capulet, Act 4, scene 5.

143 'Tis here, but yet confused. *Othello*, Iago, Act 2, scene 1.

143 If ever you chance to have a child, / Look in her youth to have her so cut off. *Henry VI, part 3*, Margaret, Act 5, scene 5 (paraphrased).

148 For this was he ordained, for this was he set on this earth. *Henry VI, part 3*, Gloucester, Act 5, scene 6 (paraphrased).

149 Grief fills the room up of my absent child. *King John*, Constance, Act 3, scene 4.

154 I am a man more sinned against than sinning. *King Lear*, Lear, Act 3, scene 2.

154 This one hand yet is left to cut your throats. *Titus Andronicus*, Titus, Act 5, scene 2.

154 I would have thee live, for in my sense 'tis happiness to die. *Othello*, Othello, Act 5, scene 2.

154 My wits begin to turn. *King Lear*, Lear, Act 3, scene 2.

154 There's not a hollow cave or lurking place . . . but I will find them out. *Titus Andronicus*, Tamora, Act 5, scene 2 (paraphrased).

157 a murdering peace. *Hamlet*, Claudius, Act 4, scene 5 (paraphrased).

157 She had been his all-the-world. Shakespeare Sonnet 112 (paraphrased).

158 And thus I clothe my naked villainy / And seem a saint, when most I play the devil. *Richard II*, King Richard, Act 1, scene 3.

162 That wild madness that's only calm to comprehend itself. Herman Melville, *Moby-Dick*, Chapter 37, "Sunset."

163 My wife, my wife. What wife? I have no wife. *Othello*, Othello, Act 5, scene 2.

165 If of life you keep a care, / Shake off slumber, and beware. *The Tempest*, Ariel, Act 2, scene 1.

166 melt into the air. *Macbeth*, Macbeth, Act 1, scene 3 (paraphrased).

170 Where is my judgment fled, that censures falsely when I see aright? Shakespeare Sonnet 73 (paraphrased).

178 and Lynette no life at all? *King Lear*, Lear, Act 5, scene 3 (paraphrased).

178 I have supped full with horrors. *Macbeth*, Macbeth, Act 5, scene 5.

179 And down I laid, to list this sad-tuned tale; / A plaintful story from a sistering vale. Shakespeare, "A Lover's Complaint," lines 2–4 (paraphrased).